Born in Scotland in 1910, Jane Duncan spent her childhood in Glasgow, going for holidays to the Black Isle of Inverness. After taking her degree at Glasgow University she moved to England in 1931, and when war broke out she was commissioned in the WAAF and worked in Photographic Intelligence.

After the war she moved to the West Indies with her husband, who appears as 'Twice' Alexander in her novels. Shortly after her husband's death, she returned to Jemimaville near Cromarty, not far from her grandparents' croft which inspired the beloved 'Reachfar'. Jane Duncan died in 1976.

D1628449

Also by Jane Duncan

MY FRIENDS THE MISS BOYDS
MY FRIEND MURIEL
MY FRIEND MONICA
MY FRIEND ANNIE
MY FRIEND ROSE

and published by Corgi Books

MY FRIEND FLORA

Jane Duncan

CORGI BOOKS

MY FRIEND FLORA
A CORGI BOOK   0 552 12879 1

Originally published in Great Britain by
Macmillan London Limited

PRINTING HISTORY
Macmillan London edition published 1962
Macmillan London edition reprinted 1963, 1971, 1978, 1983
Corgi edition published 1987

This book is set in 10/11pt Times

Corgi Books are published by Transworld Publishers Ltd.,
61–63 Uxbridge Road, Ealing, London W5 5SA,
in Australia by Transworld Publishers (Aust.) Pty. Ltd.,
15–23 Helles Avenue, Moorebank, NSW 2170, and in New
Zealand by Transworld Publishers (N.Z.) Ltd., Cnr. Moselle
and Waipareira Avenues, Henderson, Auckland.

Reproduced, printed and bound in Great Britain by
Hazell Watson & Viney Limited,
Member of the BPCC Group,
Aylesbury, Bucks

This story is for my sister-in-law,
Betty, who loves the Reachfar country.

CONTENTS

Part I
1915

Part I
1915

Her name was Flora Smith, but she was always known as Flora Bedamned, for my home district in Ross-shire has a habit of bestowing what it calls 'bye-names' on its inhabitants, some of them ugly, some of them complimentary, but all of them extraordinarily apt. Exactly how apt, I think the bestowers are often unaware.

Although I am now over forty and have, all my life, been interested in words in general and in names in particular, and although I have given a lot of thought to these home bye-names, I have never been able to arrive at any common factor among them that would indicate why they came to be given. Some bye-names derive from a physical peculiarity in their owners; some from a personal idiosyncrasy of their owners, some from a comic incident in the lives of their owners, and many are related to the lands or other material possessions of their owners. It is as if my countryside has a genius for picking out the most uncommon and unusual feature about a person and turning it into a bye-name for that person. It is, in fact, a survival, I suppose, of the original method by which surnames were given. My home countryside is rich in survivals and the bye-name habit is probably simply one more.

In the main, these bye-names are satisfyingly fitting and cling about the personality of their owners as smoothly as a well-made shoe takes to the foot it was built for. Some of them are beautifully simple, such as that of my own family. Our surname is Sandison, but we are known

9

collectively as 'the Reachfars', because our small croft is called 'Reachfar' and I, Janet Sandison, am known as 'Janet Reachfar, but she's married now and her name is Alexander'.

Other of the bye-names are delightfully complex in origin, such as that of Willie Oxypaw. Many visitors to my home have been baffled by 'Oxypaw' as a nickname, but my friend Tom, who is one of the oldest inhabitants in a countryside unusually full of old inhabitants, can give the details of the origin of Oxypaw. The real name of this family is Gordon and they came to our district around the year 1920, for old Willie Oxypaw was a lighthouse-keeper who, when he retired, wanted still to be near the North Sea, and our local village of Achcraggan is an old fishing port, right on the coast that he loved, where houses, in 1920, did not cost a great deal. He had a large family, many of them daughters, and, naturally, our local young men went to call and pay their respects to the new young ladies. The Gordons were a hospitable family and there was always tea and cake for callers of an evening, but Mr Gordon, in his retirement, was determined to enjoy himself by sampling variety, after years of tending a light that flashed, with monotonous regularity, this way and that every so many seconds.

'And so,' my friend Tom will tell you, 'the lassies would get the tea a-all ready an' the cake an' the biscuits an' a-all an' the young fellows would be sitting round, needing to get on to the fortune-telling by the tea-leaves and capers like that, an' then Bella, the oldest lassie, would say to old Willie: "Tea or Oxo, Pa?" an' old Willie would sit an' think an' think an' consider an' then Bessie, the next lassie, would say: "Och, come *on*, tea or Oxo, Pa?" an' so it went on until they chust got known as the Oxypaws an' when you think on it, they can't blame nobody but themselves.'

Maybe Tom had the right of it when he said that only people themselves could be blamed for the bye-names, but I do not think so, for the bye-names are hereditary. Old

10

Willie Oxypaw that kept the light house has been dead these twenty years and more, but his grandson, young Willie Oxypaw, is doing very well at the electrical engineering now. And Flora Bedamned also inherited her byename which, according to my friend Tom, originated with her great-grandfather who, he says, 'was a queer, lonesome wanderer of a man that came in here from away south, from somewhere about Galloway or Kirkcudbright, I believe. I was a boy at the school when he came and he was a man then of forty or more. They were building a new barn at Poyntdale at the time and old Sir Turk took him on as a labourer, but he was a clever fellow and a grand tradesman. He could do mason work, joinery, a bittie blacksmithing or anything and Sir Turk was for taking him on to the estate staff. But no. The man wouldna do it and what he said was: "Sir Turk, it's good o'ye to make the offer, but no, be damned!" And when Sir Turk asked him why not, he said: "Ah dinna like tae be tied, be damned." And that's the way he was and everything he said finished with the words "Be damned", and so he got to be known as "Jamie Be-damned".'

However, although the queer, lonesome wanderer of a man from the south did not like to be tied, he settled in our district, on the five acres of land that old Sir Turk gave him, at his request, in payment for some masonry work that he had done, and on it he built a little house, married a local girl and founded a family. The house was on the roadside, beside the sea, about a mile west from Achcraggan and, in 1915, when I was five and went to Achcraggan School for the first time, I remember walking past 'Bedamned's Corner' and thinking that I had now done two and three quarter miles of my journey to school and had only one more mile to go.

I was, of course, much too early for school . . . I find myself saying 'of course' like that as if you, the reader, must know all the quirks of the Sandison character, one of which is that, as a family, I do not think one of us has ever

11

been late for an appointment and another of which is that I, from the age of three, had looked forward every day of my life to this momentous day when I would be 'big enough' to go to school . . . And so, when I passed Bedamned's Corner, the little white-washed house, with its door in the centre, its windows on each side of the door and its three skylights in the slated roof, had a quiet, early-morning look. Smoke came from the chimney on one of the gables and went straight up into the clear, blue and gilt September sky; half of the door stood open; a pig grunted contentedly in an outhouse, indicating that he had been fed, but no washing was as yet hung out, no rag hearth-rug lay as yet on the patch of green grass and no small children were as yet romping round the door. The house had not, so far, gathered the momentum of the daily round and, as I went past, although I had never been inside the house, I could see, as if through the walls, the orderly morning scene. Mr Smith would be already, long ago, off to work; the children of school age would be eating their porridge at the table; the mother, in a low chair at the fire, would be feeding the infant, and Flora, the eldest of the school-age ones, would be spooning porridge into the mouth of the two-year-old, having already eaten her own meal. I knew all this from a sort of innate race knowledge together with the hearsay in my own home that lodged in little cavities in my brain, for I had heard my grandmother say with approval: 'Smith's is a fine big family and a very orderly house' and I had heard George – my uncle who felt the title of uncle to be ageing and unbecoming to him and would not wear it – say: 'Mrs Bedamned is a right smart wee wifie!' and I had heard him corrected by my gentle mother with the words: 'Mrs *Smith*, George, is a very fine, capable woman and worthy of the respect of her proper name.'

In these ways, I knew with certainty what the Smiths' kitchen would be like, for it would be very much like our own kitchen at Reachfar – only we did not have any children, except me – or like Mrs Davie-the-Miller's kitchen,

12

where there were seven children, for my grandmother, who was mistress of Reachfar, and Mr Davie-the-Miller's wife, who was mistress of the Mill, were also 'fine capable women', my mother said, and 'worthy of respect' and I could see for myself that they kept 'very orderly houses'.

At five years old, my mind worked within a very limited framework, and, it being very difficult to estimate the workings of the minds of other children of five, I do not know whether my mind was, in this, unusual or usual. I do know, however, that the rigid framework was there and I think it had been induced or produced by my upbringing, which was the concerted effort of that group of people known in my mind, in strong, black, capital letters against a pure white background, as: 'MY FAMILY'. This family of mine consisted of my paternal grandparents, my father, my mother, George (my uncle), my Aunt Kate and my friend Tom, who was technically a servant, in that he received a small amount of money for his constant labours about our little farm, but I did not know about Tom's being paid until I was eight or nine and by that time he was built into my family in my mind in the sense that I believed that 'every proper family' consisted of grandparents, parents, uncles, aunts, cousins (many of them never seen, owing to being born and living in Australia, Canada and other remote parts, but written to periodically) and someone like Tom. In other words, I had never thought of trying to imagine my family without Tom in it. From my point of view, he had always been there – more 'there' in the sense of hours spent with *me* than was my father for instance – and my family, in my mind, being an unchanging thing, Tom always would be there.

This family of mine was my standard and yardstick for measuring the value of other families. In my mind, my family was a 'proper' family, made up of persons 'worthy of respect' who worked hard, paid their debts, feared no man and kept an 'orderly house'. Other families round about who did not conform to these standards were not, in my estimation, 'proper families'. To me, as a child,

13

everything was as simple as that. I was a very simple-minded, slow-witted child and quite the reverse of complex.

It was 1915 when I, at the age of five, passed Bedamned's Corner on my way to school for the first time and, because it was the very first time, I was going to Achcraggan, the village where the school was, by the proper road. This meant that I had left Reachfar, my home, on the top of its hill and had walked due northwards, down to the shore of the Firth, by the cart road that led through the fertile fields of Poyntdale Estate, where my father worked as grieve to Sir Torquil Daviot. At the big gates, where the Poyntdale Road debouched on to the tarmacadam of the County Road, I turned sharply to my right and due east to follow that County Road that wound along the shore to the school on the western outskirts of Achcraggan. Bedamned's Corner was in an angle between the County Road and a cart track that led southwards, up the hill through farm lands to emerge eventually behind the black cavern which was the home of Mr John-the-Smith who shod all the horses in the district, was the Precentor in church on Sundays and threw the heavy hammer very long distances at the Highland Games.

This 'being big enough to go to school', this realisation of a recurrent dream, surpassed, I found as I walked along, all my imaginings of its wonders. Its reality made all other things strange, new and wonderful, as if it shed over them its own light, a light that came from the beautiful unknown, from over the hills and far away. It was merely, of course, that my point of view had shifted a little; that my vision had broadened slightly, but these mundane facts did not occur to my mind. No. For me, that morning, the world and everyone in it were bathed in a new light, clothed in a gay radiance, turning to my sight strange and beautiful aspects that they had never shown before because I, Janet Sandison, five years old, was at last 'big enough to go to school'.

The mile from Bedamned's Corner to the gates in the red sandstone wall that surrounded the school was a dull

14

one, insofar as any mile of Ross countryside can be termed dull. But, as a child, I was an extremist in my attitude to country and scenery – perhaps I am so still, when I think of it – and I liked best nook-and-cranny places, such as my Thinking Place among the tall firs above the Reachfar well or broad expanses, like our West Moor, from which one could see eight miles to the east, to Achcraggan and away to the North Sea beyond it or fifteen miles west to Ben Wyvis, behind whose big humped back the sun put himself cosily to bed every evening. Also, I was more interested in people than in any scenery, so as I walked along the County Road, with the sea lapping behind its wall on my left hand and the fields rich with harvest on the slope to my right, with no other person in sight at this hour of the morning – the farm workers were already away in the fields and the townspeople who might be driving bread and meat carts to the country were not yet out – I began to think of the Bedamneds.

I had made the sudden discovery, somewhere in the new and clear light of this glorious morning, that of all the children I knew, I was the only one who did not have brothers or sisters and I wondered what it would be like to be Flora Bedamned, for she was the eldest of five children and I would not be at all surprised, from odds and ends of conversation I had been overhearing at Reachfar, if, soon, she would not be the eldest of six. I had been at pains to check this last matter with my friend Tom for, even before I had been big enough to go to school, I had always resented the attempts of my grown-up world to withhold from me sundry items of local information.

'Tom, is Mrs Bedamned going to have a baby soon?' I enquired of him while we were grooming the horses in the stable one evening.

'I do not know off any leddy off the name off Bedamned,' said Tom in the sternly virtuous voice that he used when trying to be part of the grown-up world and to put distance between himself and me.

In actual fact, Tom was a little older than my father and

15

George was only a year younger than my father, but this was the sort of fact of which I took little notice, for it had no importance in the practice of life. It was a fact that I knew in a filed-away-in-a-pigeon-hole manner, just as I was aware of and filed away the fact that the world was round and not flat. *Most* of the time, for the practical business of living, the world might as well be flat, for I was never conscious of going over any hump on it and going down the other side and, in the same way, *most* of the time, Tom and George might as well be my own age, for it was on my level that they mainly lived, moved and had their being.

'Ach, poop to you and your politeness!' I told Tom now. 'Mrs *Smith* then!'

'When you go to school next month, chust you wait till Dominie Stevenson hears you saying Poop like that!'

'*You* called the red colt a weecked boogger yesterday!'

'That iss not what we are speaking about at a-all!' said Tom.

'No. We were speaking about Mrs Smith going to have a baby. *Is* she going to have one, Tom?'

'Ach, I wish to the goodness-gracious you would be quiet with your ask-aski-asking! How would *I* know?'

'You do *so* know! And she *is* going to have one! What does she want with another one? They've got five already!'

'Get over, Betsy, bonnie lass!' said Tom to the mare and then to me: 'If you can't make a better chob o' brushing Betsy's feet than that, chust leave them alone!'

'It's that red clay that's in them, Tom. We'll have to wash them.'

'Then, that's chust what we'll do. Here, get up and take her up to the duckpond and I'll bring Dick.'

With me 'doing the splits' on Betsy's broad bare Clydesdale back and Tom sitting with both his feet hanging down one side from Dick's even broader back, we ambled up to the duckpond in the moor and let the horses wade in that the clay might soak off the long white hair about their fetlocks.

'Tom, *why* is Mrs Smith getting another baby when she's got five already and we've only got me?'

16

Coldly and levelly, Tom stared at me from his place on Dick's back. 'For the dangedest, persistingest, questioningest,' he said, 'I never saw the marrow o' ye! I don't *know* why. *No*body knows why!'

'But, anyway, she's getting another baby?'

'So I'll be hearing among the women.'

'Mr Smith will have to work harder than ever to put pennies in the bank for six of them to go to school,' I said. 'Won't he, Tom?'

'Och, aye, but Jamie Bedamned will work right enough and put pennies in the bank forbye and besides. There was never a Bedamned yet that wasn't a worker and there never was one that spent a penny if he could help it. They have always been hardworking, thrifty people, the Bedamneds.'

'The *Smiths*, Tom,' I said, getting my own back.

'That iss enough of your capers,' he told me sternly. 'You are barefeet whateffer. Slide down and see is that clay softening out o' their fetlocks at a-all.'

And now, as I rounded the sweep of the bay into the little township of Achcraggan, thinking of a family of five that would soon number six and how strange it must be to be Flora Bedamned instead of Janet Sandison, I came upon Jamie Bedamned himself.

The hill on my right hand, though fertile, was steep and was the lowest slope of a hog's back of a peninsula that lay between two arms of the sea and this hog's back was a watershed. Reachfar lay almost on its spine, and to the south and north sides the water flowed away down to the firths, so that the east and west boundaries of almost all the fields were streams. On this north shore, along which I was walking, the streams came under the County Road under little stone bridges, very neat, with their freestone parapets of fine mason work; very secret, dark and exciting, underneath, if you went down on to the beach and walked into the tunnel under the road. This morning, however, in my short, new, pleated, going-to-school tweed skirt, hand-knitted jersey and hand-knitted grey

17

socks up to my knees above my highly-polished-by-Tom black shoes, I was taking part in no childish nonsense such as peering about under the 'bridgies' as we called them. No. I was walking sedately along, my back straight, my head up, as Sandisons must always walk, looking the world firmly in the eye, had there been any world to look at, but there was not until Jamie Bedamned suddenly vaulted up from the beach and over the parapet of the last bridge before Achcraggan, like a Jack-in-the-Box, nearly startling me out of my wits.

'Good morning, Mr Smith,' I greeted him with a breath of relief, recognizing him in his moleskin trousers with his hammer in his hand. I had never spoken to him before, but this morning was different from all of life before.

' 'Morning,' he said in a low, gruff voice and then, turning away, he began to tap a stone in the low part of the parapet with his hammer.

I stood watching him with interest, waiting for him to open the conversation. This morning, part of the wonder of the day was that, coming through Poyntdale Farm, I had been having conversations with all sorts of people whom I knew by sight but with whom I had never had conversations before. They had all seemed so pleased to see me, with a fresh, new sort of pleasedness, as if I were a fresh, new person instead of Janet Reachfar that they had known since I was born, the way they said: 'Well, Janet! Good morning! And so you are off to school, are you? Well, now, isn't that grand?'

It gave me a splendid feeling, a feeling such as the King and Queen must have, I thought, when they made a Royal Progress, such as my mother had told me about, when they drove along and everybody cheered and waved flags to show how pleased they were that the King and Queen were passing by. The greetings I had received this morning did not make me feel shy and lonely as I had felt when everybody applauded when, in the summer, at the Poyntdale House Garden Party, I had run in the race and had

18

beaten all the children, even the boys, of up to ten years old. *That* time, I had felt that there was a hollowness, that in spite of all the congratulations, some people were not entirely pleased and I myself thought it unremarkable and unworthy of applause to be able to run faster with my long hill-bred legs than other people. But this morning, there was no hollowness. I was satisfied that life was remarkable in that I was at last big enough to go to school and all the people who greeted me seemed to feel that I was bringing them proof of the remarkable nature of life by being big enough to go to school. I had felt, this morning, that I was a happiness in all their lives that they greeted as it passed and, in the passing, I the happiness was made happier still by the happiness of their greeting. It was surely as the King and Queen must feel – a giving and a getting all at once, a rare moment of utter synthesis.

But Mr Smith was not like the others. I had stopped, waiting for the give-and-get moment of happiness, for the smiling remark: 'So you are for the school, are you, Janet?' but it did not come. He merely went tap-tap at the freestone of the parapet with his hammer.

'Is something wrong with the bridge, Mr Smith?' I asked after a moment.

'Iphm,' he grunted and went tap-tap again, listening to the sound.

'Are you going to mend it?' I asked.

'Iphm,' he grunted again and, laying a hand on the parapet, he vaulted down on to the beach, disappearing from sight as suddenly as he had come.

I went on my way along the empty, sunlit road thinking, now, not of Flora but of her father and, with the thought, there came back to me Tom's words 'Queer, lonesome wanderer of a man' which hovered about in the bright air like some wayward, secretive little shadow. It was of the grandfather of the man to whom I had spoken that Tom had used the words, but people very often resembled the people of their families who had preceded them, just as everyone said that I was like my grandmother in nature

19

and like the Sandisons in face, but with a 'good touch of' my mother and just as Betsy, the Reachfar mare, never threw a foal without giving it four white stockings similar to her own and the narrow white blaze down the face. Yes, I assured myself, Flora's father, Jamie Bedamned, would be just the same sort of queer, lonesome wanderer of a man that Jamie Bedamned her great-grandfather had been and that was why, shut up inside his queer lonesomeness, he had not noticed that I was going to school for the first time.

When I came to the school gate – the gate that I had passed with longing ever since I could remember – and could walk, with right, into the deserted playground, I began to feel a little sinking of loneliness and, at the same time, a little uprush of panic. I began to wish that I had accepted Tom and George's offer to come with me, this first morning, after all. But, at home, in the security of the Reachfar kitchen, the suggestion had seemed silly, for, two weeks ago, my father had brought me down to meet Dominie Stevenson and the dominie had said that I was to be here at half-past nine on this day and '– it's a long way you have to come, Janet. You'll find your way down the hill and then back home to Reachfar all right?' he had asked with a teasing smile.

'Yes, sir,' I said, trying to smile too but embarrassed at this joke because I knew he was remembering how, once, when I was not quite four and had not much sense, I had come down to the school, walked into his own room where he was giving the Top Class its singing lesson and told him I thought I was big enough to come to school now. He had been very nice about it, I remembered. He was, of course, a very nice man, with a pinkish purple face, a lot of grey hair and spectacles on a black ribbon that led into the breast pocket of his hairy tweed coat. With this coat, he wore knickerbockers, knee-length grey stockings and black laced boots. From behind, he looked very much like Robbie the Gamekeeper at Poyntdale, but when you stood in front of him and he looked down at you, you felt,

20

somehow, that he could not possibly be anything other than a schoolmaster.

When I knocked at the door that day and went into his room, he bumped the end of his big wooden pointer twice on the floor, the singing stopped and he said: 'Well, now, and who are *you*?'

So I told him I was Janet Reachfar and big enough to come to school and so I had come.

'Very well, Janet,' he said. 'Just sit there at the end of the front row and we'll go on with our singing lesson.'

It had been very pleasant and, now, as I remembered it, I began to sing the song that I had learned that day:

'Early one mo-orning, just as the sun was ri-ising,
I heard a maiden si-ing in the va-alley below –
Oh don't decei-eve me! Oh never lea-eeve me!
How-ow could you u-oo-ooze a poo-oor maiden so?'

But after the singing lesson, I remembered, it was time for school to stop and the pupils to go home and it had all been rather undignified. I preferred not to think about it now. Just when it seemed to me that I had the Dominie ask-ask-asked into being persuaded that I would come to school again the next day, Tom had arrived in the play-ground with the trap and Dulcie the mare with a sweat on her and when he saw me, Tom, without even bidding the Dominie good-day or being anything *like* civil in his manners, burst out: 'Ye danged wee limmer that ye are! And your poor mother worried till she's *seeck* about ye! Dang it, I have it in my mind to take this *wheep* to ye!' and he cracked the lash of the horse-whip within an inch of my bare legs. Never in all my born days had Tom threatened me with a weapon before and I burst into floods of tears. It had been all very undignified. Of course, I was only not quite four at the time and had very little sense, but I still preferred not to think about it. So I sang over again the stanza of 'Early one mo-orning'; I forgot my loneliness and my panic and very soon the playground began to fill with children, between forty and fifty of them in all – more

21

children than you would have thought there could be in the whole wide world – some of them just five years old like me, but a dozen or so nearly grown-up people who must have been every day of twelve or thirteen years old.

When the big brass bell rang and we went inside the school, I discovered that there were six other people besides myself come to school for the first time that day and the lady teacher, Miss Inglis, told the seven of us to sit down on a long bench at one side of her schoolroom and wait, quietly, till she was ready to attend to us. I sat very quietly, watching her as she wrote some words on the blackboard for one lot of children to copy and some sums for another lot of children to do and I marvelled at how clever she must be to be able to teach two different things to two lots of people all at once – no, *three* lots of people, because she would be starting on *us* seven in a moment. I had drawn in my breath and opened my mouth to tell her how clever I thought she was when the last words that my mother had spoken to me as she sent me off from Reachfar came into my mind: 'Now, Janet, off you go. And, remember, do *not* speak until you are spoken to. Don't go airing your views the way you do with Tom and George. You go to school to listen, not to talk. Remember, now.'

I had promised to remember and I had remembered just in time.

'I know *your* name!' said the red-headed boy who was seated next to me on the bench. 'You're Janet Reachfar!'

'And *you*'re Alasdair-the-Doctor!' I said, for so he was, the son of Doctor Mackay.

' 'M not! 'M Alasdair Mackay! So sucks!' he said.

'And I'm Janet *Sandison* an' poop!' I replied.

'Now, be quiet, you two!' said Miss Inglis and we were quiet, but he pulled one of my pigtails at the back so I pinched his thigh, underneath, just at the edge of the bench, so hard that he jumped into the air.

'Janet,' said Miss Inglis very sternly, 'did I see you pinching Alasdair?'

22

'Yes, Miss Inglis,' I said

and

'No, Miss Inglis,' said Alasdair in concert.

'I hope I didn't,' she said, 'and I hope that nobody in this class tells lies,' and she turned away to her high desk at the end of the room.

'Silly fool!' Alasdair hissed at me.

'Silly fool yourself!' I hissed back.

'Now,' said Miss Inglis, 'we must put all you new people in my register of attendance,' and, looking at the boy at the other end of the bench from Alasdair and me, she said: 'I want surnames first – that is your second name. Now, you are a Gunn, aren't you?'

'Yes, please, miss,' the boy said in the accent of Achcraggan Fisher Town, an accent quite different from that of Achcraggan or the farm lands where I lived. 'I'm Gunn – Robert Watson, please, miss.'

'Splendid. Gunn – Robert Watson—' she repeated, writing the name in her big book.

'Robbie Beagle!' Alasdair whispered to me and I nodded, for 'The Beagle' was the family fishing boat of the Gunns and they all bore its name.

'Now, next one,' said Miss Inglis, working her way along the line and, as the children gave their names, Alasdair and I whispered to each other their 'bye-names' which, to us, were more real than the proper names now being registered by Miss Inglis.

'Skinner, Thomas,' she said next, and 'Tommy Clarty' we whispered, for Thomas was one of the large family of the drunken Jock Skinner the Dealer and his equally drunken and untidy wife, Bella.

'Gray, Elsie Margaret—' said Miss Inglis, writing.

'Elsie Moley—' I whispered to Alasdair, for Elsie's father was Mr Gray-the-Molecatcher, and so it went on until it came to the boy next to Alasdair.

'Smith, Roderick Mackenzie, miss,' said the boy.

'Roddy Bedamned!' said Alasdair.

Miss Inglis looked up, her face stern above the high,

23

boned collar of her white blouse. 'Alasdair Mackay,' she said, 'be silent or I shall send you out of the room.' She turned back to the boy. 'You are a brother of Flora, James and David, Roderick?'

'Yes, miss.'

'You must try to be a good worker in school like them then . . . Now, next one. Alasdair Mackay – is that your full name, Alasdair?'

'No, miss. I am Mackay, Alasdair George Adair.'

'A-D-A-I-R – that's it. Now, the last one, Janet?'

'Sandison, Janet Elizabeth, miss,' I said.

'Well, that's a fine row of new names,' she said, putting her head on one side and reading down her big book. 'Robert, Thomas, Eusdean – I hope you children know that Eusdean's name is Gaelic for Hugh and a very fine name, I think – Elsie, Roderick, Alasdair and Janet . . . Now, every morning when you come to school, I shall be standing here with my register and you will come in and sit down where you are sitting now and when I call out your names, you will stand up when you hear your own name and say: "Present, miss!" You understand? And when you answer, I shall put a mark beside your name in my register. Now, we'll do it for the first time. And I want people to be smart about it. Stand up quietly but straight and answer me quietly but firmly. Your name is a thing you ought to be proud of so be smart when you answer to it. Are you ready? Robert Gunn?'

'Present, miss!'

By the time that I had stood up and had answered in my turn, I was bursting with pride. I was really and truly, at long last, at school.

My memories of that first day in the classroom end with the answering of roll-call. I think that experience piled upon experience in a way that was too rapid for my slow brain, for the only other thing that I remember of the entire first day at school is what was known as 'little afternoon play'. The school day was broken by three intervals, the first of ten minutes in the middle of the forenoon, known as 'little morning play', the second was the lunch hour, known as 'big play' and the third was another ten-minute break in mid-afternoon, known as 'little afternoon play'. Children like me, who came from some distance to school, usually carried a sandwich lunch and also two small 'pieces' to be consumed at the two short intervals, but in my case my family had made an arrangement whereby, on most days, I went to have lunch with Miss Tulloch who kept the grocery shop. I did have in my satchel, however, an apple for one interval and a scone with jam for the other, but by the time 'little after-noon play' came along I was quite unable to eat my apple which I had saved because of a desperate need to go to the lavatory.

This situation was typical of the particular type of stupi-dity which is mine. I spent five years at Achcraggan School and three times a year new pupils came into the infant class, and fourteen times out of fifteen did I see Miss Inglis con-duct the little girls round behind the playshed at the first 'little morning play' and show them the three small lava-tories, but the first time of the fifteen times, when I should have been in the conducted party, I was elsewhere. I do not know how such things happen to me, but they invariably do. I once went to see a boy-friend off on a ship at South-ampton, quarrelled with him in the smoke-room and took myself off in a huff to take a walk round the ship. Every other visitor heard the bells ring and the stewards calling: 'All ashore!' but I did not and had to make up with my boy-friend and borrow from him my fare back from Cherbourg to Southampton. In 1939, I joined the Women's Air Force and in 1942 I was had on the mat by my senior officer and asked whether, at the end of three years, I still had not learned to read Orders and if I did read them, why was I still masquerading as a Section Offi-cer when, two weeks ago, my promotion to Flight Rank had been posted. I made some murmur to the effect that 'I just had not happened to notice' this thing in Orders.

My commanding officer was a very nice woman.

'Sandison,' she said, 'why do you always happen to notice what other people don't and not what other people do?'

I did not say anything. If I knew the answer, so many things about me would be different and better, I felt.

'Go away,' she said, 'for the love of Mike and get that ribbon sewn on your sleeves!'

So, when Miss Inglis showed Elsie Gray and me where the lavatories were, as she undoubtedly did, I just did not happen to notice and when I went to Miss Tulloch's for my lunch, I was no doubt too full of being big enough to be at school to notice any discomfort, with the result that, by mid-afternoon, I was suddenly in agony and not at all sure what to do.

'Do *not* speak,' my mother had said, 'until you are spoken to.'

My apple in my hand, I stood in a corner of the walled playground beside the trunk of the big elm tree while all the other children romped and shouted around me, and had a dreadful vision of going back into school, the worst happening and a tell-tale pool forming round the feet of myself and Alasdair Mackay. It would be such a big pool, I was sure, that it might even reach along to the feet of Roddie Bedamned and, of course, it would also spread outwards towards the immaculate buttoned shoes of Miss Inglis where she stood in the middle of the floor. Miss Inglis would look down with astonished eyes at these spreading waters, her glance would trace them to their source and she would say: 'Janet Sandison, you are not big enough to come to school yet,' and, covered in shame and ignominy, my wet clothing clinging to my legs, I would be banished from the classroom and sent home, never to return.

'That's a bonnie apple you've got, Janet,' a voice said. 'You should be eating it. Play will soon be over.'

I looked up into the face of Flora Bedamned who had left the group of big girls in the Top Class with whom she had been playing.

'I – I'm not hungry,' I said, looking down at the pretty red apple.

26

She bent nearer to me. She was a small fair thin girl, not a great deal taller than I was, for I come of a tall breed.

'Is anything wrong? Come on and play,' she said.

'I – I don't want to, thank you,' I stammered.

'Och, come now, pettie,' she said and it might have been the voice of my granny – as distinct from that of my stern grandmother – when I had fallen and skinned my knees, 'just you tell me what's wrong. Come, now!'

'Please, I want to go to the lavatory,' I said.

'Och, mercy me! Come then! Run hard!' she said, and we set off to the haven behind the playshed.

She stood outside the little cubicle until I, feeling like a different person, emerged and then she handed me my apple which she had been holding for me.

'Eat it up quick!' she said.

'Have half of it!' I said.

A hungry gleam came into her eyes but she said in her comforting granny's voice: 'No, no, pettie! You keep your nice apple to yourself,' and she began to walk ahead of me back round to the playground, but, at that moment, Alasdair Mackay ran past.

'You, Alasdair,' I said, 'lend me that knife of yours!'

'What for?'

'To cut this apple.'

He produced the knife. 'Do I get a bit?'

'Maybe. Flora's to get a bit first.'

'All right.' He handed the knife to me and we all gathered round the apple on the grass. I cut it in two halves and handed a half to Flora. The white, inner sparkle of the apple overcame her resistance and, a granny no longer but a twelve-year-old child, she took it and bit into it. I cut off a very small piece from the other half and handed it, with the knife, to Alasdair.

'I could put that in my eye and not feel it!' he said.

'And I could stick that old knife in my eye and not feel it,' I replied, and then added in the voice of my grandmother: 'Have you no manners? Say Thank you!'

' 'Snot worth it,' he replied, crunching up the piece of

27

apple. 'Look at the big bit you gave *her*!'

'Her is the cat's granny! That girl's name is Flora, Alasdair Mackay!' I said, still in my grandmother's voice, and Flora went away, slowly savouring and chewing her piece of apple, across the playground to rejoin the Top Class people of her own age.

'Suckin' up to the Big Ones, that's all!' Alasdair said.

'Oh, poop!' I said, leaving him and walking away, eating the remains of my apple.

Neither Alasdair Mackay nor anyone else, I thought, would ever know what a great service Flora Bedamned had rendered me, and my family had always told me that you must never forget anyone who had ever helped you in any way. I would not, I promised myself, as the bell rang for the last period of the school day, ever forget what Flora Bedamned had done to help me in my hour of great need.

As school became an everyday experience, however, and I dropped into my place in its routine, I saw very little of Flora and thought about her even less. Just as the old-established public schools have their traditions and customs as to the angle at which the straw hat is worn, the coat buttons that are buttoned or left undone and the umbrella carried furled or unfurled, Achcraggan School had its traditions and customs too and they were rigidly observed. We 'wee ones of the Baby Class' never entered the corner of the playground that was the preserve of the 'big ones in the Top Class' unless we were specifically asked there to add the interest of our numbers to some particular game, usually a singing game in the case of the girls. I loved the singing games, with the big ring that went round to:

'The farmer wants a wife, the farmer wants a wife,
Heigho, my daddy, oh! The farmer wants a wife!'

but very early I learned to dislike the other type of game that we of the Baby Class were called upon to join. This was a pretending game called 'Families' and the big girls would be the mothers and Elsie and I were supposed to be their

28

children, and they would bustle about, housekeeping, and then go visiting to the 'houses' of each other in different corners of their playground reserve. Flora was very fond of this game but, in spite of my memory of my indebtedness to her, after about three times of being her 'wee girl' and being told to do this and that and then being taken by the hand to go visiting with her, I formed the habit of taking myself round to the swing in the school garden as soon as a game of 'Families' loomed on the horizon and failing to hear the calling of my name. I did not like that sort of pretending. For me, there were only real families, *proper* families, like my own family and Flora's own family, and it seemed to me that for her to pretend to be my mother was simply ridiculous, undignified and unfitting. She was Flora Smith, a 'proper' person in her own right, and it was merely silly to pretend, even for fun, that she was anyone else.

So I saw very little of Flora and gave her very little thought, for school had opened up so many new, unexpected avenues of exploration in a physical as well as in a mental sense. Before I was big enough to go to school, I had not been allowed, in theory, to leave the ground of Reachfar unless I was in the company of one of my family, and although I had transgressed this law on a few occasions, as on the day I brought myself to school and attended the singing lesson, I had found, in the main, enough to occupy me within the boundaries of Reachfar. Now, though, I was licensed as it were for the three and three-quarter miles between Reachfar and Achcraggan and there was an infinite diversity of routes between these two points. I did not ever go to and come from school by the same route – indeed, very often I did not travel by precisely the same route twice in a fortnight. I could walk due east from Reachfar, over the sheep track through the East Moor, past Granny Fraser's little croft, past John-the-Smith's smoky cavern, down the rough road to the shore at Bedamned's Corner and then east along the County Road to Achcraggan. In the afternoon, I could

29

walk west on the County Road to Bedamned's Corner and from there take a long, south-westerly slant through the fields to emerge at Poyntdale Farm steading and, from there, due south, up the hill, to Reachfar. And, several times, while the warm harvest weather was still on, I walked west along the County Road after school to the 'bridgie' under which the Reachfar Burn flowed into the sea. At this point, I sat on the parapet, took off my shoes and socks, put them in my satchel and went down on to the beach to step into the water of the burn. Then, into the dark cave under the road I went, out on the upper side where the burn formed a boundary between two fields and I could paddle all the way up to the source at the spring on Reachfar ground, coming out of the water only at the point where the stream was dammed above the Poyntdale sawmill. This was the most magnificent way home of all, but only a 'way home' of course, never a 'way out' because, in spite of taking the greatest care, there was a tendency for the skirt to get wet, the hair ribbons to get caught in an overhanging bramble frond, not to mention the ever-present risk of misjudging the security of a boulder and falling in altogether, to emerge soaked to the skin and very bedraggled.

I think it was during my second week at school that I fell into the burn completely for the first time since I became emancipated from the Reachfar boundaries and had a very severe scolding from my mother when I arrived home. Around Reachfar, it was my grandmother who, normally, did most of the scolding, for my mother was very quiet and gentle and knew well that when she said: 'Oh, Janet, *why* did you do a thing like that?' and looked at me sadly out of her big soft eyes, it had far more effect on me than all my grandmother's wrath. But, this time, when I came home all wet and confessed that I had paddled all the way up the burn from the shore, my mother set upon me in a dreadful way. Her big eyes became bigger and bigger and grew darker and darker and her white face became whiter and the fine bones of it, that made you

30

think of the teacups from Dresden in the cabinet in Lady Lydia's sitting-room at Poyntdale House, seemed to stand out through the skin and she said: '*Janet* Sandison! How dare you come home like this and say you were wading up that dangerous burn! Past that horrible mill and dam! Have you no more thought for your family than to do a thing like that?. . .' And she went on and on and she was shaking, her long white fingers clutching the wet jersey that she had just skinned off over my head and I could not bear it and I ran away, out to the barn and burrowed into the straw with my dog Fly and cried and cried until Tom came and found me.

'Come now, pettie! Wheesht now, for Tom. Come, dry your face and come in for your supper.'

'No! No!'

'Come now. You'll not be able to walk to school if you don't eat your supper.'

'I'm not hungry. It's Mother! She's wild-angry at me and I *can't* come in when she's as wild-angry as that!'

'Now, now, she's not wild-angry any more. Indeed, it's myself that is thinking that she was never wild-angry whateffer. It's more that she got a fright with you.'

'A fright? Why?'

'She hadna thought on you being near that danged mill dam, ye see, pettie. That's a damnable dangerous place, ye know. There's plenty people been drowned in it – big grown-up people – not chust bairns.'

'But I *wasn't* near it, Tom! I came by the little burnie round the side and I wasn't near the dam or the mill or anything! I *wouldn't* go near them, Tom! I don't *like* them!'

'Then chust you come in and be telling your mother that, there's a lass. Here, maybe there's a few cleaner handkies in the world than this one o' mine but I'm not seeing them about here so this one will have to do. Spit a bittie on this corner till I clean your face. That's better. Come now.'

With my face smelling comfortably of Tom's tobacco-

31

flavoured handkerchief and with Tom himself behind me, I went into the kitchen and over to the chair beside the fire where my mother was sitting. I laid my hand on her knee.

'Mother, I wasn't near the dam. I never go near it because I don't like it and I'm frightened of the noise the sawmill makes. And I'm sorry I got my clothes wet, but it was only at the front because there was hardly any water at the place where I fell,' and then, looking at her, I hiccuped out another sob.

All my family was there, my grandparents, my father and my aunt, listening, Tom and George watching intently, but in a queer way the room seemed to hold only my mother and me and looking into her big eyes was like floating on warm water.

'I was not cross about the wet clothes,' she said in her quiet, gentle voice. 'You have other clothes. But you will try to be more careful another time?'

'Yes, Mother.'

'And if ever you should think of going near the dam, I want you to try to remember about tonight. Then you will never, never go to the dam. You will never, never go, will you?'

'Never, Mother.'

'That's a good girl.' She patted my hand that lay on her knee. 'Go and put on your old jersey and then we'll all have our supper.'

At supper, round the big table in the autumn evening light, with the big black iron kettle singing its song beside the bright fire, in my place on the 'bairns' side' of the table between George and Tom, I was still subdued and listened to the grown-up talk around me.

'Do you happen to know where Jamie Bedamned is working o' the now, Duncan?' George asked my father as my aunt collected the porridge plates into a pile and prepared to serve the fried haddocks.

'No-o,' my father said thoughtfully. 'I haven't been seeing him since a month, now that I think on it . . . Did you want him, George?'

32

'Mac is thinking on building a couple of loose-boxes,' George said.

'Mac', I knew was Mr Macintosh of Dinchory, our neighbour to the west, whom George served as grieve or farm manager, just as my father served Sir Torquil Daviot at Poyntdale, and George continued: 'God knows we could do with them. Since we broke in that new bit of moor ground and got the extra pair of horse and knocked up yon two extra stalls at the end of the stable, a body canna get moving in it. And the rows among the men are something fearful. Young Farquhar was taking down his harness this morning and knocked one o' ould Willie's saddles down into the drain among the dung and it's a wonder you didna hear Willie swearing down at Poyntdale.'

I could imagine, vividly, the scene in the stable at Dinchory that early morning. Old Willie, who drove the first Dinchory pair, was one of the crack ploughmen of the countryside and his harness was kept in such a way that Tom and I had a devil of a job every year to beat him for 'Best Dressed Pair' with our Dick and Betsy at the Poyntdale Show. In fact, Tom said, we would *not* have beaten him last year except that our Betsy was 'an exceptional bonnie mare that made the harness look even better than it was'. And Tom laughed now, in a malicious way, at the thought of one of Willie's treasured saddles landing among the dung.

'Aye, poor Willie – him an' his fancy harness!' he said.

But my father took a more serious view. 'Ach, it's a devil of job if your stable's not in order!' he said.

'Well, mine is like Bella Skinner's back kitchen,' said George, which made everybody laugh, for we all knew that no matter how far below George's standards the Dinchory stable might fall, it could not possibly be as messy and dirty as Bella Skinner's disorderly back kitchen.

'No-o,' my father said again thoughtfully. 'I don't know where Jamie Bedamned is working o' the now at a-all.'

'*I* know, Dad,' I ventured, speaking for the first time,

33

for my scolding and its aftermath had bound me into an unusual silence.

'*Do* ye though, Janet?' asked Tom, encouraging me, for Tom and George always took any disgrace of mine very much unto themselves. 'Was you seeing him then?'

'Yes. Every day, Tom. He's been working on the bridgies on the County Road ever since the day I went to school. He started at the east one and now he's right west at the one at the bottom of the Poyntdale House avenue.'

'Then he'll be done o' *that* job!' my father said. 'He meets Ferguson, the Ballintreach parish mason, at that bridgie – that's their boundary. Dang it, George, if you'd mentioned this last night, Janet could have caught him this morning for you.'

'You'll never be knowing where a Bedamned will be off to next,' Tom said. 'They are for ever prowling away on their lone and never speaking to nobody.'

'Surely, Duncan,' my mother said quietly, 'if you were to write a letter to him, Janet could leave it at the house when she is passing?'

There was a moment of wondering silence, before George, with his big smile, said: 'Well, now, it's myself that doesn't know what we'd do in this house if the odd one of us didn't have a puckle brains! . . . You hear that, Janet? You will be carrying a letter for us, just as if you was Bill-the-Post?'

'Och, surely,' I said importantly. 'I'll carry it in my school bag.'

'That will be the very thing,' my father said. 'George will write it after supper.'

'Well, now,' said George, 'I don't think my writer is in very good order this evening.'

'*Your* writer is never in good order!' said my aunt. 'You'd think you'd never been to school. *Can* you write?'

'Och, yes, if very sore provoked,' he told her and turned to my father. '*You* write the letter, Dunk – just tell Bedamned to call at Dinchory as soon as he can – and I might give your gun a bit clean for you.'

34

'All right,' my father said, smiling. 'And when I'm at it I might as well tell him to come to Poyntdale when he is done with yourself, George. Sir Torquil has made up his mind to extend the sawmill.'

'Oh?'

My father sighed. 'The big west beech wood will have to come down, he says. It's the war. They're shouting like the devil for hardwood.'

'What does the Laird say of the war, Duncan?' asked my grandfather, who very seldom spoke.

My father sighed again. 'He thinks it's more likely to take another five years than one,' he said.

A cloud of silence seemed to settle down over the table, as it always did when this thing called 'the war' was mentioned.

'Maybe,' George said, 'it is with the Seaforths that a body should be instead of skittering about in the Dinchory stable like an ould wife at her fireside.'

My grandmother, in her place at the end of the table, rose to her feet, went to the fireplace and picked up the teapot. Nobody moved. With the bright fire behind her, tall and stately, she levelled her defiant west Highland glance upon us all and then her eyes fixed themselves on George, her second and – I think – favourite son.

'You know what Sir Torquil and the Army chentlemen said,' she told him firmly, 'that one or two able farming men was to stop here and keep the crops going and they picked you and Duncan as two o' them that was to stop—'

With her back to the wall of her own fireside, as it were – standing before the symbol of home and family – she was, in reality, a peasant woman defending her young from slaughter.

'So let me hear no more of your idle, discontented blethering, George.' She came to the table and began to pour out second cups of tea for us all.

'If what Sir Torquil and his Army friends say is right,' said my father, easing the tension, 'we may get more than the land and the crops to keep us going. They say that this

35

is one of the places that the Chermans might pick on if they thought of making a landing.'

'Where?' said George, with a crackle as of fire in his voice.

'Achcraggan,' my father said. 'It's a flat, sandy beach and this is good fertile country – just what an army likes to advance over.'

As if operated on some dual-control swivel, the heads of George and Tom turned to the left and I saw that their eyes were raised to the four racks above the dresser where the four well-oiled, double-barrelled guns rested, gleaming in the firelight against the white-washed wall. There was a moment of silence while we all looked up at the racks, and then came Tom's voice: 'By God, it iss myself that would have a fine time of it at that back window there if them Cherman booggers wass to make a try at crossing Reachfar hill!'

'Oh, no, you wouldn't, Tom,' my father said. 'The Laird is getting the plans all ready. You and Granda and the women folk and Janet will have to drive the cattle before you, right west into the hills, when the alarm goes. Only the younger men will be allowed to stop here.'

'The younger men my backside!' said Tom. 'If it came to a good fight, Granda an' me wouldna see you among our feet! When this alarm goes off, you an' George will chust go down to Achcraggan an' halt them Chermans at the pier in the proper way an' Granda an' I will come behind an' stop any odd ones that happens to get by you. Where would we go gallivanting the red cow away over Dinchory Moor an' her within a month o' the calving? Have you an' Sir Torquil lost your brains out o' your heads an' into your asses?'

'Tom, that will do!' said my grandmother sternly.

'Tom is quite right,' my grandfather said, smoothing his long white beard with his gnarled old hand: 'There will be no driving of our cattle into the hills of Wester Ross as long as I am in it. Now, be done of your blethers, the lot of you. Come to the fire and take a smoke, Tom.'

36

My aunt, who was young and gay and many of whose contemporaries were already dead, with the Seaforth tartan of their kilts rotting in the mud of Flanders, hated talk of the war and she sprang willingly to her feet and began to clear the table, carrying the dishes through to the scullery, the only room in the house that had a window to the cold and stormy north. In a minute she was back, whispering: 'Tom, I put that hen with the late chickens round the back as you said and they're *there, two* of them!'

'Hoodie crows?' Tom said, and she nodded.

Tom and George reached for their guns and the three of us went through to the little window, a single pane of glass that opened like a little door in the three-foot-thick wall. Silently, I laid my hand on the well-oiled catch, my eyes on the two big birds with the sinister grey-feathered hoods over their heads and backs that sat, silent and menacing, on the tops of two fencing posts on either side of the little wooden chicken coop.

'Canny, Janet,' George breathed. 'I'll take the east one, Tom.'

Silently, on either side of me, the barrels of the guns slid forward like stiff straight snakes over the broad sill and, practised at this game, when the muzzles reached a certain point, I flicked the glass panel open. In the same second, with a report that, in the small room, seemed to raise the roof of the whole house, a cartridge left each gun and the two hoodie crows fell in sudden death to the grass.

'Them booggerin' Chermans wouldna have a bliddy chance!' said Tom, as I closed the window. 'Janet, go out and throw them dirty murderin' booggers in the midden.'

When I came back from disposing of the corpses, Tom and George had cleaned their guns and were putting them back in the rack and my father, at the table, was sealing the envelope of his letter.

'Mrs Smith must be pretty near her time, Granny,' my mother was saying.

'About the middle o' November, the doctor told me,' my grandmother replied.

Doctor Mackay valued her greatly as a midwife and she attended all the difficult births in the district, but at this time I knew only that the family at Bedamned's Corner was one of those whose babies my grandmother helped to get born.

'To be right, she shouldna be having this one at— Oh, there you are, Janet! Did you put a good big divot on the top o' those hoodies? If not, we'll be driven from the place with stink.'

'Yes, Granny. I put two big ones on each of them.'

'That's right. Go ben and wash your hands then.'

The shooting of the hoodie crows had been an unexpected treat, for the day for me was nearly over, and, having washed my hands, I came back from the scullery with the box that held the shoe-cleaning materials and sat down on my little wooden stool.

'All right,' said Tom, 'we'll put a right shine on that school shoes of yours the-night with you to be a postman tomorrow and a-all.'

'I've put the letter in the little front bittie of your bag, Janet,' my mother said, 'and you will just knock at the door, say good morning to Mrs Smith and tell her that this is a letter to Mr Smith from your father. You will do that?'

'Yes, Mother.'

'That's right.'

'The oldest Bedamned girl must be getting quite big now,' my aunt said, coming out of the scullery to put the washed dishes away in the big dresser. 'What's her name again?'

'Flora,' I said, 'and she's twelve. But she's not very *big* big – she's not much bigger than me. But she's *old* big.'

My aunt laughed her gay, musical laugh. 'What's the difference between big-big and old-big?' she asked.

I was puzzled. I could not think of words that would describe this, to me, so obvious difference.

'What is Auntie Kate then?' my mother asked.

I looked at my pretty aunt who was not yet twenty, dark and wavy of hair, dark and brilliant of eye, cream of skin and deep red of lip.

'She is big-big but not old-big,' I replied.

'And Tom?'

'Big-big but not old-big.'

My aunt laughed again. 'And your father?' she asked.

'Oh, he is both big-big and old-big,' I replied.

'And me?' said George, bending his head at the top of his six-foot-two to come through the doorway from the scullery to the kitchen, drying his hands on the scullery towel. 'I am wee-wee and young-wee – indeed, it's a little fairy that I am!' And with this he made a flying arabesque across the kitchen in his size eleven tackety boots, his towel flying overhead like a banner, to land with a clatter in front of my aunt and chuck her impishly under the chin.

'Och, George Sandison!' said my grandmother. 'For the love of goodness' *sake*, stop your clowning! So Flora is not very big for her age, Janet?'

'I don't think so, Granny.'

'I thought when she was a baby she would go to the mother's side. The Smiths were all big dark people, but among the Macleods of Varlich the women were all little and reddish o' the hair. She'll be a bonnie lassie, though?'

'Yes, Granny. Her eyes are blue and her hair curls a little and she's a very kind sort of person.'

'She's a Macleod right enough,' my grandmother asserted.

'She is not a bit like her father, Granny.'

'No?'

'No. Her father never speaks at all. Flora speaks a lot.'

'You and Flora should get on fine then, Janet,' said Tom.

My grandmother smiled. 'Speaking is not everything. Mr Smith is a fine craftsman.'

'An' ould Jamie Bedamned, his father, was chust the same,' said Tom, putting a high shine on the toe-caps of the shoes which I had been blacking. 'Never a word to say and a big black curlywhisker on him that would frighten a billy-goat, but as bonnie a craftsman as ever I saw . . . George, put off that clarty Dinchory boots o' yours. Janet

39

an' me chust has got time before she goes to bed to clean your boots and mine for the morning.'

About half-past eight the next morning, I knocked at the door of the tidy little house at Bedamned's Corner and when Mrs Smith came to open it, I said as I had been told:

'Good morning, Mrs Smith. This letter is for Mr Smith, please, from my father, Sandison, Reachfar.'

'Good morning! And you are Janet? Well, what a big girl! And going to school? Come in, now, and get a scone. You have plenty of time.'

This was quite the normal procedure when delivering a message in our district and I went behind her into the kitchen – smaller than ours – but just as orderly and prepared for the busy day, the fire burning brightly, the breakfast dishes already stacked on a side table, a two-year-old boy penned into a corner behind some white, scrubbed chairs, playing with some empty cotton reels strung on a string, and Flora combing with a wet comb the thick black hair of her brother Roderick who was in my class at school.

As Mrs Smith, at the dresser, spread a scone lavishly with butter and rhubarb jam, I smiled at all the children and looked about me. Yes. Her 'time' was not far off, I could see, for she had the heavy look that Betsy our mare had shortly before her foals came, but this woman had not the magnificent shining strength of Betsy. She was short – very little taller than her daughter Flora – small of bone and narrow of shoulder, so that her swollen burden seemed to pull her forward and down and to make every movement an effort of will. When she handed the scone to me, I thanked her and had an uprush of relief when she sank down into a chair beside the fire. I felt that had she remained standing, my throat muscles would have been too weak out of infectious sympathy for her to swallow the delicious mouthfuls.

As she talked, asking after the health of my mother, as everyone always did, and whether we had all our corn in

40

yet up at Reachfar, I replied to her questions, and between times I studied the dresser. I liked to study the dressers in people's kitchens, for no two were alike. Ours, in the Reachfar kitchen, was very big and of white scrubbed wood and very plain, with three shelves on its back where the plates stood in piles of different sizes, and rows of hooks on the edges of the shelves where the cups and small jugs hung. Then, on the flat top of the lower, cupboard part, there were, upside-down, piles of bowls of different sizes, and no two bowls were alike, for my grandmother got them from Hamish the Tinker, when he came around, in exchange for rabbit skins. Then, inside the cupboards in the bottom part were the great big mixing bowl – yellow outside and white within – a pile of ashets of all different sizes, a pile of pie-dishes of all different sizes, and the second-best tea-set, which was there to be handy for when visitors came, for the everyday cups, up on the hooks, were no-two-alike, rabbit-skin exchanges like the bowls.

Ours was a 'working dresser', as I described it in my mind, but Mrs Smith's belonged to the school of what I called 'bonnie' dressers. *Her* dresser was smaller than ours, painted bright blue, and had its two shelves on its back overlaid with paper that had a lace border that hung down over the shelf edges in dainty scallops. On the shelves, too, were 'bonnie' things, such as a china biscuit barrel with pansies painted on it, a glass vase with dingle-dangle things hanging from its rim and a pair of vases, urn-shaped, very narrow in the neck, with 'A Present from Aberdeen' written on their bellies in gold. Automatically I looked at the corner of the room beside the fireplace. Yes. There was the cupboard – the plates that were used every day were kept in there.

Although 'bonnie', the Smith dresser was not, however, in what I termed the 'fancy' class. I approved, on the whole, of the Smith dresser although preferring the Reachfar type, but I did not approve of 'fancy' dressers. Fancy dressers were the type owned by people who did not really need a dresser in their houses at all, but who felt that

41

they must have dressers because other people had dressers, I had long since decided. Mrs Gilchrist, the owner of the Drapery and General Warehouse in Achcraggan, was a typical fancy-dresser owner. She and her one daughter Annie lived quite alone in a funny sort of house above the Drapery and General Warehouse and they seemed to subsist entirely on cups of tea and baker's buns in a funny sort of room that had an aspidistra plant and a whatnot like a parlour, a big brass bed like a bedroom, a sink like a scullery and a big black range like a kitchen, and this room also had the fancy dresser. This dresser was made of a dark, shiny wood, something, but not quite, like our mahogany parlour table; and when I questioned Tom about it, he said it was not mahogany but a wood which, in the voice he used for things which he called 'cheap trock', he called 'varnished deal'. Anyhow, it was very, very hard-bright and shiny and carved all over itself, with rows of wooden holes hanging down from the edges of its shelves and holes shaped something like ferns in its cupboard doors that had red pleated silk behind that you could see through the holes. On its shelves you never in your born days saw the like of what it had. It had a picture of Queen Victoria looking very cross in a purple plush frame, and one of John Knox looking even crosser, almost jumping out of his pulpit and out of his sober frame of black plush. Then it had three shoes made of china, a shoe made of silver with a blue velvet pincushion sticking up out of it, another shoe made of clay stuff with two pink china kittens looking out of it, then a silver horseshoe that was small enough to go in our Dick's ear, and very silly-looking, with 'Good Luck' written across it in metal letters, and various other things that were all either shoes or kittens. I questioned Tom about all these shoes, too, one day after he and I had been up there and he said: 'Ach, I suppose they will be shoes that ould Teenie will be buying whiles that didna fit her, for she's terrible bad with corns an' bunions, so she chust put them on the dresser.' That, of course, was some of Tom's nonsense that merely meant

42

that he could not explain about the shoes any more than I could. All in all, though, it was a terribly fancy dresser and I could not abide it . . .

When I had finished my scone, Flora and her three brothers were ready to leave for school, so we all left the house together, saying 'Ta-ta!' to the little one called Hughie, who was still penned in behind his chairs, banging away contentedly with his cotton-reels. I remember thinking, away back inside my head as we walked along, that I was not very sure if I would like to have a lot of brothers like Flora if having them made your mother look so tired. It was not nice when your mother was tired. My own mother got very tired far more easily than I or the rest of my family did, and somehow, when she was tired and had a headache, the house was less happy, and of course my grandmother's temper became very short, so that George, Tom and I were scared into silence and afraid to open our mouths.

'The bonnie one is lying down!' my grandmother would say to us in a low, vibrant voice, fixing us with fierce, protective eyes. 'Stop clumping about like a lot of unbroken colts!'

'The bonnie one' or 'Ealasaidh Dhu' or 'Dark Elizabeth' or 'Her with the eyes of a deer', who seldom asserted herself, never argued and spoke nearly always in a gentle, questioning voice, determined the atmosphere that prevailed in the house of Reachfar. The old stronghold of the Sandisons had fallen completely, in 1908, before the soft-eyed stranger that my father had brought within the gates . . .

'Mr Macintosh of Dinchory wants your father to build two new loose-boxes for him,' I told Flora as we walked along.

'Does he?' she said, but I could see that she was not at all interested.

'Has your father finished with the bridgies now?' I asked.

'The bridgies?'

'Yes – he was mending them.'

43

'Was he?'

We pursued our way in silence. Maybe, I suggested to myself, being one of the Top Class, Flora did not want to be bothered with a Baby Class person like me talking to her, but I did not really think that this was true. Flora liked to talk and she began to tell me about a new Sunday dress that Mary Mathieson-the-Shepherd had got. I half-listened only and went on thinking how queer it was that Flora did not seem to care where her father worked or what he did. I was always very interested in what my father and George were doing, for I was proud of their positions as grieves; and although I knew that I must not brag or have a 'big boasting mouth' about anything, I also knew that when people asked me: 'Is Poyntdale at the harvest yet?' I ought to be in a position to say: 'No, but my father says that they will be cutting the roads first week', or some business-like thing of that sort. In our family everybody took part in everything, like Tom and George, on Sunday afternoons, when the rest of the family went to Sunday sleep, having a run through my school reading book.

George, reading the way we had to do it in school, was enough to make a cat laugh. Alasdair Mackay and I, you see, had been able to read before we went to school, but Miss Inglis, who knew everything and what to do about everything, was prepared for people like us; so while Tommy Clarty struggled with the cat and the mat, Alasdair and I were each given a beautiful, different, much more grown-up book. Mine had in it, among others, the story of the Three Bears and I taught Tom and George to read properly. Tom could do it in a way that would have made Miss Inglis say: 'That was very nice, Tom', but I could not think what she might say to George, who started off, very loudly: 'THE THREE BEARS', and, then, in a smaller voice, read on: 'Once upon a time there were three bears take-a-breath a big bear longish pause a middle-sized bear short pause and a very small bear stop and take a breath these bears . . .' If I told him once, I told him a hundred times that you must say the things like 'take a breath' and 'short pause' in to yourself and not aloud, but he never could remember and then, bless my soul, if I did not discover that he thought the 'pause' was 'paws' so that the longish pause was the paws of the big bear and the short pause the paws of the middle-sized bear.

'And what, then, about the *wee* bear, you stupid clown?' Tom asked.

'I thought *it* was so wee it had no paws at a-all!' said George.

You were never sure, half the time, with my Uncle George as to whether he was taking a rise out of you or not, but somehow we came to accept the fact, in spite of our explanations to him, that when it came his turn to read from my book he would start off: 'Cinderella once upon a time short pause . . .' and that henceforth this would always be his way of reading aloud.

'What are you going to be when you are – when you are done of school?' I asked Flora now.

I had been going to say 'when you are big', but I had a feeling that Flora felt that she was big already and I did not wish to be tactless.

'A dressmaker,' said Flora.

This silenced me. In my family I had never heard of anyone wanting to be a dressmaker. Dressmaking was something that you did in the winter evenings when you had plenty of time, and my Aunt Kate and my mother would spread on the kitchen table the beautiful pink silk from Mrs Gilchrist's Drapery and General Warehouse and cut out a new dance dress for my aunt, who would take the top off the sewing machine and sew up the long seams while I, if I was very careful and had very clean hands, would be allowed to help my mother to gather its flounces with very small stitches. I had never heard of anyone going to be a dressmaker any more than I had heard of people going to be scone-bakers or cow-milkers. These were things that came to you naturally, like your finger-nails growing, and if that was all you wanted to do there seemed to me to be no point in going to school at all.

'But you like *school*, though, Flora?' I questioned her anxiously.

'No. Not very much,' she said.

This was odder than ever. These Bedamneds could not be a proper family like mine after all, even if they did keep an orderly house.

'But Miss Inglis said you were a good worker in school,' I told her.

'Oh, you have to *work*,' said Flora. 'Everybody has to *work*!' And then we were at the school gates.

Coming home that afternoon, on a long, south-westerly slant as a crow would fly from Achcraggan to Reachfar, by a series of field boundaries and field paths which had little bridges across all the burns that were so tempting but earned me such scoldings, I gave some more thought to Flora Bedamned. Indeed, I think I thought about her and her family and her home quite a lot during the next few days. I think that this was my earliest realization that there were home disciplines other than the Reachfar discipline; that all families were not like mine. The more I thought about it, the more the subject widened until its ramifications became terrifying, which sent me back into my short-past experience to try to find something that remained unaffected by this great new light of knowledge. All that this led to was the discovery that I had always known, but had disregarded the knowledge, that the Skinner family, with its quarrelsome, drunken father and mother and their messy house and yard, was different from mine; that Mrs Gilchrist and her daughter, with their malicious tongues and their fancy dresser, were different from my family; and that Sir Torquil Daviot and Lady Lydia at Poyntdale House, with their children who went away to schools – boarding schools and public schools they were called, although not public at all, where the children slept and had their food and everything – down in England, were actually a family too, although so unlike my family that I had not hitherto thought of the Laird's household as a family at all. And all these families

46

were different from each other as well as being different from mine, so which of them were 'proper' families? They could not *all* be wrong and, with utter certainty, the Sandisons of Reachfar could not possibly, at all, in any way whatsoever, be wrong. It was all very puzzling. It was better to concentrate on the smaller differences among people.

'Tom,' I said in the barn on Saturday evening when he and I were cleaning and oiling the reaper knives to put them away until next harvest, 'did you ever in all your born days hear of anybody that didn't like school?'

'Och, aye,' Tom said, 'plenty o' them. To tell you the truth, I was not that terrible fond of it myself.'

If it had not been Tom who spoke I would have been shocked into silence; but if Tom had not been that terrible fond of school, I was certain that such a failing could not be really sinful.

'Why not, Tom?' I asked.

'Och, it kept a body in the house too much,' he said. 'I can mind on sitting down yonder in the Dominie's room at the school – not Dominie Stevenson, of coorse. It was Dominie Gregor, then, that was that fond o' the Bible that it's a minister he should have been I am thinking. And we would be sitting yonder and it a fine spring day and the Poyntdale and Seamuir men out at the sowing and the sun shining and the first yellow bloom on the whins and the Dominie laying off like to split himself aboot the devil being thrown out o' Heaven by this mannie Milton.'

'Tom Reachfar! That's a pack of lies! The devil was never in Heaven!'

'Oh, but he was *so* in Heaven in the first of it! *Paradise Lost* the poetry is called, because o' the devil getting thrown out and losing Heaven, ye see. Och, aye, when you get up into Dominie Stevenson's room you'll be hearing about it likely . . . Chust hand me the oilcan for a meenute, there's a dirty sticky bittie on this blade . . . But to hear ould Dominie Gregor droning away at it was chust as good as a sermon, although very tedious on a fine

47

spring day and you only a young loon. He was a terrible man for all the droning, angry kind o' poetry, I mind, and none o' them cheery, lilting bitties like you will be teaching to me and George. He had another one – aye, I mind on it yet.'

Tom rose from his seat on the corn kist, the long reaper knife held, one end on the floor, the other end about level with his shoulder, and the evening sun struck the sharp edges of the big teeth of the knife as he declaimed sonorously:

> 'So a-all day long the noise of battle rolled
> Among the mountains by the winter sea;
> Until King Arthur's table, man by man,
> Had fall'n in Lyonnesse about their Lord.

Ay – let me think now . . .

> A bro-oken chancel with a bro-oken cross,
> That stood on a dark strait of barren land.
> On one side lay the Ocean, and on one
> Lay a great water, and the moon was full—'

Tom sat down and resumed work with his oily rag. 'That's the bitties of it that I mind on. On a good spring day, when the men was at the sowing and we had to stand up and say that, one after the other, about poor King Arthur an' this sad, cold place with the broken cross an' it barren an' not fertile at a-all like about here, I used to be wishing that it was ould Dominie Gregor himself that had been killed in the battle. No. I wouldna say that I was that terrible fond o' school myself, but why was you asking?'

'I was just asking.'

'I see.' He held the knife like a gun, teeth upwards, closed an eye, sighted along it and then laid it aside. 'You wouldn't be getting tired of the school yourself, though?'

'Oh no, Tom!'

'That's fine. Ye see, it's different for a lassie. If she'll not have schooling, there's no chob much she can go to but service, an' some o' the leddies is not like Leddy Lydia

48

an' their servant lassies hasn't the lives of dogs.'

'Maybe somebody that didn't like school could be a dressmaker – or something, Tom?'

'A dressmaker? It's not *me* that would care for a chobbie like that!' He rose to put the knife in its storage place on the high rafters and laid it down on the corn kist while he fetched the high ladder. In the middle of the barn floor he struck a preening attitude. 'An' all the fancy leddies saying: "Chust a little tighter *here*, Miss Sandison, an' chust a little lower *there*, Miss Sandison", and making you pick back a-all your work and finding fault with it. No. I wouldna be bothered with the like o' that.'

'No, nor me either, Tom.'

'I would chust think not! A person needs a *right* chob, like working the good ground with a fine pair o' horse and seeing the corn come into brear or the like o' that. And if you are a lassie, look at the things you can be doing like that friend o' Leddy Lydia's that's a lady doctor with the soldiers at the war! Mind you, there's a lot of schooling in being a doctor. But apart and not takin' into account at a-all the chob you will be doing when your schooling is over, the schooling itself is a fine thing. I am pleased now myself, after all, that I stayed with old Dominie Gregor long enough to be able to read and write and count and not be what they will be calling illiterate, like some people.'

'What is illiterate, Tom?'

'Not being able to write your name and having to make a markie like a cross no better than the big cockerel could do with his claws in the midden. And reading is a fine thing too – you would hardly believe the wonderful things a person will be learning chust from reading and very inter-*est*ing things, too, forbye, like this old chentleman, Lionardo da Vinsy in Italy long ago that I was reading about in the encyclopaedja the other night.'

'Who was Lion – what you said, Tom?'

'He was an old scholar sort of chentleman an' could do a bittie at the pentin' and the stone-carvin' and the science and, indeed, a bittie of chust nearly anything as far as I could make out, but I will tell you what I think is so interesting about him. You mind on yon flying machine that went over here when we were at the hay and Dick bolted and broke the pole o' the mower?'

'Yes, Tom.'

'Well, according to a-all I was reading in the papers and people was telling me, them flying machines was new contraptions. Well, that's a pack o' lies. Lion-ardo da Vinsy invented a flying machine away in Italy hundreds of years ago . . . Mind you, that chust shows you that a person can read *lies* too, especially in the newspapers. A paper that comes out every week with new stuff for reading in it is bound to have some lies in it because it is myself that is thinking that there is not enough new stuff in the whole wide world to fill a whole newspaper every week.' My uncle George came into the barn, sat down on the corn kist and began to fill his pipe. 'Well, George, so it is yourself home then. We was chust talking about schooling and education in cheneral. Can you mind anything you was learning at school? Spell "barrow" for me, now!'

'B-O-X, barrow!' said George smartly, which was an old joke that always made us laugh.

'If you was a lassie, George,' Tom continued, 'would you ever think of having a chob like being a dressmaker?'

'Not me!' said George firmly. 'I have no law myself for chobs that do not lead to anything. Where is the use of spending a lot of time in making a bonnie dress that some rich leddy will tire of in a week? I would rather grow a fine puckle tatties an' then watch the old sow eating them . . . Of course, I suppose *some* people have to be dressmakers, them that's not fit to be anything better,' he conceded.

'Then for me, them that wants to be dressmakers can do it,' said Tom. 'A person always does best the things they like to do.'

'But *some* people,' said my grandmother at the door of the barn, 'don't care to be doing anything very much in the way of work! It is half-past five and a Saturday evening and I'm not seeing the Sunday sticks in the woodshed yet!'

50

'We was chust going to be seeing about them, Mistress,' said Tom.

'Iphm. If you three worked more and talked less this would be a better place,' she said and stalked away along the yard.

'Why do people have to work?' I enquired of my friends, for this was another point that Flora Bedamned had raised.

'We-ell, a body has to make a living,' said George.

'But some people work at things that *don't* make a living!' I said, thinking of Flora and school. 'Why do they?'

'Och, that's the ones that's chust made a danged bad habit of it,' said Tom.

'That's right,' George agreed. 'There's some that makes such a habit o' working that they canna stop even when they try. Now, there's no danger of *me* getting like that. Ye know, Tom, I often think it would be chust fine to have enough money to be able chust to sit at the fire and take your smoke all day an' be able to have a dram now and again when it came over you an' never do a hand's turn o' work from morning till night.'

'Aye, maybe.' Tom was thoughtful. 'Mind you, though, I've noticed that if I have to sit for too long my backside gets sort of itchy.'

'Oh, but you could be going out for a bit walk when you was tired of the sitting.'

'Where to?' Tom asked. 'If you went down Poyntdale way the men would all be working and have no time for yarning.'

'Well, a body could give them a bit hand with the hoe or whatever they would be doing and have a bit yarn chust the same.'

'But then you would be *working*, George!' I said.

He began to scratch his head with the stem of his pipe and after a moment a gleam of inspiration came over his face. 'Aye, but *then* you would be working chust to *amuse* yourself!' he said.

A smart drum-tap of heels came along the yard towards the barn door.

'The Ould Leddy!' said Tom, and the three of us shot out through the back door of the straw barn and set to work on the Sunday sticks, not to amuse ourselves but to prevent my grandmother from being unamused.

I suppose that all children assimilate experience and acquire knowledge of their world in different ways, but when I remember myself as a five-year-old I always think of my mind at that time as being like a white bowl containing some clear water above a sediment of indeterminate colour which lay at the bottom. Any new idea which came to me was like a blob of coloured fluid being dropped into this water. At first, its colour very intense, it lay on the surface and then, gradually, it was invaded, dissipated, assimilated by the surrounding water until, a short period of time later, I would consciously remember the actual moment of experience, as when Flora said that she did not like school very much, and look into my mind for the coloured blob, only to find that it had disappeared. But although the coloured blob had gone, down in the sediment at the bottom were its dissolved elements, a little sum added to my knowledge of Flora, so that now, when I looked across at her playing in the Top Class section of the playground, a new feature was added to her. She did not like school and she wanted to be a dressmaker. Because I knew these things and because, in them, she was so different from myself, I found her by far the most interesting person among my colleagues. I thought that she was quite unique, having the firm conviction that I myself was the norm and that all the other pupils except Flora were like me. No other one among them, I was completely certain, had a dislike for school and wanted to be a dressmaker. Only Flora was as different, as interesting and as extraordinary as that.

I began to make a habit of waiting, in the mornings, at Bedamned's Corner till the children came out so that I might walk to school with Flora and I would walk back by the County Road with her in the evenings too. I cannot say that I was fond of her, and she irritated me in many ways, particularly with her tendency to take me by the hand and 'mother' me, but I was so interested in her difference from myself that I was magnetized towards her for several weeks, almost against my own will. But no more new and dramatic knowledge of her emerged. Indeed, she was rather dull by my standards, for she had no conversation that ranged from Leonardo da Vinci through the Old Testament prophets and tales of old worthies of our own countryside to the best feeding for a sow in farrow, which was the type of conversation on which my friends George and Tom had brought me up from my cradle days. However, my interest in Flora took me in around the Bedamned household a good deal, for I would always stay on in the afternoons until I was forced to leave to get home to Reachfar before dark and, because of this, I was there on the afternoon of the tragedy.

Like most of the houses in our district at that time, the Smith house had no laid-on water supply and the water was carried into the house in buckets from a spout of pipe that poked out of the hillside about fifty yards behind the house, to fall into the stream that flowed under the road to the sea. In the afternoons, when Flora, the boys and I came home from school, there was no question of our playing. All the Smith children had certain tasks to perform, and I helped Flora with hers, so on this evening we two went up the hill a little way, up the Smiths' little field, to untether the cow and move her to a fresh patch of pasture. From above we looked down on the little stream, the little pool in it which the pouring spout from the spring formed, the little white-washed house and outbuildings and the curling ribbon of the County Road beside the grey waters of the Firth. I saw Mrs Smith, walking slowly and heavily, come out of the house with a bucket in each hand and take the little upward path to the water-spout.

A few minutes later, when Flora and I had moved the cow and were coming back down to the house, we saw Mrs Smith lying, face downwards, her hair in the mud, at

53

the edge of the pool, and she was moaning, a terrible sound, a sound that seemed to be using every ounce of strength that was in her, weak and feeble a sound though it was.

'Oh, Mam!' Flora cried, running to her, kneeling down beside her and starting to cry.

As if I had taken root among the short green turf that bordered the stream, I stood staring, my mind momentarily stunned, and then, after a second or two, it was fleeing swift as an arrow and as straight, as it always did in frightening moments, home to Reachfar and the thought of my grandmother . . . I had never seen my grandmother make an uncontrolled action, and I have never seen a train of events that she could not control. . . . The arrow flight had taken my mind to the Reachfar kitchen and she was there, tall and straight, standing on the hearthrug with the fire behind her. What would she do? She would come – she would come to help Mrs Bedamned! With the speed of a mountain hare I was off, south-westerly across the face of the hill for Reachfar, but half way across the first field came the thought: 'Friday! Tom took her to Achcraggan today!' and, again like a hare, I turned in a rapid swerve and made off down the hill for the County Road. I do not think I had gone half a mile when I saw the trap coming towards me, the little trap mare spanking along, the purple bow in my grandmother's second-best hat nodding against the early October sky.

'Granny – Flora's mother – she fell at the spring – she's awful sick—'

'Pick Janet up, Tom, and get on to Bedamned's Corner,' said my grandmother.

I sat, panting, between them, and at the Smiths' house my grandmother said: 'Janet, jump down and hold the mare's head. Tom, come with me.'

All the Smith children were crying now – Flora and Jamie, the nine-year-old boy, up at the water-spout beside their mother, and the three younger boys in a little huddle by the door. The two-year-old Hughie, with his round, fat

54

face, would stop crying for a second, look at his bigger brothers and then begin to bellow again more loudly than ever. I felt that he did not know why he was crying, but always did what the bigger ones did and tried to do it more thoroughly than they could. My grandmother and Tom came past, carrying Mrs Smith between them, quite easily, and she looked very small and strangely distorted and misshapen compared with my tall, spare grandmother, who had a hand under her ankles and a hand under her thighs while Tom had a hand under her shoulders and one under her back. Mrs Smith was quite flat – it was strangely frightening to see – until I realised that they had a broad board from the hen-coop underneath her which made the flatness, broken by the great hump of the belly, more reasonable, somehow.

The howling cries of the Smith children were upsetting the mare, and I was very glad when Tom ran out of the house and said: 'Get up, Janet! We're going for Doctor Mackay!' and I was more glad still, even although I knew it was selfish, when the mare swung out of the yard on to the County Road and galloped away eastwards, so that the crying of the children was lost on the wind and in the sound of the sea.

I do not remember much of the next day, except that our house at Reachfar was very queer because my grandmother was not there, and off and on all day Tom or my father or George were away with the trap, fetching and carrying for the Smith house. A bundle of sheets went away and a bundle of towels, and when the trap came back the one of my family who had been driving it was always very silent, at first, and then began to talk in a queer, artificial way, about the warships in the Firth or some outside sort of thing like that, but as soon as I was out of real earshot, I could hear them all talking in undertones, and on the Saturday night my mother had been crying, I was sure, and so had my Aunt Kate. That was when I came in for supper. And on Sunday morning, when I came down for breakfast, my grandmother was still not home, and this

55

was something that had never happened before in all my born days, something so unusual that it was frightening now. *Never* had I known our house at Reachfar without my grandmother down at breakfast, full of energy at the start of the day, directing everything, ordering everybody about, asking if nobody around this place intended to get anything done at all today. I had managed, I felt, to put up with her not being at home for one morning, but two mornings and the second one the Sabbath Day – there was something dreadful in that. I began to feel more and more frightened, frightened in a queer way as I would be if the sun forgot to rise over the North Sea out east. This was cataclysm. Deep inside me I began to blame the Smiths. These people, who did not like school, wanted to be dressmakers – they were interrupting with their queerness the even flow and symmetry of the stable life at Reachfar. Spooning my porridge into my mouth at the big table with the empty place at one end and the silent people about it, I made up my mind that I was going to use my worst swear-word and say '*Dirt* on these Bedamneds!' the moment I was outside.

But before I had finished my porridge my grandmother was there in the doorway, her white hair hatless, her face seeming very thin, her long black lustre coat hanging unbuttoned from her shoulders. Behind her stood burly Doctor Mackay, a small stubble of reddish whisker showing on his jaw which was usually pinky-brown and shiny clean. Somehow all of us at the table had risen to our feet and were standing in our places as my grandmother put a hand on the back of her own chair.

'The doctor brought me home,' she said. 'It is all over. Kate, lay a place for Doctor Mackay.'

'The little wifie—?' my grandfather asked, down the long table, between us all.

'She's gone – a little after four o' the morning.'

'The baby?' my mother whispered.

'The baby will do,' said Doctor Mackay. 'A lassie – little but strong.'

56

'Poor little craitur!' my father said.

'George,' my grandfather said quietly, 'go ben to the parlour for the whisky. A dram will do the doctor good, and a little mouthful won't hurt your mother either.'

There is only one more scene from this Sunday in 1915 of which I have a memory picture, for with the return of my grandmother and the departure of Doctor Mackay my child's world returned to its norm and the remainder of the day, I suppose, conformed to the pattern which was comfort and security but was not material for detailed memory. In the afternoon I had been out, with Tom and George as usual, I suppose, and I do not know where my father and grandfather were, but I ran alone into the house where the three women – my grandmother, my mother and my aunt – were gathered round the Sunday fire in the parlour. I ran through the porch that guarded the door, turned left towards the parlour – the kitchen was to the right – and as I reached the threshold there was a tableau of my mother sitting on one side of the fire, my grandmother on the other and, standing between them but facing my grandmother, my young aunt, the firelight on her pale skin, flashing red in her dark eyes, her dainty jaw a clean-cut, out-thrust, little sabre of defiance: '. . . a skilled craftsman and too busy to lead a water-pipe into his own house! Say what you like, Mother, if you ask *me*, Jamie Bedamned killed that woman as surely as if he put a shot in her!'

The situation was serious. I hardly breathed as my grandmother, who could usually quell us all with a look, rose slowly and majestically to her feet, this time to deal with her youngest-born.

'Nobody asked you, Kate! What is over is over and words won't mend it! Go *at once* and make the supper!'

My aunt darted through the doorway past me like an angry swallow in full flight.

'So there you are, Janet!' my mother said. 'Did you have a nice walk?'

57

Part II

1920

Part II
1920

By 1920 I was a big girl of ten years old in the Top Class, and Flora Bedamned, who had been such a one when I was in the Baby Class, was an old woman of seventeen, for after her mother's death she never came back to school but stepped into the place that her mother had vacated. For her father, her four brothers and her baby sister she had cooked the food, cleaned the house, washed the clothes, milked the cow, fed the pigs and the hens and carried the water down the five years. Sometimes, on my way to school, I would see her around Bedamned's Corner. I at ten was as tall as she was at seventeen and, I am sure, a great deal heavier. She reminded me always of the only tree on the east moor of Reachfar, which was a bleak hill sloping to the north-east, facing the razor-edged sleet that swept in from the North Sea in winter. This tree, a spindly, ill-thriven fir, had a twisted trunk that leaned mainly to the south-west in obedience to the drive of the wind, except that near the top it took a defiant twist back to the north-east, just as Flora's head poked upwards at the top of her twisted body with its right shoulder lower than the left from carrying heavy buckets in the right hand. The tree had no branches left, nothing to burgeon in the spring, except a few scrawny twigs at the top that were as lacking in the form and symmetry of fir branches as was Flora's thin, wispy hair, maltreated as it was, tied up with a piece of tape and drawn tightly back from her meagre little face. The roots of the tree were wrenched half from the ground and rose in lumps round the base of the trunk like deformed feet in surgical boots, just as the men's black tackety boots that Flora wore at the ends of her spindly legs looked like weights that were all that held her to the earth. Both Flora and the tree showed every evidence of their battle with the winds of circumstance, and it was impossible to look at either without wondering why they had not, long ago, been overwhelmed.

I did not even know Flora now. She was far, far away in the grown-up world while I was still secure in the world of the child, my family world of Reachfar. But I was not separated from Flora only by the day-to-day things that separate any ten-year-old from any seventeen-year-old. In my mind, with its peculiarly rigid framework of set ideas, Flora had no claim to belong now, in any sense, to a proper family. She had no mother. She was an orphan. About her people said: 'Poor Flora!' She was a being apart, an object for pity, and this made an unbridgeable cleavage between her and someone like me. I was Janet Reachfar, with my 'proper' family, with all its members present and correct and Tom for makeweight like a firm rock wall behind me, a wall with no gaps in it for the winds of the world to blow through; while Flora belonged among the unfortunates, those with the broken ramparts, such as Murdo Fraser, whose father had been lost at sea during the war, or Mary Anderson, who had been born a baby-without-a-father when her mother went south to work in a munitions factory. It was not that a person like me was arrogant about these people with broken ramparts, nor did I hold them in scorn, but I could not see them without feeling sorry for them, and I was afraid that they would see or feel my pity and be hurt, as I would be hurt, my pride dropping a trail of gouts of blood, were anyone to pity *me*, a Reachfar Sandison. Although the ramparts of my life were levelled to the ground, I felt, please God let nobody show me their pity, but there was the inner conviction that my ramparts could not fall. And so I avoided people like Flora and Murdo and little Mary Anderson.

62

After the Christmas holidays of 1919, when the year had turned into 1920 and I was not yet quite ten years old, Alasdair Mackay and I were halfway through our second year in the Top Class, for Dominie Stevenson had to keep us at Achcraggan School for an extra year because we were too young to go on to Fortavoch Academy, although, scholastically, we had both passed its entrance examination the summer before. The Dominie was giving us extra lessons that would help us when we went to the Academy, and among these were Latin, a little algebra, and a few excursions into English literature, all of which made us very uppish in our attitude to the other pupils, who studied none of these learned subjects. Alasdair and I, without words, regarded ourselves as only a shade below the scholastic standard of the Dominie himself; quite definitely an academic step ahead of Miss Inglis, and gods who sailed upon aery clouds above the earthbound heads of the remainder of the pupils in the school. We were quite certainly abominable, and would have been more abominable still but for the heaven-sent nature of our respective families.

Alasdair was the late last-born of a big family of clever brothers and sisters, whose eldest brother was already a doctor in Edinburgh, while the brothers and sisters were all studying medicine in one of its branches. The vacations, with their influx of incipient doctors, nurses, dieticians and anaesthetists, were a godsend in setting Alasdair down where he belonged. In my case the operative factor was the George-Tom combination. At the first sign of over-preciousness on my part George would say: 'I am getting the devil of a queer smell aboot here, Tom,' and they would both begin to look around them and sniff and look at the soles of their boots as if they had trodden in a cat's mess.

'Yes, man,' Tom would comment, 'I am getting it myself now that you mention it,' and then there would be another sniffing and wrinkling of noses. By this time I would be furiously aware of blushing scarlet, with which

63

George would say: 'It's not so bad now, Tom.'

'No, George, it seems to be clearing away.'

'I was thinking it was a whiff of silly conceit that was in it, Tom – there's not a worst stink on the face of the earth than the stink of silly conceit.'

'No, indeed, George – it's worse nor cat's dirt . . . Chust lend me your matches for a minute. My boxie is empty.'

And to bring things back to normal and make my peace with them, I would offer – as no person who was sillily conceited would do – to run into the house and fetch Tom a new box of matches, or into the barn to fetch the oil-can, or anywhere to fetch whatever item he had declared himself to be short of.

As long as I gave off no smell of silly conceit, however, George and Tom were as interested in the Latin as they had been in my first school reading book. They were willing to co-operate with my algebra when co-operation was required, but the thing that interested all three of us most was the discovery that we had made, that there was a very important scholastic subject which was called 'English' and this subject was nothing other than the language that we spoke every day, the words that made it up and the books that had been written using these words, to perpetuate the thoughts of certain men and women for hundreds of years.

'It's a very wonderful thing,' said Tom, 'that's what it is. It is myself that was never thinking about this English before. Of coorse, I always knew it was English I was speaking and not the Gaelic, but it never came over me before that somebody must have made up all these words for things like plough and barrow in the first of it. It chust shows you that if a thing comes to you easy you never put a right value on it, like. Here we are, getting all these words handed down to us for nothing, from the old people of long ago. It is a very wonderful thing when you think on it.'

On a wet Sunday afternoon, in the straw barn, while the

64

rest of the family were at Sunday sleep, George, Tom and I contemplated this great legacy of our language, and the more we thought of it and remarked upon it, the more marvellous it became.

'Ye know,' said George, 'if there was no words, poor Reverend Roderick, the minister, would have to be a ploughman or something, for he couldna make a living at the preaching if there was no words to preach.'

'If there was no words,' said Tom, 'he couldna be at the preaching whateffer because it's not chust his own words that he'll be preaching, but the words of that old Abraham and Moses and them that was thinking and saying what's in the Bible. And if there was no words, the Dominie couldna be teaching Janet all this about English that we are learning and all them derryvations. Now this derryvations is chust about as inter*est*ing a thing as I've heard about for a long while, George. Do you not think so yourself?'

'Yes, indeed, Tom, and right reasonable, when you think on it. When you think on that Romans coming here with their Latin tongue and some of it getting mixed up in our English that we'll be speaking, it is chust like when the Ould Leddy will be putting a puckle cinnamon in the currant duff and giving it a bit flavour of Africa or some foreign place here on Reachfar hill. And there's another thing that is inter*est*ing about words. Have you happened to notice that some of them is a lot bonnier than others?'

'What way is that, George?'

'Well, take Jock Skinner's name, now. Skinner is not a bonnie word at a-all. Do you think that is because Jock himself is not bonnie or is it chust an ugly word whateffer?'

'Skinner,' said Tom, listening to himself say it.

'Skinner,' I said, also listening.

'It is not a bonnie noise of a word,' Tom concluded, 'besides making you think on beasts being skinned at the slaughter-house, poor craiturs, as well as that ould skinflint Teenie Gilchrist and that big long skinny pole o' a man Sandy Peerie. Of coorse, there might be some very

65

nice people off the name off Skinner for all that. But no, I wouldna say it was a bonnie noise of a word.'

'Flora is a bonnie word, isn't it?' I asked.

'Flora?'

'Flora!'

Tom and George listened to the word as they spoke it, considering it.

'Aye,' said George, 'aye, I like that one now. Flora.'

'Aye and me, forbye and besides,' Tom added.

'And it's not bonnie because of Flora Bedamned,' I said. 'It's just bonnie for itself.'

'That's so,' Tom agreed. 'Nobody could call Flora bonnie, poor trachled little craitur, but a nice lassie for all that.'

'Well, she has a bonnie name whateffer,' said George.

'It's derived from the Latin word for "flower",' I told them.

'Do ye tell me that now?' said Tom. 'That's a funny thing, now. It was myself that was always thinking that the Macleods of Varlich had the name o' Flora among them because of Prince Charlie's leddy, Flora Macdonald.'

'I suppose Prince Charlie's leddy got it handed down from them old Romans,' said George. 'But I always thought it was the Gaelic myself. Och well, there is not much of flowers or Prince Charlie's leddy either about poor wee Flora Bedamned. Maybe names don't mean very much.'

'But I'd rather be called Sandison than Skinner!' I said.

'Och, if Skinner was your born name you'd be quite pleased with it, likely,' said George. 'There's a lot in what a person is chust used to. Although, mind you, there's some devilish queer names, like that army doctor that came to Poyntdale in the war that was called Major Marchbanks although to read it you would have said it was Marjory Banks.'

'A very queer name altogether, that,' Tom agreed, 'Major Marjory Banks, as if it was a lassie that was in it and him a major in the army.'

'Major is the Latin word for big,' I contributed.

66

'That makes it foolisher than ever,' said George, 'for yon doctor was a wee craitur of a mannie with wee short leggies on him and big lugs like a donkey.'

'So *that* was what they meant about Davie the Plasterer's auntie's operation!' said Tom.

'What was that?' George asked.

'Yon time they said she was off to Glasgow to have a *major* operation! They meant it was a big one?'

'Very likely,' I said.

'Och, well, well, she died of it whateffer, the poor craitur,' said Tom.

The algebra George and Tom looked upon as being, on the whole, of less interest and discussion value than the Latin and the English, although worthy of respect because it was much used in the 'ship-building and the engineering trades, among the skilled craftsmen and architects and the like', but it was what they called 'outlandish' enough to be laughable as a foible developed by scholars in an attempt to mystify the layman.

George and Tom had always spent much of their time together in friendly argument. The division of duty among the men of my family was that my father and my grand-father were the administrators, the deciders of policy, and George and Tom were the carriers through of that policy. George's charge as grieve at Dinchory carried less respon-sibility than did my father's on the great estate of Poynt-dale, so George had more working time to devote to Reachfar. On an evening or a Sunday, then, my grand-father and my father would decide to divide off the moor-land pastures in a certain way; for instance, and in due course, George and Tom – with me to help them – would go out to run the fences. After we were out of sight of the house, but before we did any work at all, we would have a prolonged discussion as to whether we would start at, say, the east side or the west side.

'The way I look at it,' Tom would begin, 'is that if we start driving the posts from the east side we will be work-ing towards home a-all the time.'

'But it's a devil of a long road to go away east there this evening, Tom,' George would counter. 'It looks like rain and it will soon be dark whateffer . . . Have you a fill of teebacca about ye? I must have left mine in the house.'

With the advent of the algebra, the modus operandi of running a fence took on a highly academic flavour with: 'Say the bittie round the old quarry is x yards long and we need a post every yard there or the calves will be through and fall over the quarry face, that's x posts, and we made it y yards for the bittie from the big black rock to the north corner, so that's x posts added to y posts.'

'No, no, Tom, man – a post every *two* yards will do for the bittie down to the corner. It's only the Seamuir hay that's on the east side and if the calves break into it Captain Robertson will never miss what they eat. So that makes x added to y divided by two.'

'No, no, not at a-all – it's chust the y divided by two an' the x lot left hale and whole!. . . Was I telling you that Captain Robertson was devilish fou' when I saw him in Achcraggan on Friday?'

Actually, when I think of these discussions now, it would be discovered, when the argument was over, that somehow the hole for the straining post of the fence had got dug. There was something of the sleight of hand of the confidence trick about George's and Tom's method of working, but in their case it was the skill and ease, not primarily the speed, that deceived the eye. There was no fluster or panting or rolling up of sleeves or spitting on hands with them. In memory, I see them always standing gazing around them, puffing at their pipes, arguing or chatting, but on Reachfar ground there are to this day the walls that they built, the roads they made, the easily swinging gates that they constructed and hung. I can remember being present at the building, the making, the constructing and the hanging, but the detail I remember is the algebraic argument or the gossip of the countryside.

*　　*　　*

68

When Alasdair and I went back to school in January of 1920, as if we were not uppish enough already with our Latin, English and algebra, circumstances conspired to make us even more so.

It is a statistical fact, I believe, that the birth-rate invariably rises during a war, and in January 1920 the babies born in Achcraggan district in 1915 – and they were many, which leads me to wonder if people who live by agriculture tend to breed in the spring – were five years old and ready to come to school. The general unpreparedness of Great Britain for any occurrence that is the logical outcome of trends and pressures is also – although not a statistical matter – well known, so that in January 1920 twenty-three new pupils descended on Achcraggan School instead of the normal invasion of three to eight. Dominie Stevenson and Miss Inglis, however, were not dismayed. Alasdair was given six boys, I was given six girls and Miss Inglis took the other eleven and combined their teaching with that of Classes II and III as was her normal procedure, while the Dominie took the brighter ones of Class III up into Class IV and into his Big Room to relieve the congestion. So Alasdair and I became teachers in the forenoons, and in the afternoons Miss Inglis took charge of the whole boiling while Alasdair and I retired to the Dominie's room for our Latin, English and algebra and reverted to our proper status as pupils.

Now, about forty years later, I can still remember the names of the six little girls in what I called my 'teaching' class, as distinct from my 'learning' class in which I was the pupil of the Dominie. They were Isobel Mackenzie, Mabel Fraser, Margaret Macrae, Mary Dorset, Edith Clayton and Georgina Smith.

Three of these names have an interest in that they are a minor example of the effect of war on our remote district. Mabel Fraser derived her Christian name from the English mother of the wife that Malcolm Fraser brought home from London; Mary Dorset's surname came from the naval petty officer from Portsmouth that Mary Mackenzie

69

married, and Edith Clayton was called after a sister of Mr Clayton from Yorkshire, who had been a corporal in the army and stayed on in Achcraggan to go into the painting business that was owned by his father-in-law, Hector Macniel. But, much against my will, for the rivalry between us was keen, I had to give Alasdair best over the names business. My girls had what we called a 'wide-world-ness' about them that extended right down to Kent and Portsmouth at the very south of England, but among Alasdair's six boys he had one called Guido Sidonio, for Bella Gilmour had married, down in London where she was in service, an Italian sailor who had, early in 1918, been lost at sea. When Alasdair and I were going through one of our short periods of truce we both referred to this boy as 'Guido' but when we were at war, which was most of the time, Alasdair, in an insufferable way, said '*My* Guido', and I, I regret to admit, said '*Your* Eyetie Tally-wally'.

For the first two days my pride in my teaching class knew no bounds, and my family became quite worried by my air of extreme responsibility which alternated with severe outbursts of 'silly conceit', but by about the third day I myself was growing very worried indeed. The reason for this was Georgina Smith. On the first morning of school, with Alasdair and myself in attendance, Miss Inglis had gone through the traditional procedure of the register, and when it came to Georgina's turn she would say nothing but 'Georgie'. Miss Inglis, of course, knew that she was one of the Bedamneds.

'Georgie what?' she asked.

'Georgie.'

'Where do you live?'

'Georgie.'

'Come now, Georgie – your address is Smith's Corner, isn't it?'

'Georgie.'

And at the end of two mornings of my teaching and two afternoons of singing, sewing and games with Miss Inglis, no one had heard her utter any word other than 'Georgie'.

70

But there was something that worried me much more than the monotony of the Georgie. She was a big, dark, lumpish child and not small thin and wispy as Flora had been, yet her size was not the healthy sturdiness of the boys of the family. Flora had been very pretty as a child, but Georgie had a strange ugliness. She frightened me. She was like an outsize, ill-fashioned hobgoblin, a sort of parody of a human being, made by some power with the powers of God, I thought, but a power that was not good at its job. My grandmother would refer to a piece of work that was badly done as a 'proper botch' of a job, and that was how Georgie looked to me – a proper botch of a little girl. It was difficult to say exactly what was wrong about her, because she was *all* wrong, somehow. She had two eyes, a nose and a mouth and all the other usual features, but the eyes had a blankness and the nose and mouth were too close together, with hardly any room for a lip between. Her voice, saying its one word 'Georgie' which she pronounced 'Chorchie', was more like the snuffle of some little animal than any human sound, and she walked and ran with a curious crab-like gait, as if her legs were hung one from her abdomen and one from the end of her spine, instead of from the right and left sides of her pelvis.

I can find a few words now, nearly forty years later, to give a rough description of the physical nature of Georgie, but at ten years old I could find no words at all; and even if I had been able to find them, I think I would have been afraid to use them to tell even George, Tom, or my mother, for something about Georgie terrified me as if an evil spell emanated from her. At this time of day, a long time after, I think that this emanation from her, this aura that hung about her, was simply a manifestation of my instinctive consciousness of her idiocy, for Georgie – the baby that survived her mother's tragic death in 1915 – was an idiot, although I did not recognise her as such at first, for I did not know that such creatures existed.

At the end of about two weeks Georgie had become a sort of obsession with me. As I walked home from school

71

through the bleak January rain, by the shortest flying-crow route, her queer, blank-eyed face was in the trunks of the gnarled hawthorns of the hedges; her distorted running movements were in the bare, twisted branches of the trees; her thickly animal voice snuffling 'Chorchie, Chorchie' was in the squelch of the field mud under my moor boots; and when I went to bed and the candle in my friendly attic was blown out, that emanation, that aura that was all about her, invaded the room.

On a Saturday night I went to bed as usual, not having seen Georgie all day, and I hoped that the 'thing' of her would not come that night, but it did and I had to wrestle with it, for it was winding all about me and writhing like the snake curls on Medusa's head and I knew that if it could rise up as far as my eyes I would be turned to stone and lie there on my bed for ever and ever like the man in the picture of the Crusader's Tomb in my history book. And then, just as the coils were about my neck, I heard my mother's calm voice say: 'All right, Janet. All right, lovie. Come then, see Tom and George and everybody here.'

And it was true. My mother, my father, Tom and George were all in the room and the big brass lamp from the kitchen was standing beside my bed.

'And here's a biscuit,' George said, 'and move over and let your mother in there to be warm and chust be telling us a-all what you were dreaming about.'

'Yes, indeed,' said Tom, who was wearing his big ploughing overcoat and his boots without the laces tied, as he sat down on the end of my bed and took his pipe and tobacco from the coat pocket. 'I'm danged if I'll go back to my bed till I hear a-all about it. Chust sit down and take a smoke, George.'

'What was the dream about, Janet?' my father asked.

'It wasn't a dream. I wasn't sleeping. It's Georgie.'

'Georgie?' my mother asked. 'Wee Georgie Smith, you mean, Janet?'

'Yes.' I shivered against the warmth of my mother's white winceyette nightdress.

72

'What about Georgie then?'

'It's the thing of her. It comes every night. It's a thing that comes to you and makes you blind and deaf and dumb and – and – you get like Georgie.'

I went on and on talking, trying to make them understand but without hope of success, but I knew that as long as I talked they would not go away. Eventually, though, George gave a huge yawn right where he sat on the end of my bed and said: 'It's myself that's tired o' the very name o' this Georgie. I think she's a stupid little craitur myself and shouldn't be in school at all. I doubt I'm too sleepy to walk back to my own bed. Janet, would you chust put your mother out of there and let me come in, maybe?' He gave another enormous yawn.

'Yes, if you like, George,' I said.

My mother slipped out of the bed and George came into her place. 'Be off out of here the lot of you!' he said. 'And let a man have his sleep. And take that danged lamp out of here. Janet, my back is cold. Pack in there and be warming it for me.'

I did as I was told; he emitted a snore that shook the rafters, and I watched the lamp and the people go out of the room, but the thing of Georgie did not come back. There was only George's big warm back on one side and the wall on the other and I felt safe at last.

The next morning, which was Sunday, it was dry and most of us went to church as we always did except when the road was impassable with snow, so today it was my mother who stayed at home to look after the dinner – she seldom came to church in winter – and my father who stayed to look after the animals and write letters; so it was what I, in to myself, called 'good church' because both Tom and George were there. If my grandmother had known of my mental term 'good church', and had been told what it meant, she would not have approved.

Our minister, the Reverend Roderick Mackenzie, was a scholarly son of the Western Isles and all his journeyings and sojournings at the universities of Edinburgh and

Oxford had failed to change the soft sea-murmur of his Hebridean speech which could rise to Atlantic gale force and fury as he hurled from his high pulpit anathema against the mortal sin that was for ever threatening his flock. Nor had his travels and studies eradicated his Hebridean accent, which was at its most pronounced on the consonants 'j' and 'g', the former being softened to the sound of summer waves on shingle and the latter hardened to the thud of stormy seas against rock. In the Reverend Roderick's voice the great names of the Bible were transmuted, seeming thereby to gain added importance and reverence, to Chehovah and Chudah, Cheesuss and Kod and there was a cheery friendliness about Cherusalem and Cherico that George, Tom and I did not find in Jerusalem and Jericho which were merely places far, far away.

On wet Sunday afternoons, when we could not go for a walk while the rest of the family went to Sunday sleep, the three of us would retire either to the straw barn or to Tom's or George's bed, if it was very cold; and having made ourselves comfortable, with the men's pipes going really well, we would treat ourselves to the morning sermon all over again. Tom, although born in Achcraggan where the speech was less soft than that of the minister, could none the less 'do' the Hebridean voice to perfection and was now also very accomplished at interpolating a quotation here and there from the Latin, which was one of the Reverend Roderick's methods of impressing on his congregation that he himself was practically a minor prophet who had been endowed with the gift of tongues. George, Tom and I, therefore, did not have to be dragged unwillingly to church of a Sunday. I think my grandmother accepted our willingness as about the only sign of saving grace that we ever demonstrated, for, of course, she was unaware that we were, in modern jargon, merely theatre scouts in search of material.

The Reachfar pew was in the front row on the middle side of the gallery that ran round three sides of the big,

74

bleak church, an excellent position from every point of view, and the other three-quarters of this front row was the pew of Poyntdale House. This meant that Lady Lydia and my grandmother could see who was not in church that day and take appropriate action if they decided that it was required. It meant that Sir Torquil and my grandfather could see if Mr Findlay of Ardnaclaggan was in his pew down below, because, if he was, it meant that his young mare had foaled all right. It meant that my aunt could see all the new hats and dresses that anybody had and be able to discuss them with my mother when she got home, and it meant that George, Tom and I, directly opposite and a little above the level of the pulpit, had an uninterrupted view of the Reverend Roderick in his impressive, bat-winged gown, with his dark eyes flashing fire above his strong black beard.

Although a great scholar, the Reverend Roderick did not lead a remote, Il Penseroso existence, divorced from the life of his congregation. The manse was something of a 'high, lonely tower', it is true, black and forbidding in its circle of tall trees where the rooks nested, but the minister did not spend a great deal of time in his manse. He was unmarried and maintained a trap and two fat ponies which were driven on alternate days, and these were tended to a sleek shine by the handyman who was known as 'Malcolm the Minister', although he had been born about seventy years ago as Malcolm Grant. I pointed out to Tom once that Malcolm should really be called 'Malcolm the Minister the Third', as the Reverend Roderick was his third minister, but Tom said it was the minister who should be known as 'the Minister the Third of Malcolm's'. When we took this to George for arbitration, George took the view that Tom's way would not do because the minister was not exactly Malcolm's and that my way would not do because it was the ministers who died and not Malcolm, so Malcolm had just better remain 'Malcolm the Minister' with no numbers to him, as a minister more or less made no difference in his life, and,

75

anyway, he was only called Malcolm the Minister to differentiate him from Malcolm the Shepherd and Malcolm the Roadman, so nothing was done about the alteration of the title.

One of the greatest and most recurrent sins against which the Reverend Roderick had to do battle in Achcraggan Parish was malicious gossip, and in January of 1920 there was a great deal of talk going on about a young woman called Violet Boyd who had given birth to an illegitimate child and subsequently committed suicide. The gossip had rendered the Boyd house a virtual prison for her surviving sisters who could not walk along the street in comfort or peace because of the speculating, malicious glances that followed them and the serpent hiss of tongues in every doorway and corner.

On this Sunday, the preliminary psalms, paraphrases and prayers over, John the Smith the Precentor put his tuning fork away in the rear pocket of his frock-coat and sat down in his little corner under the pulpit and the Reverend Roderick rose to his majestic height in the pulpit, placed both hands on top of the big, black Bible that lay on the oak lectern, swept his fierce eagle glance twice round the church over us all and said: 'On this Lord's Day, my text iss from the Book off the prophet Isaiah, at the third chapter and at the eighth verse.'

From the tone of his voice, the look of doom upon his face, the congregation knew that they were sinners on the verge of chastisement and there was a slow, procrastinating, furtive riffling of Bible pages as we all turned up the text, as if, by our slinking delay, we could postpone – or even escape – the wrath to come. As, with a feeling of dreadful guilt, I found the place, I could imagine the stern eyes in the pulpit and I was afraid to lift my head, and I was sure that the only person in church, from Sir Torquil down to the smallest child, who did not feel as I did was Georgie Smith, who, being big enough for school, was now also big enough for church and sat beside her father in their pew on the ground floor.

76

Having given us, with a godlike air of patience that flowed among us like wreaths of grey mist, what he considered to be ample time, the Reverend Roderick cleared his throat, the fluttering of pages died to silence and, compelled by some awful power though sore afraid, we all looked up at the pulpit. With one hand holding the band of his gown, the other resting on the closed Bible, the Reverend Roderick squared his shoulders, raised his bearded chin and said: 'Listen, now, to the words off the prophet Isaiah: "For Cherusalem iss ruined, and Chudah iss fallen; because their tongue and their doings are against the Lord, to proffoke the eyes off His klory!" This Lord's Day I am going to speak to you about tongues that are against the Lord, yes, tongues that are a proffoking of Kod's kreat klory!'

I sank back in my place between George and Tom with a sigh of relief. *This* week I had not provoked a single person with my tongue, and not once had rung out the familiar exasperated phrase: 'Ach, Janet, be off with your continual ask-ask-asking!' so I was in the clear.

On a Sunday when he was fighting hand-to-hand like this with mortal sin, the Reverend Roderick's sermon took three-quarters of an hour, so I do not remember all of it, but the 'Thirdly', in which he worked up to his thunderous peroration, was, as it were, a Pageant of Sinful Tongues Down the Ages. Beginning with the wicked tongue of the serpent in the Garden of Eden, he came on through the long centuries to 'Many-tongued Rumour' in Spenser's *Faerie Queene*, and from there to Shakespeare, when he gave a performance of Iago dropping his sly poison into the ear of Othello that many a great actor might have envied. Then, having demonstrated nearly every aspect of the evil of tongues, he paused, then raised both gown-winged arms in a broad sweep and said quietly: 'And I haff not yet spoken off the wickedest tongue off them all.' The voice gained power and range. 'Wass it not a tongue that sent our blessed Lord Cheessus to death upon the cross?' The voice rose to a mighty thunder-roll that

77

rumbled over our heads, struck the back wall of the church and reverberated back, clamorous about our ears: 'Yes. The traitor's tongue off Chudas Iscariot! . . .'

In mid-breath, the Reverend Roderick stopped and, turning, began to open the little door of his pulpit while his eyes looked down to the ground floor of the church. My glance followed his and there, lying in the aisle, was Georgie Smith, contorted, writhing, her limbs jerking in terrible convulsions. Doctor Mackay hurried forward from his pew near the back, picked up the jerking, marionette-like body and disappeared with it into the vestry, followed by the minister and Jamie Bedamned. Sir Torquil, in his pew next to ours, rose to his feet.

'Members of the congregation, Jamie Smith's little girl has been taken ill. You will all, please, go home. God bless and keep you all, Amen.'

That Sunday was a 'fine before seven, rain before eleven' day, and when we came out of church the whole country-side was sodden and shivering under a hard, steady down-pour. My grandfather drove the trap, the rain dripping from the brim of his tall black hat, and my grandmother and my aunt sat beside him, huddled under the oilskin lap-robe, their black umbrellas making a dark little tent. From under the seat of the trap, before they left the stable of the Plough Inn, my oilskins and moor boots were pro-duced, and so were the oilskin coats that George and Tom wore when carting turnips on a dirty day. Our good Sunday coats were folded and put under the lap-robe, together with my Sunday shoes, and my grandmother said: 'All right, be off then, the three of you! Go the driest, quickest way you can.'

It was being a very interesting Sunday indeed, I thought, but Tom and George seemed to be more depre-ssed than interested and they did not seem to want to talk very much, which was always a pity from my point of view. Not until we were nearly home by the shortest south-westerly route, when we were in the shelter of the trees in

78

the Home Moor of Reachfar, did either or them say anything of any consequence, but then George stopped underneath the big Scots fir that I called the 'Stalwart Tree' because it was so big and strong, and said: 'Janet, did that wee Georgie Smith ever have a fit like that in school?'

'No, George.'

'Then why were you frightened of her?'

'I was *not* frightened of her!'

No Sandison was ever afraid of anyone or anything or, if you *were*, it should never be mentioned. The proper way to behave about a thing like that was to Take No Notice, and it was pure rudeness to mention such a thing, like speaking about the limp of Cripple Maggie the Tinker, who could not help being born with one leg shorter than the other.

'It is myself that *is* frightened of people that takes fits,' said Tom, 'and I do not care who will be knowing it, what's more. It is very, very frightening and not natural, taking fits like that.'

'That was it, Tom!' I said. 'Georgie didn't take fits in school, but she isn't *natural*!'

'I know what you mean,' George said. 'It's not that a person is frightened, ecksactly, but there's chust a queer kind of feeling. Och, well, the poor little craitur will have to stop out of school now till Doctor Mackay makes her better.'

'Will she, George?'

The relief – oh, the relief! My teaching class of the other five little girls and no Georgie! The bliss – oh, the bliss!

'*Will* she, George?'

'Surely!' Tom confirmed. 'Having fits is a sickness, like having the measles or a broken leg. You never saw anybody in school with the measles or a broken leg, did you?'

In spite of the pouring rain that dripped from the dark green fir trees, in spite of the sodden moss of the moor path that squelched round our boots, my spirits rose and I

79

became happier and happier. It was as if, since school started after Christmas, I had had bound to me a heavy black load that had threatened to overpower me and press me down into the darkness under the earth, and now, miraculously, this load had been swept away. I began to sing and the three of us tramped the rest of the way home through the sheets of rain to the tune of 'Onward, Christian Soldiers'.

It was impossible to go for a walk that afternoon, so when the rest of the family went to Sunday sleep, George, Tom and I retired to Tom's room, took off our shoes and got into Tom's bed, under the quilt, George at the bottom and Tom and I at the top, all very warm and comfortable.

The quilts – for George and I had similar ones in our rooms – had been made by us women of the family, my grandmother, my mother, my aunt and me. George, Tom and I called them our 'odds-and-ends' because they were made completely out of odds and ends. Their top sides were of scraps of brightly coloured cotton, left over from all sorts of things, sewn together firmly and then each seam covered with feather-stitch in brightly coloured pieces of my mother's left-over embroidery silk. Their bottom sides were of crochet in all different colours of left-over pieces of wool, and in between the patchwork and this there was a layer of patchwork made of blanket, the left-over corners of blankets, whose centres had worn out, all sewn together. The whole was held together by a border of cotton round the edges, and an all-over pattern of left-over small buttons of all sorts, which were stitched together in pairs, one on the patchwork side, one on the crochet side, the stitches going right through from one button to the other.

As a rule, on a wet Sunday afternoon, underneath somebody's odds-and-ends, we preached over again the Reverend Roderick's sermon of the forenoon, but on this day none of us seemed to want very much to remember church of that morning, so when Tom and George had got their pipes going well, Tom said: 'A dirty long grey day like this a-always puts me in mind of ould Dominie Gregor, someway, George, and yon terrible dreich, droning poetry he used to be at.'

Tom took his pipe from his mouth, sat up straight instead of lounging back against his pillows and with a stern face began to declaim:

> 'So a-all day long the noise of battle rolled
> Among the mountains by the winter sea—'

The rain drummed on the windows and the roof and the wind howled round the gables.

> 'On one side lay the Ocean, and on one
> Lay a great water, and the moon was full.'

Tom lay back, relit his pipe and George said: 'Aye, you're quite right, Tom. He was a devil of a man for the dreich dour poetry. I don't mind on that one you was reciting, but there was another one that he had that used to make me think there was bodachs on the road home through the moor. Do ye mind on this bittie?'

George now sat up straight, holding his pipe in his hand, and recited:

> 'Like one that on a lonesome road
> Doth walk in fear and dread,
> And having once turned round, walks on,
> And turns no more his head;
> Because he knows a frightful fiend
> Doth close behind him tread.'

He lay back, replaced his pipe in his mouth and said: 'Mind you, he was a great scholar, Dominie Gregor, but it's a minister he should have been.'

'That's chust what I've a-always been thinking,' Tom agreed. 'Now Dominie Stevenson is a nice, cheery sort of man and chust the thing to be a dominie.'

'Dominie Stevenson has some sad poetry too,' I said and began in my turn to recite:

81

'Home they brought her warrior, dead,
She nor swooned nor uttered cry,
All her maidens, watching, said:
"She must weep or she will die".'

'Ochee, ochone!' said George. 'That's worse nor ever and terrible miserable. Maybe it would be better if we gave up the poetry the-day.'

'I know what we'll do,' I said. 'We'll sing. You two have got to learn to sing properly in parts.'

'Parts?'

'Yes, like we do in the Top Class. I'll do the high-up bit, like the girls do, and you two will do the low-down bit like the boys. Of course,' I said in a superior way, 'at school we have the piano and it goes tinkly-tonkly-tonkly-tink like the birds singing.'

'That's quite easy,' said George. 'You do the high bit, Tom will do the low bit, and *I'll* be the piano and the birds. What's the song?'

I gave a rendering of the first stanza of 'Early One Morning'.

'A very bonnie air,' said Tom. 'Chust a minute now, till I get my note.'

He opened his knife, struck it against the brass rail of the bed, held it to his ear in imitation of John the Smith the Precentor with his tuning-fork and intoned in a deep bass: 'Doh! Doh! Doh!'

'All right,' I said. 'Ready? One, two!'

Tom and I:	'Early one mo-orning just as the sun was ri-ising,'
George:	'Tinkly tonkly tinkly cockle-doodle doo-oo-oo'
Tom and I:	'I heard a maiden si-ing in the va-alley below'
George:	'Tra-la-la-lassie lee-lee-lee-lee'
Tom and I:	'Oh don't decei-eeve me, Oh never lea-eeve me'
George:	'Eee-ee-ee-ee-eeow, Eee-ee-ee-ee-eeow'
Tom and I:	'How could you you-oo-ooze a poo-oor maiden so?'

82

George: 'Ow-ow-ow-ow-ow-ow-ow-OW-OW! Ochee ee-ee! Ochone!'

We were delighted with it. Again and again we did it, our voices growing louder and louder and George's sound effects becoming more dramatic with every repetition until just at a very loud 'Cockle-doodle-doo!' in mid-stanza the door flew open and my aunt stood there, the hat that she should *not* have been trimming at Sunday sleep in her hands.

'For pity's sake, you three!' she said. 'Stop that row! It's *Sunday* and not even a hymn that you're bawling! Do you want *Granda* to come up to you?'

'Well,' said George, his eyes on the hat, the pink ribbon and the Sabbath-forbidden needle that she was holding, 'we don't as a rule intend for to get our friends into trouble. You wouldn't have a few sweeties aboot you, in your room anywhere?'

The next morning, I discovered that Tom and George were quite right, as they usually were about everything, for Georgie was not at school that day, nor did the 'thing' of her come to threaten me in bed that night. Indeed, it never came again on any night, for Georgie never came back to school at all. Until the Sunday when she had the fit in church it had not been known, even by her family, that she was epileptic, and Flora and her brothers had been too young – and too hard-worked and busy, probably – to notice that she was 'not natural' as I had become aware that she was when she came to school. Children accept many things, if they grow up alongside of them, that another mind, seeing them for the first time, finds unacceptable and, where the Smith children had accepted their baby sister as she was, I had looked upon her with unaccustomed eyes and felt her to be beyond the bounds of normal acceptance.

With Georgie no longer at school every day, I forgot all about her, for there were many more interesting things to think about. If I gave any thought to the Smith family at all, it was only to push them aside and away out of sight. There was something 'queer' about them; 'funny' things

83

happened to them, like their mother falling at the spring and dying like that, leaving them all orphans that people pitied, and then Georgie being 'unnatural' at school and ending up by having a fit in church during the sermon. *Other* families did not have such things happening to them; my own family, well regulated and proper, would never countenance such things. No. There was definitely something 'queer' about these Bedamneds and it was better to avoid the very thought of them.

Spring began to come, and this was to be the most wonderful spring of all my born days, for, early in March, I would be ten, which would make me old enough to move on from Achcraggan School to Fortavoch Academy, but also to come in March was another event which was so strange and wonderful, of a texture so different from any other event to which I had looked forward that I was almost afraid to contemplate it at all. My mother was going to have a baby, and, up in my Thinking Place in the dark-green gloom of the tall fir trees above the well, new aspects of this miraculous event kept occurring to me every day. I was to have a brother or a sister. There would be one more new person in my family. There would be a cradle in the house. Of course, the cradle had *always* been there, up in the west attic, ever since I myself had grown too big for it. It was made of wickerwork and had a soft, cushiony, blue quilted lining. But a cradle in the west attic was not the same as a cradle beside the fire with a baby in it. All sorts of people would come to see the baby, and Sir Torquil, very big and broad in his riding clothes, would bend down and tickle its cheek and put a silver sixpence under its pillow for luck as he did with everybody's new babies. The baby was such a tremendous thing that I did not dare speak directly about it, because it was far too important for words, and yet when you are thinking of a thing almost constantly your thoughts must overflow in some way, so I spoke of things that were connected in my mind with thoughts of the baby, but I did it so slyly and cleverly that nobody would ever know that I was thinking of the baby at all.

84

'Alasdair, do you like boy babies or girl babies best?'

'I don't like any of them – squallin' brats!'

'Squallin' brat yourself! You're the baby of your whole big family!'

'So are you!'

'I'm not! I'm the *eldest*! Yah! Yah! Wee Baby Mackay!'

And then: 'Tom, did Sir Torquil give *me* a silver sixpence when I got born?'

'Aye, he did that and not chust the one sixpence, either.'

'How many?'

'I'm not sure, but forty o' them whateffer.'

'But forty is a whole pound!'

'Aye, so it is.'

'Where is it?'

'Where would it be but in Mr Foster's bank?' said Tom. 'Like all the other pennies that's put by for your eddication!'

And very gently, in a small voice: 'Mother, do you like pink ribbons or blue ribbons best?'

'I like both, Janet . . . Would you like to sew on these two little buttons for me?'

'Yes, Mother.'

'All right, and don't put the needle right through and make a hard lump. Babies have very soft skins.'

My tenth birthday came along. Two days later my baby brother was born, and two days after that my mother died. I tell this in this sudden way because that was how it happened to me and I can tell it in no other way. I suddenly became an orphan like the Bedamned children, and my baby brother and I were members of a 'queer' family, the children of a mother who had died.

As I have said in another story I have written, I have no memories of that year 1920, for the period between my father telling me of my mother's death on a bright, windy morning in March and walking across the moor with Tom and George on a Sunday in July, more than three months later. Apparently, from what my people have told me, I

85

behaved normally during these three months and more – I did my little jobs around Reachfar, I went to school and played and quarrelled with Alasdair, and went around as usual with Tom and George, but I do not remember any of it. I can only believe that the essential part of me, where emotion is felt, where experience takes root and memory is born, had, by some merciful intervention, gone into a state of suspended animation.

When I came alive again, it was to find that the face of my world was to undergo a great change. My father had taken a post as a farm manager in south Scotland and I was to go south with him and go to school there, while my baby brother would stay at Reachfar with the rest of my family. By Tom and George I was reconciled to the outward aspect of this great change, for they told me of the wonders of Cairnton Academy, the school which I was to attend and which my father had already seen. They told me too what a distinctive way of life mine would be.

'The most of the people when they go away from the Highlands, here,' said Tom, 'goes away for good and a-all and makes their homes in the south or London or Canada or Australia, but it is not like that with you and your father at a-all. You are going down there purely to get what eddication they can give you and your father is going to get a lot of good money on this dairy farm, now that Sir Torquil is finding things so hard at Poyntdale since the war. And you will be up home here every school holidays and George and me meeting you at Inverness and your father will be up every summer. It will be a fine way of life, I am thinking, and if I was a little younger I would wish it was myself that was going.'

'Not me!' said George. 'I wouldna like to go – the like of me is too stupid for big cities like Glasgow and the quick way the people in the south will be speaking. If I was to go, it's chust a burden on Duncan I would be with my foolishness, and I think it's better if you and me chust stop here, Tom, and let Janet go with him, to be company, like.'

86

But they could not reconcile me entirely to the loss of the countryside I loved, and they could not lift from me the weight of the divine vengeance that I felt upon me, for they did not know of it, and throughout August, until we left for Cairnton, I wandered about Reachfar and the district feeling, much of the time, already an exile who had been banished for her sins, very much as the devil had been thrown out of Heaven. This banishment had come upon me, I was aware, because of the 'evil tongue' of my inner thoughts about the Bedamned family; because of the contempt in which I had held them for the 'queer' things which had happened to them; because of my ingratitude to Flora to whom I had sworn eternal gratitude for her help to me on my first day at school. This that had happened to me was divine vengeance – an eye for an eye and a tooth for a tooth. No doubt, now, the people of Achcraggan round their doors of a morning were talking of me as a 'poor, motherless wee lass' and pitying me and my baby brother as 'those little orphan craiturs up at Reachfar', as they had spoken of Flora and her brothers and baby sister. Somehow, somehow, I must make reparation to Flora for the wicked things I had thought of her and her family. Somehow I must fend off the arrows of divine vengeance. I knew that nothing I could do would bring my mother back, but I could show the angry Almighty that I had learned my lesson so that perhaps He might drive His chariot of wrath back into His thundercloud and send no more bolts of vengeance down upon me.

And so, although it was my school holidays and summer and I would soon have to leave Reachfar and go to Cairnton, I went down to Bedamned's Corner as often as I could and helped Flora with her unending toil. It was a very strange thing, but the very first afternoon I spent down there I began to feel better, as if the thundercloud of the divine wrath were lifting and rolling away, as the ordinary thunderclouds did, to be lost in the vast sky over the North Sea. Nor was I, now, repelled by or afraid of Georgie, not even one afternoon when she had a fit on the

87

kitchen floor. I helped Flora to pick her up and fetched a spoon from the table drawer that Flora might put the handle of it between her teeth. And then I went to Achcraggan to ask Doctor Mackay to come.

My grandmother and my aunt were, I think, quite pleased about me spending my time at Bedamned's Corner, for they were busy, with my little brother John added to all their normal summer work, and I think, too, that they felt that with the Smiths I was in the company of other children, so that I would not notice so poignantly the gap in the Reachfar household.

I did, however, notice that gap and I noticed too the great change that my mother's death had worked in my grandmother. She seemed, suddenly, to have developed a look of patience which is one of the main characteristics that differentiate the old from the young. It was as if she, too, had learned a severe lesson, the lesson that there were some things that even her tremendous force of character could not control. I do not mean to convey that her spirit was broken, for that was unbreakable, but hitherto she attacked everything, be it the 'proper' way to lay a teaspoon in a saucer or one of the great moral issues of right or wrong, with a similar fire and force. Now, the teaspoon's position seemed to be of less importance; and instead of bustling about from dawn till dark and whipping the rest of us into a bustle with her tongue the while, she would sit, when she had a spare half-hour, in serene, calm content beside John's cradle, her proud, bright eyes soft with a humble tenderness as she looked down at her infant grandson.

Inevitably, as the storm in my mind died down, as I reoriented myself, I suppose, to this new world without my mother in it, I began to draw comparisons again between Reachfar and the house at Bedamned's Corner. I was older now, observed things that were different and observed them in a way that was different from my observation of five years ago. I think I speak truly when I say that the main characteristic of Reachfar as a house was its

88

air of orderly thrift and plenty in an atmosphere of family peace and good fellowship, and at five years old I had thought that all 'proper' homes were like this; but by 1920, when I was ten, I had come to know that all families were not as fortunate as were we Sandisons and that all homes did not have the peace of Reachfar.

The Smith home presented, probably, the greatest contrast that our district could provide to Reachfar. Flora, undersized and only seventeen years old, was physically and mentally quite unable to get through the amount of work that lay before her when she rose in the morning, even if she had not had the additional burden of the idiot Georgie on her shoulders. Georgie was always wandering away; there was the constant anxiety that in some hidden corner she would fall down in a fit and lie there untended. Jamie, the oldest boy, who had been nearly ten five years ago when I went to school, was now fifteen, having been taken away from school at the age of twelve to help his father. Davie, the next boy, was now twelve and he also went away to work with his father every day. Then Roddie was ten, like me, and Hughie was seven, but they were boys and more interested in rabbiting and fishing than in helping their sister, nor had they any consciousness of a need to do penance, like me, so when Flora sent them to the spout for water they would leave the buckets in the pool and disappear as completely as if the earth had swallowed them.

All day Flora and I washed clothes, cleaned the house, chopped sticks for the fire, fed animals, cooked meals and herded Georgie. When Mr Smith, Jamie and Davie were working anywhere within two miles of the house they came home for dinner, and these days I used to dread. Flora was always different on the days that her father was coming in at midday, and about five each evening, when I felt this 'difference' in her as it came near to the time for him to come home for the night, I used to leave and go home to Reachfar. She was always flustered and in a hurry, but for the hour before the arrival of her father she

89

was more flustered and hurried than ever and she gave off a queer miasma of uneasiness, as our Betsy the mare did, when she had to cross with her cart a certain little wooden bridge that she did not like.

When my grandfather or Tom came into our house from the steading outside at suppertime they always came in as if they were happy to come, with a 'Well, well, it's been a grand day and making a fine evening!' or some remark like that, and the womenfolk, busy preparing the meal, would smile a welcome and say: 'You can take the hot water in the little kettle to get that oil off your hands,' or make some other suggestion for their comfort or well-being at the end of the working day. And, of course, when my father and George came in from Poyntdale and Dinchory, they were welcomed back from the outside world with 'Well, did you get well away with the hay today?' or 'Has the new mare had her foal yet?' And of course the fire would be bright and the meal all ready to serve as soon as the last man had come in and had washed his hands.

But it was quite different at the Smiths'. In spite of all Flora's fluster and hurry and my best efforts to help her, the dinner would not be as it should be when 'the men' came in, for Flora had no idea of laying a table in any case, but put a heap of plates and a heap of cutlery at one end of the wooden slab and let everybody except her father help themselves from the pots on the fire. That is, if there *was* a fire, for it frequently happened that Georgie would get away during the bustle of preparation and by the time Flora and I had found her and had got back with her, the fire of quickburning wood – the Smiths bought no coal – would have gone out and we would be faced with a heap of grey ash and probably the next lot of wood would be either green or wet and would not burn.

Then Mr Smith would arrive, big, dark, morose, and sit down at the table, his hands dirty, his tweed cap on his head, staring in front of him, waiting for his food, word-less. Flora would put something on a plate, put it before

90

him, and he would cover his eyes for a moment in a silent grace before meat, then eat the food, get up and go out. Jamie and Davie, the two working boys, would now stuff the last of their food into their mouths and in a scared way, wordless also, get up and follow him, and the three would go away back to work, the boys two paces behind their father, nobody speaking.

The 'bonnie' dresser of Mrs Smith's time was now just a wooden ramshackle, its paint chipped and scarred, untidy and neglected, with pieces of string and heaps of bent rusty nails where once the vase with the glass dingle-dangles and those that were a present from Aberdeen had sat. All that remained of the 'bonnie' things was the electro-plated lid of the china biscuit barrel that used to flaunt the painted pansies, for the lid was unbreakable and all the breakable things had fallen to the fluster of Flora, the roughness of the brothers whom she could not control or the destructive mischief of Georgie. I do not suppose that Mr Smith ever noticed their disappearance. When he came into the house he seemed to be in it but not of it, and yet when he went out of it he left behind him a gloom that it was difficult to dispel.

I had been helping Flora every day for quite a time, Sundays excepted, when, on a Friday evening, I saw Mr Smith and Davie approaching along the County Road and told Flora that I had to go home now.

'All right,' she said, in her resigned way.

'Your father and Davie are coming,' I warned her. 'Jamie's not with them, though.'

'No. He's got a job by his lone the now, up at Seamuir. He's getting big. He can work by his lone now at a thing like making a drain,' she said and bustled away, the queer 'difference' upon her of her father's advent becoming more marked.

I made my way up by the water spout and set off across the fields, thus avoiding a meeting with Mr Smith, and on my way home I thought of Jamie, and how fine he must

91

feel working 'by his lone' and out of the bleak shadow of his silent father.

The time for my father and me to go 'away south' was now becoming imminent, and the nearer the spectre came, the more Tom and George made fun of it. It was their way of making the great change and the separation more acceptable to us all, and it succeeded, for the actual day of the departure came upon me almost unawares, so that I had no time for long farewells and lingering last looks at special spots such as the Thinking Place on the moor above the well.

So, on this evening, as we all sat round the supper-table, with John, already bathed and fed and gurgling happily in his cradle at my grandmother's right hand where my mother had been wont to sit, with my aunt on the baby's other side, George looked across the table and addressed the cradle as if John were a proper grown-up person, for this was the only way George had of speaking to anyone, no matter what age they might be.

'Jock, lad,' he said now, 'it is time you got on with this growing you have to be doing, man, for when you are big enough to go to school, it is myself that is going back there with you.'

'Well, now,' said Tom, 'I hadn't thought of going back to school myself, George, but maybe it is a very good idea. What made you think on it?'

'Well, Tom, it is this way. By the time John there is big enough to go to school, I am thinking that I will be an ould done useless mannie, not able to wheel a barrow, but I will have the Lloyd George pension that will keep me in teebacca and I'll have my bed and board here at Reachfar and I think I'll chust go back to school and maybe come out as a doctor.' He looked round at us all. 'And then I would be off down south like Janet here and make my fortune.'

'Where could *you* ever be a doctor, George?' I asked, while my family laughed and even John gave an extra loud sleepy gurgle.

'Why would I not be a doctor?' he asked indignantly. 'Come now, Mrs Anderson, I would say, chust be showing me your leg. Dear me, dear me. It's the counterextrascrewmatics that's in it, Mrs Anderson, and then I would be writing the medicine on the bittie paper in the Latin and a-all.'

We had reached the point where George had decided that it might be better to be a schoolmaster in his old age, when there was a clump-clump of heavy feet in nailed boots in the yard outside and a tall black form went swiftly past the window.

'Who was that?' asked my grandfather as my father rose to go to the door and the dogs' growling from under the table became audible. They had probably been growling for some time but we had all been laughing so loudly that we did not hear them. Before my father had his chair drawn back from the table, the feet came clumping in through the porch and along the passage to the kitchen door. We all kept still, our eyes on the closed door. There was something eerie about that unexpected, lonely tramp of feet that lay outside of and foreign to our cheerful family circle round the big table, and the strangest thing about it was that there was no voice. Any neighbour coming on an errand or a friendly evening visit would have been calling out as he neared the window: 'Anybody at home? How are you all the-night?' or some friendly thing like that. No friend came voiceless like this, with no greeting but this tramp of invading feet. I felt uneasy, the men of the family were all frowning, and my grandmother bent to the cradle and picked up my brother as the door was unlatched and pushed back so roughly that it rebounded a little way from the wall it struck. Mr Smith stood there, in his plaster-stained mason's clothes, his tweed cap on his head, his arms hanging down limply from his bowed shoulders in a curiously menacing way and his fierce dark eyes fixed themselves on *me*.

'Where's my money, ye thievin' wee bitch?' he growled.

All four men of my family were now on their feet, closing in round him in a semi-circle.

93

'What money?' my father asked.

'My ninety-three pound! *She* took it!'

'Bedamned,' my father said, 'you're out of your mind!'

'No other one has been in my house!' he growled.

The men of my family stared at him, stared at each other, then turned to stare at me. I stood up in my place at the table, looked straight at my father and said: 'I did not touch any money, Dad.'

'In my kist in my room, it was,' said Jamie Bedamned. 'No other one but her comes about my house and she'll come no more. Where's my money?'

Suddenly my dog Fly came out from under the table, raised her eyes to the window and gave a short, sharp bark. Had John been in his cradle she would not have barked – that was why she had merely growled with the other dogs when Jamie Bedamned came – but now she was telling us that there was another stranger's foot on Reachfar ground.

'Somebody else is coming, Dad,' I said.

'George,' my father said, 'go out and see who that is.'

George went out and my father turned back to Jamie Bedamned. 'Jamie, come and sit down and tell us what has happened. I am certain that Janet wouldna touch your money, man – nor anything else that wasna her own. Come and—'

'I want my money! Nobody comes near my house but her and she'll come no more!'

The phrases were like a ritual with him, as if he had said them over and over until he could speak no other words and it was as if he had built them into a wall – like one of the thick walls he built of stone with his hands – in his mind, so that he could not hear or interpret other phrases that were spoken to him.

'She'll come no more!' he repeated.

'And that's the only true word you've spoken this night, Jamie Bedamned!' flashed my grandmother over the fair, goldy head of baby John. 'Where would *my* granddaughter turn thief for your wee bittie money?'

94

'Ninety-three *pound*! She's the only one that comes to my house and she'll come—'

He made me think of Georgie, with her 'Chorchie, Chorchie', only where Georgie snuffled, the father growled. He broke off as George appeared in the doorway, with Flora beside him, her face be-slobbered with tears, her wispy hair in rat-tails about her face, her spindly legs literally shaking in the too-wide men's boots that were laced with string about her ankles. In his hand George held a soiled piece of white paper.

'Jamie,' he said, 'this tells you where your money went,' and he held the paper towards Jamie Bedamned.

The forward-bent, dark-bearded face swung round to look at George. 'Eh?'

It was a queer sound, like a lost echo, and the dark eyes, too, looked lost as if the ritual of 'Ninety-three pound! She'll come no more!' had gone away, leaving a vacuum behind it.

Tom snatched the paper from George's hand and read aloud the pencilled words written there: 'I took the money from your kist. I am going to America. I will never come back. Jamie.'

Tom glared into the dark face with its lost eyes.

'It's your *own* that robbed ye, Bedamned! Your own son! And God knows I don't blame him! If ever a man deserved—'

'Tom!' said my grandfather in his quiet voice. 'That will do. Sit down, Bedamned, and take a cup of tea.'

But with eyes that swept once round all of us and all the walls of the room as if looking for something that they did not hope to find, Jamie Bedamned turned slowly out through the doorway and we all listened to the clump-clump of his heavy boots die away along the front of the steading. It was only then that we became conscious of Flora, who stood, her bent arm over her eyes and between her face and the wall, as the bitter sobs shook her twisted body right down to the skinny ankles in the too-wide boots.

95

'Tom,' said my grandmother, 'carry the cradle ben to my room. Kate, take the bairn ben – he's sleeping. George, go to the parlour for the whisky bottle. Janet, make some fresh tea.'

Then the voice changed from the commanding voice of my grandmother to the comforting voice of my granny.

'Come, Flora, lovey, come to the fire and get a droppie tea. Mercy me, you must be fair done, running all the way up here like that. Come, now.'

'Jamie! Jamie!' sobbed Flora.

'Come now, Flora, pettie. Just drink a little of this and then we'll speak about Jamie. There's a lass. I am sure Jamie is a fine big fellow now.'

'Yes, Mrs Reachfar. He's a fine big fellow. And – and he's not a *bad* boy!'

'Mercy on us, but *surely* he's not a *bad* boy! Jamie is a fine boy and he's your brother and he'll not forget you, lassie. Jamie will never forget you!'

Part III
1930

Part III
1930

In our district the people who were law-abiding, and they were in the majority, would tell you, when they came to know you well enough to have confidence in you, that my grandmother had Second Sight; and the few who were less law-abiding, whether they knew you well or not, would describe her to you as 'the witch, Mrs Reachfar'. She encouraged rather than otherwise both beliefs as to her nature, for she seemed to feel that those who stood in awe of the law were none the worse of some less material governance to stand in awe of, while those who had no respect for the law were immeasurably the better of being frightened out of their wits and into some sort of respect for *some*thing. She was reputed to be able to see into the future and to be able to foretell, with accuracy, future happenings, but when, in 1920, she told Flora Bedamned that her brother Jamie would never forget her it seemed that my grandmother had made one of her remarkably few mistakes. The years came and the years went, and never another word was heard of young Jamie Bedamned, who had run away to America with his father's ninety-three pounds.

By 1930 I was a young woman of twenty, my grandmother was in her late seventies and Flora Bedamned was an even older woman than my grandmother although, in years, she was not yet thirty. I had seen her seldom in the ten years that had passed, for since the night of her father's call at Reachfar I had never been back to Bedamned's Corner, so that I saw Flora only when I happened to pass along the County Road into Achcraggan, which was not often, for I usually went by the more attractive field routes. I do not wish to imply, though, that there was a feud of any kind because of Jamie Bedamned's wrongful accusation made against me. Before Flora left Reachfar on that night in August 1920, escorted by George and Tom, we knew enough of her father to make us sad for him rather than angry with him.

'Father is very hard on the laddies,' Flora said. 'He's not so bad with Georgie and me, but he is awful hard on the laddies. Jamie said that if he hit him again he would run away, but I never thought he would do it.'

'But why did he hit Jamie?' my father asked. 'Jamie is a fine hard-working boy.'

'It was last night. Jamie asked for some of his money to buy Sunday boots,' Flora said.

'His own money?'

'Aye. The money Captain Robertson paid him for mending the gate pillars at the big East Park. And my father leathered Jamie and—'

'But what for?'

'Sunday boots is vanity – that's what my father says. He's a good man, my father, hard-working, good-living and thrifty.'

Loyalty is a highly prized attribute in the Highlands and nobody – and least of all a Sandison – would attempt in any way to undermine it, so my father agreed quietly: 'Yes, your father is a very hard-working man, Flora,' and said no more.

So there was no family feud – it was merely that the drift of life carried me away from Bedamned's Corner. Only about a week after Jamie Bedamned had come to Reachfar my father and I went to Cairnton, and there we remained, coming home only for the holidays, for six years. At the end of that time my father, who had remarried, came home to work at Reachfar – my grandfather and Tom were getting old enough to find the work too much for them – but lived in a house in Achcraggan

100

that belonged to us, for Jean, my stepmother, and my family did not get along together. I remained in the south, in lodgings, for a further three years, to take my degree at Glasgow University, and often thought during the winter of 1930 that I need not have bothered, for the Great Depression was hovering like a death bird over the land and there was no employment for people either with university degrees or without.

My degree in my pocket, unwanted on the labour market, aged twenty, I came home to Reachfar and would have been entirely happy there, and to remain there for ever, except for the said degree, which is one of the typical contrarinesses that life presents to its victims. From childhood I had felt that one of the greatest blisses on earth would be a university education, and having, by the thrift and self-sacrifice of my family, achieved it, it at once began to take on the character of a very painful boil just at the point where the collar rubs upon the neck.

There is a variety of points of view about the purpose of education which I do not intend to write a thesis about here, but there were two conflicting points of view about my education in particular within my family. In the beginning I had set about acquiring the education without thinking out why I wanted to acquire it, but by the time I had acquired what little I did acquire I had arrived at a point of view about it. You will remember from the earlier parts of this chronicle that George, Tom and I gave a considerable amount of time to the study of Latin and to the study of derivations of English words, and I think you may agree that we are three very simple and basic thinkers. Well, the word 'educate' is related to the Latin 'educere', meaning 'to lead forth', and by the time I was twenty I had decided, quite basically and firmly, that the purpose of my education was to lead me forth to make the best contribution I could to the weal of the world, compatible with my own enjoyment of what the world had to offer. If I had ever had the courage to put this into words and tell George and Tom about it, they would have been my supporters,

101

but I had not the courage or the words then, and, meantime, the rest of my family had their own view about this education of mine which they expressed very freely and frequently. This was that its purpose was to enable one to get the best job available and do as much financial good as possible for oneself.

In 1930, no jobs being available and I having no particular desire to do anything other than work around Reachfar and eventually try to write poetry – both ambitions being quite unsuitable for disclosure to my family – my life went into the doldrums, as it were, for some six months – from mid-July 1930, I think, until early February 1931, to be moderately exact. As a Master of Arts with a diploma in shorthand, typewriting, book-keeping and a few other odds and ends, I had a very nice time milking cows, baking, feeding pigs and hens and doing all the other things that Sandison women had always done around Reachfar, but my grandmother and my aunt, although appreciative of my help about the place, were disappointed that all the education had come to nothing but one more Sandison woman doomed to spend her life 'tied to Reachfar'. My father, George and Tom were disappointed too, and I could feel a similar disappointment in my silent grandfather, although he never took part in the discussions about the labour market and my future which were almost a nightly occurrence when we all sat round the fire. These discussions used to make me feel that I had gone back to the age of nothing to ten; back to the time before my brother was born, for I was once again 'the only bairn' in the house, my brother now having gone down to live with my father and stepmother at Jemima Cottage in Achcraggan so that he might be nearer to the bus that took him, every day, to Fortavoch Academy.

No situation in life is as simple as the minor problems in algebra that Tom, George and I used to work out ten years ago. This was not a straightforward case of x equals the trade depression plus y equals Janet's education adding up to the sum z which was the zero of my family

102

disappointment. My family in itself was no simple algebraic quantity such as a. Oh no. My family, the Sandisons, including my young brother and Tom, although numbering seven people, was no simple $7a$ either. Not at all. My family had seven different points of view, seven different kinds of disappointment, and seven different ways of expressing that disappointment, and a seven-fold, cussed persistence in repeating *ad nauseam* that 'it was a shame that Janet should be wasting her time here at Reachfar'.

There always comes, in a situation like this, the moment of crisis, the moment when the last straw is added to the camel's load, and in this case it came through some words spoken by my Aunt Kate. She was now about thirty and the reigning beauty of our small countryside, accustomed to being sought after by all the most eligible young men and to picking and choosing between them, but we of the family knew that the one who could bring the wine-dark blush up over her cool, haughty cheek was a certain Malcolm Macleod of Varlich, up the glen to the west, who was a cousin of Flora Bedamned, being the son of her mother's brother. Malcolm had gone south to Glasgow in his youth to work in the offices of a shipping line and was now working in a small branch office in Aberdeen, but I had gathered from George and Tom that if my aunt would 'take him', Malcolm wanted to go away south again, to the main office, where there would be more scope for advancement for a clever and ambitious young man.

My aunt, however, dilly-dallied, blew hot and cold, went on flirting about the countryside with this one and that one as was her wont, going to the Northern Meeting at Inverness with Farquar Stewart and to the Choir Dance in Achcraggan with Peter Sangster, while the countryside watched her goings-on and had much sly entertainment at the dance that Kate Sandison was leading poor Malcolm Macleod. I watched all this take place and felt that I quite understood what was actuating my aunt, for she was so young and gay in her manner that I regarded her, now that I was twenty, as my own contemporary, and I felt sure

103

that, like myself, she simply was not quite certain that she wanted to get married yet at all. In this, I discovered many years later, I was quite wrong. Kate knew only too well that she wanted to get married and that she wanted to marry Malcolm, but she did not see how she could do it and go away, leaving my grandmother alone and unaided at Reachfar after I had obtained the post I had been educated for. This was the reason for the dilly-dallying and the kicking up of flirtatious heels, but her Sandison pride would not let her make it known, even to Malcolm, and he, in a fit of the pet, went to Edinburgh for a holiday, came home married to his cousin and shortly after that went away down south for good and out of our ken.

My aunt's Sandison pride held firm and with defiant dark eyes she went about the district, affecting not to notice the pseudo-sympathetic looks of the neighbours, some of whom felt genuinely unhappy and some of whom were maliciously pleased that she had been jilted, but no Sandison I have ever known has been an angel, and my aunt, on the stamping ground of the Reachfar kitchen, after Malcolm went away, became a complete devil.

One morning, while I was turning the handle of the churn, I was carolling happily but with no consciousness of the words I was singing: 'Oh, don't decei-eeve me! Oh, never lea-eeve me!' when she turned on me like a spitfire and said: 'What *you*'ve got to sing about, the Lord only knows! If *I* had had your sort of chance *I* wouldn't be clarting about making butter on the top of this godforsaken hill!'

I tried to be peacefully placating, but it was of no avail. My aunt was bent on an outlet for her frustration and she was going to have a row right reason or none.

'But, Kate! There *are* no jobs – down south or anywhere else!'

'There *are* no jobs!' she repeated after me, miaowing the words like a squealing kitten. 'There are plenty of jobs for people with any guts!'

Panting with rage, she glared at me, and, panting from

104

my exertions with the heavy churn, I glared back, straightening my spine and pushing the hair back from my forehead.

'Look at you!' she spat. 'Master of Arts, fluent French and all the rest of it, with your hands all greasy and your hair in your eyes and no more guts than a louse! You're – you're as bad as FLORA BEDAMNED!'

'What is going on in here?' said my grandmother, coming in from the milkhouse at my aunt's last shout. 'Be quiet at once, the two of you! Since when did Reachfar women begin to behave like tinkers in Dingwall market? Kate, get upstairs and do the bedrooms!'

My grandmother having put some distance between my aunt and me for the remainder of the forenoon, I took myself off after dinner-time with the idea of putting distance between us for the afternoon as well, to give my aunt time to cool down. She had always been a mercurial person, going from rage to tenderness inside a moment and from laughter to tears in the same breath, but I had never known her, before this, to be so continuously ill-tempered and black-browed. 'She's – she's black-*advised*!' I told myself, walking through the moor, thinking. 'She's just like Jamie Bedamned!'

Looking back at myself as I was that day, I see myself as a very slow-witted creature, very backward for my age of over twenty in human understanding, but my development had always been slow, despite my parrot-like quickness of brain for the absorption of bare facts and academic information. Even with a mild, so-called, love affair behind me, I was completely unawakened to any knowledge of sexual emotion, and the mental turmoil which my aunt must have been suffering, as she struggled with the old problem of her love for her Malcolm as against what she believed by tradition to be her duty, was something that was utterly out with my own experience and beyond my childish comprehension.

An academic education, I have concluded, is, in a case like mine, of little help in the immediate business of living.

105

I was the first of my family to receive such an education, and it was a new development among people of our class; a new graft, as it were, on to a virgin stock and there must be a lapse of time before a stock accepts a graft and before the graft begins to feed from the stock. At twenty years old, I was a stock of sturdy peasant blood on to which this academic education had been grafted; I was a stock willing in spirit to harbour and feed the scion which had been attached to me, but, surrounding me, there was much hard bark of native growth which the scion must penetrate before deriving substance on which to feed; and coming up from my roots in the rocky soil of Reachfar there was a strong flow of bitter race experience, a sap that was bitter and harsh as food for the delicate new graft. At the age of twenty to twenty-one, and indeed for many years after that, I think, the education that I had received was not a part of me; it was no more than a new graft in the state of suspense between the 'taken' and the 'untaken'; a scion which any harsh wind of circumstance could have blown from the foster stem to wither away and be forgotten while the hard bark closed over the incision which it had taken fifteen years of school and university to make.

Historically, I imagine, the middle of the twentieth century will be noteworthy for the advance and emancipation of what were, before then, the backward peoples of the earth, and a people being the macrocosm of that microcosm, the individual, I feel that it is not unlikely that in the advance out of backwardness whole races will go through a process similar to the process that applied to me as an individual, a process when what is known as academic knowledge is one thing, but the business of living is quite another; a stage when literature is a branch of learning quite divided from life; a stage of divorcement between what has been learned by the brain and what has been assimilated into the mainstream of the spirit. It is an uneasy and terrifying time to live through, a time when the instinctive reaction is into physical activity absorbing and brain-drugging to the point of violence.

Walking across the moor that day, I tried to bring to bear on my aunt the light of my slight knowledge of the -isms and -osophies in an effort to understand why she had turned so bitter against myself, but the light was too faint to be of any avail in these dark places. I tried to think of a means by which I could discuss the subject with Tom and George, but at the back of my mind there was an uneasy, instinctive knowledge that this thing in my aunt was something that they would not want to discuss; something that would embarrass them and that they would prefer to ignore. Yes. I think I was conscious, but in a very dim way, that sex was at the root of the trouble. And sex – sex among human beings, that is – was, of course, a subject that was never discussed. The pretence was that it did not exist.

If the twenty-year-old is subject to puzzles and worries, however, she has compensations too, and in my case I had spirits that could not stay low or depressed for very long. I was healthy; the familiar, native East Moor of Reachfar was springy under my feet; the sharp air of the early year was clear and sparkling as spring water; and the kitchen that held my black-avised aunt was soon a mile and more behind me. I began to feel better and then began to feel very well indeed as I stood on my hilltop looking down to the Firth and away to the northern hills. I began to feel that all the world was mine, with the year at the spring and the day at the morn.

Having walked as far as the source of the Reachfar Burn, I began to follow its course northward and towards the sea, and when I came to the point where it went into its deep gorge under the overhanging brambles I stayed on the higher level and walked down along the grass verge at the side of a stubble field. Although it was late January only, it was, as I have said, a beautiful spring-like day, very clear and sparkling, but warm in the sun, and the stream at the bottom of the gorge was chuckling to itself, as if happy to be hurrying on its journey to join the party of dancing little waves and frolicking sun-sparkles making

107

merry in the great waters of the Firth down below. Dancing in the light wind, throwing sticks for Moss, the collie, to retrieve, I began to sing, as I used to sing when I was a child, and to a quick-time version of 'Early One Morning' Moss and I took the last slope down to the County Road at a brisk canter.

Moss was really George's dog, for Fly, my own collie, had died when I – and she too – was sixteen, for we were almost exact contemporaries. Moss was a different type of collie from Fly. Fly had been of the small Shetland breed, but Moss was a big hill collie, black and white, very wise and capable of great speed and endurance. He should not have been with me at all, for the rule was that he did not leave Reachfar except in the company of George.

I have heard it said that dog-lovers grow to resemble their dogs, or is it that the dog takes on something of his master? At all events, Moss was a dog of very definite character which, yet, was in no way obvious if you merely watched him trotting along behind George. But then, George, if a stranger met him walking across the moor at Reachfar, would look just like any other countryman, quite unremarkable, for it was the way of George to go unremarked, and even in our home district he was completely overshadowed in the minds of the local people by his brother Duncan, my father. In a similar way, Moss was overshadowed around Reachfar by the other two dogs, Fan and Spark. Moss had no pretty habits to attract attention to himself as Fan and Spark had. Moss was simply always there at the right time, such as when hens had to be put out of the garden or a rat popped out of the pig-sty drain. He would put the hens out of the garden neatly with a minimum of fuss and he would destroy a rat in a similar way and then retire to his favourite spot at the barn door and lie down again. When Moss was mentioned at all by us humans the words spoken of him were always the same: 'You don't want to anger him, though', and this was a little extraordinary, for it was very seldom that Moss had been seen to be angry. I myself had seen it only once,

108

which was when a young man who was visiting us sought to demonstrate a ju-jitsu hold on George. The young man had moved swiftly, as ju-jitsu exponents do, but he did not obtain his hold, for Moss moved more swiftly still, took a double hold with his teeth about two inches deep on the young man's left buttock which required six stitches by Doctor Mackay and put an end to all ju-jitsu demonstrations at Reachfar for good. The anger of Moss was a little like the anger of his master, George. It did not rise very often, but, when it did, it created an effect which was permanent.

So, finding myself at the edge of the County Road with this dog character at my heels, I decided to turn up the hill again, for I was afraid we might meet someone on the road who might anger him, but when I turned to call him I discovered that he was displaying every aspect of being extremely angry already. His ears were laid back, his upper lip was curled upwards showing his brilliant white fangs, the strong hair on his shoulders was bristling like spring wire, and from his deep throat there came a hideous, menacing growl.

'Moss! Heel!' I said in my deepest, most commanding voice. Ten yards away from me, he stood stiff-legged but did not move except that his nose twitched before he growled afresh. I looked east and west along the hill face and along the County Road, but could not see a soul in sight. It was then that my own nose became aware that the clear air down here was sullied by a horrible smell of burning hair and scorching flesh, and in the same second I saw a wisp of smoke issuing from the end of the 'bridgie' that led the County Road over the Reachfar Burn. As soon as I moved, Moss was off like a flash, across the fence, across the road and down over the bank to the beach, but he checked at the bottom of the bank in a tangle of old wire that someone had thrown there and I was able to hurl myself on top of him and get a grip on his collar. Then he tore himself free from the wire and, dragging me behind him, he leapt down to the sand at the end of the bridge.

Inside the tunnel was Georgie Bedamned and she had a mongrel dog tied to a heavy tree root that had been washed in by the tide. She had a fire burning; she had a piece of red-hot wire in her hand; she was torturing the dog. One can see a great deal in a few seconds. I saw hours of agony for that stray mongrel, and I saw too the lewd, sexual writhing of Georgie's body which was naked from the waist downwards as, once again, she approached the scarred and terrified animal with the red-hot wire in her hand. Suddenly she saw Moss and me. She dropped the wire, which hissed in the stream in the middle of the tunnel, seized the bundle of skirt and other clothing that lay on the sand and darted out, making off with incredible speed with her crab-like gait, eastwards, along the beach. I felt sick. I suppose I loosened my grip on Moss's leather collar. At all events, in a streak of black and white he sprang through the air, there was a horrible howl from Georgie and the next thing I knew was that I once more had both hands in Moss's collar while Georgie, blood coursing down her skinny mis-shapen leg from the ugly wound in her bare buttock, took to her heels and soon disappeared round a curve of the grass bank by the shore. Moss, having growled until she was out of sight and out of his hearing, then put his paws on my chest and licked my face, as gently as any lady's lapdog. I went back into the tunnel, released the burn-scarred mongrel, which darted, whimpering, away westwards along the sand, and then I began to vomit into the clear water of the Reachfar Burn, where it spread in a small delta among the pebbles. Moss sat beside me until the spasm was over and then licked the cold sweat from the backs of my hands.

It was long past suppertime before I went home with some story of having gone for a longer walk than I had intended and I went early to bed that night, but I did not sleep. It was, of course, not possible to tell of what I had seen; even if I could have found the words, it would have been loathsome to me to re-create that scene in the minds of any of my family. It was something, I felt, that must be forgotten, buried; but how to forget it, how to bury it? I fought with the knowledge that the stain of it would always be there in my mind, like some hideous pock-mark on my vision of the face of humanity, like some dreadful cruelty perpetrated by the merciful God in whom I had been trained to believe. The idiot Georgie was not to blame for what she had done, for she had merely been obeying the perverted instincts with which she had been born accursed, but why had any creature been so cursed? And why in such a way? The thing I could not eradicate from my mind was the atmosphere of perverted, orgiastic sexuality that had pervaded the little tunnel when Moss and I appeared at its entrance. In my memory, it seemed, there would remain for ever the picture of Georgie's deformed face, further deformed by a mask of lust, the picture of Georgie's distorted body, further distorted by motions of unnatural lewdness, and echoing from behind these pictures was the sound of the animal voice, more animal than ever as it snuffled the 'Chorchie! Chorchie!' in an effort to express her bliss in this orgasm of cruelty and debauchery.

When I came downstairs the next morning the January sun was rising as sharply brilliant as it had been the day before, but to look to the east, where it was coming up over the sea, was to know that between me and it lay the house we called Bedamned's Corner. To go with my aunt to the byre for the milking and take my place under the glossy side of Big Maggie and touch her warm udder was to remember the exposed, pasty-skinned, wriggling belly of Georgie Bedamned. To see the big Wyandotte cockerel, high-stepping down the yard with the sun on his tail plumes that the morning breeze was ruffling, was to remember Georgie's avid lust in the hidden place under the bridge so that the clear sunshine and fresh air of the morning became the half-light of the furtive, foetid dankness of the tunnel and the smell of burning hair and scorching flesh. For the first time in my twenty years of

111

life it seemed to me to be desirable to get away from this place, Reachfar.

It was about two days after that that Lady Lydia came up to ask my grandmother to help her find a nursemaid for her married daughter in Hampshire and I offered myself for the post. There may be a divinity which shapes our ends – I have an open mind – but the ways of that divinity are strangely devious. After Lady Lydia's visit and it being settled that I would go to Hampshire, I had a few more days at home and I found myself thinking a great deal about Flora, whom I had hardly seen for ten years, and I thought, with bitterness, of the love and care and endless watchfulness that she had expended on Georgie down the days of her idiot life. Although, bodily, I was escaping into another life, I knew that my mind would never escape from this question of why, why, why. I would be 'ask-ask-asking' for the why and wherefore of Georgie for the rest of my life.

'Tom,' I said one morning when he and I were in the granary alone, bagging oats. 'How are the Bedamneds? I haven't seen any of them since I came home from Glasgow.'

'Och, chust the same,' Tom said. 'The three boys is a-all up and working now, but the housie is as miserable, and poor Flora chust as trachled with work as ever. And Georgie is dafter than ever, although she's bigger and taller than poor Flora now. How old will she be – Georgie, I mean?'

'Fifteen. She's five years younger than I am.'

'Aye. That's right. Poor Flora has her hands full with her, whateffer.'

'Does she still have these awful fits?'

'No. They tell me she doesn't get them at a-all now, but the way she is now is worse, if anything.'

'How do you mean, Tom?'

Tom put his hand into the bag we had just filled and let a handful of grain run through his fingers while he looked

112

down at it. 'It's the men she's after now,' he said. 'When the harvest was on at Seamuir, she came on to the field among the men and was for taking a-all her clothes off.'

'Tom!'

Although I pretended to be horrified at something that was new to me, I was comforted to know that Flora must know something of the ugly side of Georgie.

'It's a terrible thing for poor Flora. It's in some kind o' a home or an insteetution place she should be, but in spite of four men's money coming into the house Jamie Bedamned won't pay the few shillings a week that the home would ask from him. The Laird has been at him two or three times about it, but you know what Jamie is. You might as well speak to a stone.' My mind – I think *both* our minds – went back to that night ten years ago when Jamie Bedamned kept repeating his ritual: 'Ninety-three pound! She'll come no more!'

Tom shook out another bag, handed it to me to hold the top open and began to fill it with the big, bright, square shovel. When it was partly filled, not too heavy for me to lift, I swung it on to the scale platform, and as it sat there Tom brought the weight up to a hundred-weight and a half. It was a clean, fresh-smelling job that I liked, that had also the satisfaction of being a step in the supply of a human and animal need, a normal need, for a basic foodstuff.

'But surely, Tom,' I said, 'Jamie Bedamned could be forced to put Georgie into some place or another. It would be for her own good, wouldn't it? And for Flora's good, too?'

'People is very funny about things like that,' Tom said. 'Flora is as fond of that eediot as if she was the bonniest and cleverest lassie in the countryside. If she was to be taken away, Flora would miss her something desperate. An' then, eediots is not as stupid as a lot of people think when it comes to getting what they want for themselves. Georgie knows in some way that Flora is soft about her and she behaves herself good when Flora can see her. And Flora thinks she has no more sense than to take her clothes

113

off in the harvest field, but Georgie knows what she's after by it, right enough.' Tom bent very low over his shovel and the heap of oats. 'She tried it on with myself once when I met her and me coming home from Achcraggan and I'm not the only one she's tried it on with. And it's as if she knew none of us could face wee Flora to tell her a thing like that.'

'*Some*body ought to, Tom!' I burst out. 'It's horrible!'

'Ach, we all chust take no notice and keep out of her road if we can. Poor Flora!'

'But – but some man might – might take advantage of her!' I said, bringing up from my childhood a phrase which I had once heard.

'Och, no man in his senses would go near the like o' Georgie, for God's sake!' said Tom in disgusted protest. And so the one opportunity to tell of the horror I had seen slipped past, for there seemed to be no point in disgusting Tom more than he was disgusted already, especially when nothing, apparently, could be done about removing Georgie to a home. Besides, there was the question of words, words to explain, to describe . . .

'She's as cute as a bag o' monkeys, that Georgie,' Tom went on. 'She is most damnable destructive. She'll work away at a fence post till she has it out of the ground and the wire down, she'll leave gates wide open all over the place, she'll kill any chickens or ducks she can lay hands on an' chust leave them lying about. And we all know it's her work that's in it, but dang it if you'll catch her at it! *And*, of coorse, dang it if she'll do any of her mis*cheev*yous destructiveness round about Bedamned's Corner! Not her! She'll not lay a hand on Flora's ducks or ould Jamie's shaky ould rickles o' fences!'

'If somebody *could* catch her Jamie Bedamned would *have* to send her away,' I said.

'Ach, I don't know. Anyway, she never comes up this way. It's on Poyntdale she's such a devil of a nuisance, but ye know what Leddy Lydia is with her: "Poor thing, it is only a *phase* she's going through and, anyway, Torquil,

114

you have no *proof* it was Georgie!'' Proof! As if any person in their sober senses would do the capers she does! And then Leddy Lydia gives her another hat or dress or something an' you'll meet Georgie on the County Road dressed as if she was for the Northern Meeting Ball. I was ever o' the opeenion that people that is vain o' themselves had a bittie o' the eediot in them, an' Georgie is chust the proof of it.'

The last time I had seen Georgie, she was not dressed as if for a ball and I fled away from the memory of her again.

'Nothing has ever been heard of young Jamie, Tom?' I asked next.

'Not a word. And it's myself that's not surprised. I think if it wasna that he's sorry for Flora, young Davie would be off too, long ago. Indeed, it would be the price of ould Jamie if Davie and Roddie and Hughie was to be off, taking Flora with them, an' leave him with Georgie. I bet you he'd put her in a home *then* soon enough, the mean ould devil! Indeed, I don't know how the laddies stand it – they slave and work from week's end to week's end, they never have a penny to call their own and not as much as a bittie fire in the house unless they cut the sticks for it. And Jamie in the kirk every Sunday in yon ould black coat o' his father's that's as green wi' age as a young larch in spring and not a Christian thought in his hard, black head. It's enough to make a body spew . . . Where's the bag needle? Sew this one for me and that's the last o' the lot for Dingwall . . . Flora was quite clever at the school, wasn't she?'

'She was a worker more than clever by nature, I think.'

'And was there any brains among the boys?'

'Roddie was average to good, I'd have said. He was in my class. He'll be twenty now. Are they all at the mason work, the boys?'

'Och, aye. Ould Jamie trained them and keeps them under his hand, like.'

'And it's a pretty hard hand. I wonder why they stick it? Flora, I suppose.'

'God knows. Davie is working at Poyntdale the now. The

115

roof o' the big barn came half off in that gale in November.' Tom sighed. 'It's changed days at Poyntdale, a young loon patchin' up the big barn. I can mind on the day when a squad o' twenty would be up there, putting on a new roof if it was needed, before the storm was right over.'

'I can remember those days too, Tom,' I said and we sewed bags in silence for a little.

'You should go and see Flora before you go off south, Janet,' he said next. 'Nobody never goes near there – people are kind o' frightened o' ould Jamie.' He looked up and giggled mischievously. 'Indeed, with us here, it is the other way. Jamie's kind o' frightened o' *us*!'

'Why?'

Tom bent to his work again. 'Och, I don't think he's ever got over the fool he made of himself yon time about the money. He's awful civil to your father or George or me, whateffer, and God knows he's not civil to many people.'

'Tom, do you honestly think that Jamie Bedamned is quite right in his head?'

Tom looked straight at me over the top of the bag of oats.

'He's as right in the head as any Bedamned ever was,' he told me, and then he straightened his back, took out his pipe and went to the door of the granary. It was a loft that ran above the stable and loosebox, entered by an outside stairway that came up the east gable of the steading. At the top of this stairway there was a small railed platform or landing, and Tom now put one buttock on the rail and stared away north-easterly in the direction of Bedamned's Corner. With his back to me, he said: 'The Bedamneds are all right in their heads – except for Georgie, of coorse – it's in their hearts and their souls that they're wrong.'

'What do you mean, Tom?'

He turned his head towards me. 'It's kind of hard to explain, to explain right. They keep to the Ten Commandments and they do a-all the things that decent people do.

116

They don't steal. Jamie worked hard to keep his ould mother and father until they died – that is what is meant by "honour thy father and thy mother" I am thinking? And they do a good job at the mason work, and they pay their debts and go to the kirk on Sundays. If you was to tell anyone that had never seen Jamie Bedamned these things about him, he would think to himself, most likely, that this fellow Jamie Bedamned was a fine man – a decent, honest, hardworking, good-living fellow. And so he is – on the outside of him. But when I am looking at the black eyes o' Jamie Bedamned, I start to think on a wicked horse, like yon dirty brute that Mr Macintosh got cheated over at the sale down south and brought home to Din-chory. If it had been any other man in the countryside but George at his head yon day they tried him in the binder for the first time, there would be another grave in Achcraggan churchyard. A good horse *likes* the job he is trained for if he gets justice at pasture and in the stable, and a good man *likes* to work at a job he can do and he likes to live decent and pay his debts, but Jamie Bedamned is like yon wicked horse, he doesna like any of it or any*body*. The horse, poor brute, was stupid enough to show the badness that was in him and got a shot through his head for his pains, but Jamie Bedamned, being a man and not a horse, is cute enough to hide his badness. Aye, he's a-all right in his head, right enough.'

'Were his father and grandfather like that, too, Tom?' I asked quietly.

'I never liked the look in the eye o' *any* Bedamned,' he replied, 'but I was younger at the time and never took special notice o' the older ones.'

'What are you two blethering about *now*?' my aunt asked from the bottom of the stairway where she had arrived on her egg-collecting round.

The Reachfar hens, I should mention, were non-algebraic and quite without conformity like the rest of the family. They would lay in the nests provided for that pur-pose only 'when taken real short', as George put it, and

117

much preferred the horses' hayracks, the sack heap in the barn or the whin bushes in the moor as laying places.

Since I had found myself a job and my departure was imminent, I think my aunt regretted having used me as a whipping-post and outlet for her frustration and hurt pride, but this does not mean that she had suddenly become an angel of sweetness and light. She no longer quarrelled with *me*, but she was not interested in any subject of conversation that did not give rein to anger, indignation or some of the other feelings with which the crisis in her own life had filled her, for at that time she *had* no other feelings to bring to anything.

'Did I hear the name of Bedamned?' she asked now in a warlike voice, depositing her basket of eggs in Betsy's cart, which was lying, trams on the ground, before she began to come up the stairs.

'Janet was chust asking was there ever any news o' young Jamie,' said Tom as she seated herself on the top step.

'No, no news! And no wonder! And good luck to him! And if these other three laddies had the guts of herring they would be off too! As for that Flora, skittering about round ould Jamie Bedamned's tail with her "Yes, Father; coming, Father" – she's enough to make you ashamed that women were ever born!'

'Och, away with you, Kate!' said Tom, who, wiser than I was, probably knew that in her diatribe against Flora my aunt was releasing some of her own pent-up sense of being doomed to spend the rest of her life saying, 'Yes, Mother; coming, Father', around Reachfar.

'Dammit, where could the lassie run away *to*?' Tom went on. 'And where would she go? What could she do? She's never seen anything but Bedamned's Corner.' His voice altered its tone. 'It's not as if she was like *some* people, that could get married any time they wanted to or take a job at any sort of thing.'

'And what would getting married be but skittering round another tail?' snapped my aunt. Her dark eyes stared

118

away rebelliously across the Firth for a moment, then softened, and her voice softened too when next she spoke: 'Poor Flora! You should go down to see her before you go south, Janet. Nobody ever goes near there except one of us – Granny or me, sometimes.' She smiled at me. 'It's not a very nice place to go to, even if you pick your time and go when old Jamie's not there. It's so bare – and kind of miserable.' She shivered and then added: 'I feel so sorry for that laddie Davie, the oldest one. He's delicate looking – he's more on the mother's side than the Bedamneds'.'

'He's working down at Poyntdale the now,' said Tom, 'sorting the roof o' the big barn.'

'I don't think he likes the mason work,' she said. 'But, of course, down there it doesn't matter what people like – they just have to do what ould Jamie says. Look at Roddie – he wanted to join the Seaforths and try to get into the pipe band. Alasdair Mackay taught him to play the pipes on the quiet and he's a grand piper, but, oh, no! He had to be a mason, under ould Jamie's thumb, and say: Yes, Father; coming, Father! *I'd* Father the old brute if he was anything to do with *me*!' The noise of a cart on the track came rattling down from the moor and she sprang lithely to her feet. 'Lord, there's Granda and Duncan coming back with the firewood – it must be nearly three o'clock tea-time!' She glared balefully out over the clear, sunlit hillside to the Firth. 'This weather's too good for January! We'll be up to our behinds in snow in April, I'll bet you!'

She ran down the stairs, snatched the eggs from the cart and ran along to the house.

'When things will be going against people like your auntie,' said Tom, 'even the weather will be wrong, though it will be putting its backside out of choint to give us a little sun in Chanuary!'

It was on the morning after Tom and I had bagged the oats, I think, that my father came up from Achcraggan as usual but brought with him an unusual piece of news.

119

'I met the policeman along at the Smiddy,' he said. 'He's on the lookout for a stray dog.'

We were all in the kitchen at the time, just finishing breakfast, and I, as always, was sitting on the 'bairns' side' of the table between Tom and George, with the dogs underneath, at our feet.

Life at Reachfar is like one of those Highland rivers that has a flat, pebbly, shallow side where the water sparkles along and a deep second channel at the other side where the water slides quietly past in the shadow of a shelving bank. The shallow side is the small-talk and surface relationship of day-to-day; the deeper channel is the flow of the deeper relationships in our family. But the river in both its channels contains the same water, and sometimes a little wave crosses from the pebbles to the deep channel, and sometimes a surge from the deep channel breaks over the pebbles.

As my father spoke, I felt my mind tauten into wariness, and even as I became wary I felt a surge of feeling transmit itself from George to me. Neither of us spoke or moved.

'Sheep-worrying already?' Tom asked, and my aunt added: 'The worrying doesn't usually start until the lambing season.'

'No.' My father sat down by the fire and began to light his pipe. 'It seems that Georgie Bedamned has been very badly bitten.'

'Och, poor craitur!' my aunt said.

'It is myself,' said Tom, 'that feels sorrier for the dog, poor beast!'

'Tom!' my aunt protested.

I stared straight across the table top at the red fire, saying nothing while my father, my aunt and Tom discussed the news, until I heard George say: 'All right, Moss, here's your bittie!' and the dog's head came up between his knees to receive the little corner of oat-cake that George gave him each day after breakfast. Then, quietly, George left the table and went out, the big dog at his heels as usual. I felt myself under a strange compulsion to follow them, which I did, and found George leaning against the barn door, filling his pipe, while Moss sat at his feet.

'You and Moss took a bit walk the other day,' he said, watching the flame of the match go up and down above the bowl as he drew upon the pipe.

'Iphm,' I said.

'Was you seeing anybody when you were out?' he enquired conversationally.

'Nobody – of any consequence,' I replied.

'Did anybody – of any consequence – see *you*?'

'I don't think so, George. Why were you asking?'

He looked away into the distance, to the dark fir trees up on the moor. 'I've known Moss to take a bit snap at people,' he said quietly, 'if sore provoked.'

'So have I,' I said, equally quietly.

He eased his shoulders away from the barn door and stood upright. 'Och, well, if Soutar the Bobbie comes this way the-day, you could tell him you were out that day but saw nothing – of any consequence. That damned Georgie likely deserved the bite she got – she's inclined to tease beasts when she gets the chance, like the day she put Granny Fraser's old cat in the water barrel. Maybe she'll have more respect for dogs from now on . . . Well, I'm going out round the sheep on the West Moor . . . Heel, Moss!'

He strode away up the yard, Moss exactly one foot behind his heavy boots, and I went back into the house.

When the policeman called, we gave him a cup of tea, my aunt and I, and he was very amused because Fan and Spàrk barked by way of saying 'Thank you' for pieces of biscuit. Working dogs like ours were not registered or licensed, and the policeman did not seem to be aware that Reachfar had a third dog, called Moss, who had no pretty tricks with pieces of biscuit. Moss was not mentioned.

'The beast must have been some stray,' the policeman said as he was going away. 'Farmers don't keep weecked dogs.'

'Of course not!' I said.

'To tell the truth, a bit of a nip won't do that Georgie Bedamned any harm,' said my aunt. 'She's a wicked little devil.'

'Between ourselves, she is that,' the policeman agreed. 'But it's sheep-worrying more than Georgie that's on Sir Torquil's mind, I think, if there's a stray going about.'

'I see,' my aunt said. 'Well, we've no sheep-worriers on Reachfar. We can't afford them, can we, Fan?'

Fan waved her plumed tail and so did Spark.

'No, I can see that,' the policeman said and, having patted the dogs once more, he went away.

It was a custom of our countryside that anyone who was 'going away south to work', as I was now, made a round of farewell calls on their special friends and acquaintances, and during my last few days at Reachfar I conformed with this and went, one morning, to Achcraggan to call on Dominie Stevenson, Mrs Mackay, the doctor's wife, and one or two others.

Social calls in Achcraggan were not confined to a polite twenty minutes, and although I had gone to the school specially at the time to catch the Dominie at 'little morning play', he showed a fine disregard for his Education Authority employers by setting his classes tasks they could do by themselves and retiring with me to the schoolhouse with the words: 'And if I hear any noise before I come back, I'll take the cane to the whole boiling of you!' In his study, he produced a bottle of whisky and a decanter of sherry and a tin of shortbread and he and I sat down to put the world to rights for about two hours.

Nevertheless, when I took my leave of the schoolhouse I decided that I was not going back to Reachfar without doing a few more of my calls, so I went next to the doctor's house where Mrs Mackay would not be in the least put out at an unexpected guest for lunch; and as I walked along the shore road, which was parallel with the main thoroughfare of the village, but so little used now that the fishing trade in Achcraggan had died away, that it might

122

have been miles away from any centre of habitation, I was thinking about the Bedamneds again and of what the Dominie had said.

In my family, as a child, I was notorious, as I have said, for what was known as 'ask-ask-asking'. All normal children ask questions, but I had – and still have – a tendency to get my mind fixed on a particular subject and I cannot rest – nor let anyone else rest – until I have reached what seems to me to be the bottom of it, and I was now in a bad state of this kind over the Bedamneds. I do not remember deliberately introducing the subject over the Dominie's sherry and shortbread, but there is little doubt that the first mention of it came from me, obsessed by the subject as I was, although once introduced the Dominie had much more to say on the matter than I had.

Many people were content to describe Dominie Stevenson as 'that drunken ould bachelor' and to leave matters there, but no man, even the most insignificant, can be described as simply as that. And there was nothing insignificant about the Dominie. Indeed, I think he drank because he was constructed upon a scale too large and grandiose for the small and paltry age that succeeded the 1914–18 war; he drank so that he could escape from petty officialdom and that his mind might soar, a free spirit, into the upper realms of broad ideas which were its natural home. Dominie Stevenson believed in Youth and he believed in the Future, and this last seemed, in his mind, to be a place just over the horizon which Youth could build into a Golden City of Eternal Bliss. His own eyes were too old and tired to see this place, with its nuggets of gold lying around awaiting the hands of Youth that would build them into palaces; with its spread canvases and acres of paper, all waiting for Youth to turn them into beautiful pictures and inspired works of literature; with its secrets of medicine and engineering all lying packed in boxes, waiting only for the hands of Youth to open them and the minds of Youth to bring them into the service of mankind. When Dominie Stevenson looked down from his great

123

height at a five-year-old child he did not see the latest of the big Mathieson brood or the little red-headed Sandison of Reachfar whose mother had died at his birth. No. Dominie Stevenson saw a potential knight in shining armour, a keen-eyed adventurer into the land of the Future who needed only one thing, a thing which he had a right to claim, a thing which Dominie Stevenson would fight with all his strength to give him, the thing which Dominie Stevenson called 'a chance in life'.

'Good young people, all these Smiths,' he said to me over his whisky that day, 'and not one of them allowed the ghost of a chance. Oh, there was nothing special about Flora as a scholar, but life owed her more than to be born into slavery. And Georgina was a tragedy. Your grandmother and Doctor Mackay wasted their gifts the day they saved *that* life.'

This was the sort of thing that Dominie Stevenson was not afraid to say although it outraged many of the sanctimonious minds that surrounded him.

'But with that boy Davie, Jamie Bedamned has a mortal sin to answer for, if any one thing that I believe is true.'

He poured himself some more whisky and stared into the red heart of his study fire.

'I knew that young *Jamie* was fairly clever at school,' I said, 'but I didn't realise that Davie was anything very special.'

'Young Jamie fiddlesticks!' he barked at me. 'Young Jamie was just old Jamie over again – that's why he had the ruthlessness to do what he did, steal that money and run away. Mind you, he was not as ugly in the temper as his father – there was a little Macleod sweetening in his blood from the mother, but the ruthlessness and the striving for himself were in him, strong in him. But Davie was different. Davie was never out for what he could get but was out to give. And I am sure that he had some great thing *in* him to give.'

'Yes, Dominie?' I encouraged him.

'Yes!' he barked, his bushy eyebrows drawn down over

124

his fierce old eyes. 'Davie had one of the finest, most sensitive minds that ever came to this school and I've seen quite a few good minds come in through that gate in the wall out there! But it isn't a mind any more that Davie has – Jamie Bedamned killed it and turned the corpse into Davie Bedamned, stone-mason and plasterer!'

The Dominie's voice had deepened to a shaking, subdued shout of rage, and as he reached again for his whisky bottle I put my sherry glass on the table and, rising, went over to look out at the school playground on the other side of a little strip of garden. When I turned away from the window, the Dominie was again staring into the fire and was calmer now. He had become a little drunk, I think, a little insulated against present realities.

'I have to go, Mr Stevenson,' I said.

He looked up at me. 'Funny thing about youngsters,' he said. 'No two of them are alike. Davie Smith was always frightened of heights – no head for it. And you and that Alasdair Mackay were devils to climb when you were young.'

'Were we?'

I did not remember any climbing exploits.

'*Were* you!' he jeered at me, wrinkling his nose at me in a disgusted way. 'Alasdair never had any imagination, of course. *You* had a gleam here and there, but it never seemed to affect your climbing head. You don't remember the day the two of you were astride the roof-tree of the church at dinner-time?'

'Oh yes, I believe I do, vaguely.'

'Vaguely! And the whole town of Achcraggan gathered round and women crying and screaming and men running with ladders and the minister praying and the doctor swearing and I – I always think of myself first – I was wondering how I was going to explain this to your grandmother . . . How is she?'

And so, thinking of the Bedamneds and Davie, now, in particular, I walked from the shore road in through the back garden gate and round, with last-minute formality,

125

to the front door of Doctor Mackay's house.

The doctor's house, though larger and more rambling than most of the Achcraggan houses, conformed to the local pattern and had the usual porch over the front door, with a pitched, slated roof, and at the peak of this was a weathercock, a handsome bird, with a tall comb and a luxuriant plumed tail. He had always been known to Alasdair and me as 'Blithe Spirit' because of 'Hail to thee, blithe spirit, bird thou never wert . . .' and today Alasdair was astride the roof-tree of the porch with a can of gold paint in one hand, a brush in the other and a smear of paint down one side of his nice, ugly face.

'Hullo,' I said, 'how's Blithe Spirit?'

'Well enough, but a little rusty. What's this I hear about you going to nurse Lady Islington's offspring, is it true?'

'Quite true.'

'God have mercy on the poor brat! Here' – he handed down the tin and the brush – 'hold these for me.'

'Why aren't you back in Edinburgh?' I asked as he climbed down. 'Has the Varsity sacked you at last?'

'Going back on Monday. Let's go in and have a beer before Mother gets back from the shops.'

Over lunch at the Mackays' big table in the shabby old dining-room, after the doctor and Lachie, the spaniel who assisted him in his practice, had come in from their round, I told of my visit to the Dominie and, naturally, the subject of the Bedamneds arose again.

'Stevenson exaggerates a lot of the time,' the doctor said. 'It's possible that Davie Smith was a clever enough boy, but the Dominie sees every young goose that goes to his school as a potential swan.'

'Anyway, Daddy,' said the spirited Mrs Mackay, 'that's better than seeing every child as a potential few shillings a week which is all Jamie Bedamned does!'

'Doctor Mackay,' I said, 'will Georgie Bedamned ever get any better?'

He shook his head. 'Speaking very unprofessionally, Janet, and only among ourselves here, poor Georgie can

126

only get worse, I'm afraid.' He sighed. 'That's the saddest house in the countryside. These are bad times and there are houses a lot poorer – the Bedamneds can always get work, it seems. I suppose Jamie sees to that. But there's no house as damned *miserable* as Bedamned's Corner.'

'By the way,' Mrs Mackay said, 'how is Georgie's leg? I met Nurse Morrison this morning and she was saying she had never seen such a wound.'

'Nurse is young and hasn't seen much,' said Doctor Mackay easily. 'Georgie's all right – a good clean tear, that's all.'

'Is this this dog-bite I've been hearing about?' I asked.

'Iphm.'

'Has anybody any idea how it happened?'

The doctor bent his bright twinkling eyes on me. 'No. Flora didn't know it was a dog-bite until I came along. By that time she had reported to Soutar, the policeman, that Georgie had been assaulted, so I had to put things right with Soutar.'

'How were *you* sure it was a dog-bite, Dad?' Alasdair enquired from a medical point of view. 'How can you be sure? What did you go on? *Georgie* couldn't tell you anything!'

'In my job – and yours, if you play a little less rugby and attend a few more classes – there are two main things you go on – what you see now and what you've seen before,' the doctor said. 'Up to now, Georgie was very fond of teasing Lachie here – putting her tongue out at him through the car windows and rattling her fingers on the glass and so on. She won't go near the car now. That's one thing. The other thing is that I once' – his eyes flickered across my face and back to Alasdair – 'before saw a similar dog-bite that took a similar six stitches, that's all. Quite simple.'

'Poor Georgie!' Mrs Mackay said. 'I hope they trace the dog.'

'They won't,' said Doctor Mackay confidently. 'As I told Soutar, there's a couple of hundred big dogs who

127

could have done it in this district – it could have been any of them. And I wouldn't waste your sympathy on Georgie, Mother. She's a vicious fiend in many ways. Lachie could tell you that if he could speak . . . Georgie is a real Smith, a big strong lump physically. It'll take more than a dog-bite to kill her. She's heavier than Davie – that boy went to the mother's side.'

'That's what the Dominie said when he was going on about him,' I said.

'I don't remember much about Davie Bedamned at school,' Alasdair said, 'and, of course, since I went to the Academy and then to Edinburgh, I haven't seen him at all.'

'He's two years older than we are, of course,' I said.

'I know.' Alasdair frowned. 'But I remember the bigger one, Jamie, the one that stole the old man's money and ran away. I don't seem to remember Davie playing football or anything down in the Big Boys' Bit,' he ended, grinning at me.

'That's true,' I agreed. 'I suppose he was a quieter type than some I could name.'

'I only remember him one time distinctly,' Alasdair pursued. 'We were playing cricket with an old tennis ball and Davie hit it up on to the roof of the schoolhouse and it stuck in a drainpipe. He wouldn't go up for it – scared of going on the roof – and there was a fight.'

'Who went for the ball?' the doctor asked.

'I did. Got caught, too, and got a walloping. That's why I remember it.'

'Serve you right,' said his father. 'You two were no better than a couple of monkeys at that age – always climbing over everything,' and he began to recount all over again the episode of the church roof.

'The Dominie was on about that this morning, too,' I said. 'Do you remember it, Alasdair?'

'I don't think I remember actually being up there,' he replied. 'But I remember Mother here giving me hell when I got home for causing an uproar in the town.'

'The whole thing was ridiculous,' said the doctor. 'The two of you were perfectly safe, but I was afraid the yells of the women would make one of you lose your nerve and fall and I gave Mrs Gilchrist the Draper a good round cursing and made her go home. Then the minister had nothing better to do than give *me* a telling-off for using bad language to Mrs Gilchrist! I've never spent such a half-hour in all my life. I could have killed the two of you with my bare hands and that was neither the first nor the last time I could have slaughtered you both, let me tell you! Oh, well, Janet, these days are done and you're off to young Miss Grace, are you? What's her husband's name again?'

'Islington. Sir Adrian Islington.'

'That's it. Not much of a job for the like of you, but it takes you nearer the centre of things. You'll never get anywhere, stuck away up here. And it's only temporary, isn't it?'

'Yes. The real nurse is ill, that's all.'

'So artificial Nurse Sandison takes over,' said Alasdair.

'Poop to you and your artificial!' I said. 'Half-a-doctor Mackay!'

At the age of five I thought that people of nearly twenty-one were what I called 'Real Grown-up Persons', but this was a mistake, for Alasdair and I, although nearly twenty-one, were not at all grown up even yet.

After leaving the Mackays, I made one or two more short calls and then made my way westwards along the street, speaking to my friends the shopkeepers and one or two old retired fishermen and my friend Bill-the-Post, who, in spite of the sharpish January wind, were at their stance at the pier-head, waiting patiently opposite the closed, inhospitable, unlicensed-hours door of the Plough Inn, and then I left Achcraggan behind, planning which of the many routes I would take back to Reachfar. Then, on an impulse – it was still only about three in the afternoon – I decided to go by the County Road as far as Bedamned's Corner, go in and see Flora and, incidentally, ease my conscience about the dog-bitten Georgie.

I have always been stimulated by the company of my friends, and I think my day spent among so many people that I liked had made me feel mentally stronger and less haunted and sickened by the thought of Georgie, so that, as I set out along the County Road, I even had some idea of telling Flora something of what I had seen in the little tunnel under the bridge to try to bring home to her how necessary it was that Georgie should be under some sort of restraint. As I walked along the road by the sea, I felt more normal than I had felt since I had vomited at the small estuary of the Reachfar Burn and I even began to plan, in actual words, what I would say to Flora, words that would portray the iniquity of Georgie without giving away the fact that she had been bitten by Moss. The fact that I had been to school with Flora and that she was so much younger than my grandmother, my aunt and Mrs Mackay made the words to describe Georgie easier to find, and there was also in my mind the idea that the down-trodden Flora would be easy to dominate mentally, so that I, Janet Sandison, would be able to tell her what I had seen and what must be done to avoid a repetition of it in the future and brook no argument. Flora Bedamned was accustomed to being dominated, used to being bent to the will of others, and her natural reaction would be to bow her head and listen to what I had to say and accept it without question, so I thought.

The little house was built facing south-west, with its gable to the north and the sea; and as I approached it, it presented its blank east wall, broken only by one small window which, I knew, was in the little bedroom that opened off the kitchen. The wall around the over grown garden was broken in many places and falling down in some; the oblong, stone-built chimney on the north gable of the house – the chimney of the 'parlour' that would never be in use – its mortar loosened by gales and rain, had lost several of its topmost stones so that it stood like a broken rampart against the redly darkening sky. The walls of the house themselves, instead of being stoutly rough-cast and white-washed as they once had been, were like a diseased skin, the rough-cast battered away by the weather, the mortar between the stones crumbling out, and several slates were missing from the roof. Like a scar on the pitted east wall, a broken rope hung at an angle, one end attached to the roof edge, the other lost in a tangle of run-out, thorny gooseberry bushes.

Cold, bleak, grim, desolate, the little house seemed to cower under the winter sky as if under its battered shelter there lay a secret that it must conceal or fall into ruin in the effort. As I came nearer to it, my mood of confidence began to disintegrate into a tangle of horror, mental nausea and panic fear. This was induced, somehow, by the house itself and was not generated primarily by the thought of Georgie, what I had seen her do or the difficulty of approaching Flora on the subject.

I should say here that I think my main motive behind my desire to have Georgie removed to some institution was that she was a blot on the fair face of my countryside, a corrupt menace who despoiled the very earth she trod – this was how I saw her. I do not claim for an instant that I cherished any humane motives for the well-being of Georgie herself. I had always found her loathsome and now, for me, she was more loathsome still. An animal with her type of deficiency, born in our community, would have been quickly and painlessly destroyed, and my attitude to Georgie was exactly what my attitude would be to an abnormal animal – what our countryside called 'an objeck', like a calf with five legs. We did not commercialize such creatures and charge the more morbid a penny for the sight of them. We quietly destroyed them, buried them and spoke of them no more.

But the nearer I came to the crouching, grey little house, the more difficult it became to think in clear-cut terms of rights and wrongs, natural people and 'objecks'. Georgie might be an 'objeck', but she was a human one who lived in that little house, and her sister Flora had loved her, cherished her and worked to keep her clean and fed and

131

safe for fifteen years. And the house, like a crouching, cowed animal, seemed to say to me: 'And I have sheltered her! I have sheltered her!'

Walking straight-backed, Sandison-fashion, along the road towards it, I began to feel that I was arrogant, guilty of the sin of spiritual pride in my arbitrary decisions as to what should be done with the youngest child of this unhappy house. According to Tom, Flora was aware of many of Georgie's excesses, did her best to keep them in check and loved her in spite of them. Who was I to interfere? Flora's unhappiness was already great enough. Why make it greater by describing to her a scene which would only haunt her imagination for ever as it was likely to haunt my own? From now forward Georgie would probably avoid dogs, the only animals likely to be tame enough for her to catch. And there was the final telling truth that Georgie, though an 'objeck', was a human one, and all my training had been directed towards an appreciation of the importance in the scale of creation of the human being. Was not this Georgie that same infant for whose life my grandmother and Doctor Mackay had fought through those two nights fifteen years ago?

None of this, of course, was clear in my mind as I walked along towards the house. The only things that were clear were that I did not want to go there, did not want to speak of anything to Flora, did not want to enter that sinister little house. And so I told myself that it would soon be dark, that I had not time, that what Georgie did was none of my business and that, in any case, in a few days now I would be hundreds of miles away from this countryside on which this black blot of a house and a family lay. I turned up the road that ran behind the house, beside the broken garden wall, that would take me out at the cross-roads on the hilltop where John-the-Smith's friendly, red-hearthed smithy stood. I had to call on John-the-Smith, anyway, I told myself. He was a closer friend than Flora Bedamned.

But when the house was behind me, over my right shoulder, I thought of that broken rampart of a gable chimney standing against the red-stormy, blown-cloud winter sky. I stopped in my tracks and I shivered, and in the noise of the sea on the beach I heard the words:

'Like one that on a lonesome road
Doth walk in fear and dread,
And having once turned round, walks on,
And turns no more his head;
Because he knows a frightful fiend
Doth close behind him tread.'

I looked up the hill ahead to where the smithy stood just beyond the brow and fought down a panic urge to run. Then I thought of Reachfar and my grandmother and how my aunt would laugh, scathingly, at this exhibition of 'herring guts'. Squaring my shoulders, I turned round and stared defiantly down the hill at the house which appeared from this angle as a blackish heap of stone against the grey winter sea.

I could now see all round it from above where, before, I had been seeing a silhouette against the darkling, angry sky, and as I looked panic drained out of me. At the front of the house stood two cars and one of them was Doctor Mackay's; the two younger boys, Roddie and Hughie, stood in front of the door, and even in this poor light they looked strangely forlorn; and by the rain-water barrel at the end of the gable nearest me, Flora stood in an attitude of worn-down dejection, with Georgie beside her. Out of the past time, out of the fifteen years that I had known this house, out of the very ground on which it stood and like a miasma that hung in the air around it, came the feeling of another Bedamned tragedy. Without thought, I began to retrace my steps down the hill, back the way I had come.

I went to Flora, behind her, where she stood with her forearms on the water barrel, her head bowed down upon them, and laid my hand on her shoulder.

'Flora,' I said.

She looked up. She was not crying, but her face was stark with a dumb, dry despair.

133

'Chorchie! Chorchie!' snuffled the idiot girl, jumping up and down in excitement, jerking her arms and legs, pulling up her skirt to show me her bandaged thigh.

I turned on her furiously, with the intention of silencing her if that was possible, but as soon as I looked at her I stopped to stare. Her face looked exactly as it had done when she was approaching the stray dog with the red-hot wire, avidly greedy, with the eyes flashing, the mouth and nose slavering and drooling and the animal voice panting excitedly: 'Chorchie! Chorchie!' Even the movements of the body and limbs were similar, the tensely jerking arms and legs, the belly and hips writhing. Of a sudden the memory that had been haunting me so horribly became meaningless, as meaningless as Georgie herself, for I understood that all feeling and emotion were alike to her. It seemed that she herself felt nothing, but derived this excitement – this same excitement – from some dim awareness of feeling or emotion in another. It was as if there was of Georgie herself nothing but a small spark of latent sexual excitement; as if she had no mind but some shrivelled kernel; as if she had no seat of emotion but some single, decayed, blunted nerve so that nothing penetrated to her consciousness by any channel except some extreme of suffering or emotion experienced by another creature, to which she responded with this grotesque likeness to a debauch of sexual lust.

As I stared at her in the grey silence while these ideas formed vaguely in my mind – they took shape waveringly, as a rainbow forms between storm and sun – she began to quieten, her limbs ceasing their jerking, the fire in her eyes dying down, the flow from mouth and nose becoming less until she backed slowly away and leaned against the wall of the house, looking limp and spent and unreal, like a clockwork toy whose mechanism has run down. Where, before, I had been looking at her impersonally as an object I must understand, I now gave myself a shake and glared at her deliberately, willing her to stay still, daring her to move. A look of fear came into her face – perhaps she was

134

remembering in a dim way and relating me to Moss who had bitten her – and with a whimper of: 'Chorchie! Chorchie!' she slid, back to the wall, around the corner of the house and disappeared into the tangled back garden. I turned back to Flora, laid my hand on her shoulder again and said: 'Flora, I'm Janet Sandison.' She nodded. 'Flora, is someone ill?'

'It's Davie,' she whispered harshly. 'He's dead. He fell – off the barn roof at Poyntdale. They brought him home – dead.'

I could think of nothing to say, nothing to do. 'Flora, is there anything I can do?'

'Nobody can do anything,' she said and stared in front of her with those blind-looking eyes in her prematurely withered face. 'Nobody can do anything,' she repeated and then, turning away from me, she sighed and said: 'Maybe it's for the best. He never liked the mason work whatever.'

Something bitter rose in my throat and, with it, the desire to be physically violent – to shake Flora or go into the house and strike her father. But physical violence was not possible, and I felt that I could no longer stay in this grey, hopeless place. I pitied Flora without having real sympathy for her; I loathed Georgie, but without having pity for her, and I hated the thought of Jamie Bedamned but was denied the right to give expression to that hatred. Full of rage, loathing and hatred, I stared at the brooding, darkly secret tangle of the garden and said: 'Flora, you are sure there is nothing I can do to help?'

She merely shook her head and sighed. Then she laid her arms on the top of the barrel again, put her face down on them and sighed once more.

'I'm going home to Reachfar, Flora,' I told her. 'I'll be down to see you in the morning.'

I do not think she heard me.

When I told my dreadful news to my family, some of the black silence which had shrouded Bedamned's Corner seemed to descend upon the cheerful Reachfar kitchen, for,

135

for a long moment, nobody spoke, but they all stood, stricken into sudden arrestment, so that the broad smile remained on George's face, incongruously, while his voice ceased in midword. It was my aunt who broke through the evil spell by clashing the frying-pan she was holding down on to the top of the big stove and saying: 'The laddie! And that devil Jamie Bedamned is left to live!'

'Kate!' said my grandmother. 'Mind your tongue, lassie!'

In a seething sort of silence my aunt went about her work of preparing the supper, but sparks seemed to radiate from her light feet as the heels of her shoes tap-tapped across the floor.

'If only a body could *do* something!' she burst out at last.

'There is a small thing we could do, Kate,' I said and turned to my grandmother. 'Granny, Flora won't even have anything to wear for the funeral and I don't believe she'll be able – able to arrange things. Could Kate and I maybe give her some clothes? And go down there and see that the house is in order for the funeral and things like that?'

My granny – not my grandmother – looked at me out of her wise old eyes. 'Surely, lassie. The two of you can help Flora in any way there is and give her anything you like of what you have.' She looked away from me into the red heart of the fire. 'It will maybe be the first time that anybody ever gave Flora anything. There's some that's born just to give – and never get.'

My aunt could hardly wait to get the supper over, so intense was the energy of her anger and rebellion and her need to fight back, and she went into one of her moods of what George called 'ramming our supper down our throats and nearly taking the hammer to the dishes to save washing them'. And when the meal was over, she and I went upstairs to set upon our joint wardrobes. It did not take me long, in my own room, to lay out in a pile the few garments that I could spare, for I had not a large wardrobe,

136

and I picked up the bundle and went with it to my aunt's room, where she was sitting on her bed, staring out at the dark beyond the window. I looked around, but the doors of her cupboard were closed and nowhere did I see a bundle of clothing similar to the one I was holding.

'Are you glad *now* that you're going south and away from this place?' she asked me suddenly and fiercely.

'Not specially,' I said and laid my bundle on a chair.

Almost physically, I felt my mind retiring, drawing away, pulling a casing over itself as the small shellfish on the sands of the Firth did when you went near them. Wasn't it enough for my aunt that I was going away south to the land of opportunity? Wasn't it enough for her that I was committed to leave Reachfar? Must I be glad about it as well? 'What do you *see* in this confounded place?' she asked. 'Why do you want to *stay* here, when you are free to go?'

She was impatient and angry, not receptive but encased in resentment; but even had she been at her most sympathetic and understanding, I could not, at that time, have found words that she would understand to explain what tied me to Reachfar. I myself did not know, in words, what I 'saw' in Reachfar. I did not know, in words, what urged me to stay there. I took refuge in flippancy.

'Och, in spite o' the Higher Eddication an' the chance to make a fortune in the south, I'm chust a crofter at heart with the cow sharn up to my backside! . . . Well, what about these Bedamneds?'

She stared at me out of her dark eyes for a long moment and then, with a sigh as of defeat, opened the door of her clothes cupboard. I had a sense of victory, of security inside my little citadel of flippancy, of pride in the secret self that I could keep hidden there. It was easy to keep the world outside, even the close, near world of my family, and let that world *stay* outside now. In the course of a few moments I had changed from a vulnerable child into a hard-shelled young woman, the young woman who was to lark along with hardly a serious thought through the decade

137

of the 1930s and the war that came at the end of it . . .

When my aunt had added a dark grey coat and skirt and one or two other things to the bundle I had brought, she disappeared up the little narrow stairway into the roof and I heard her go along to the west attic, which was the lumber-room. After a moment, she returned with a hideous black feather boa, which was about five yards long with big silk tassels at the ends.

'For the love of Pete!' I said. 'What are you going to do with that thing?'

She giggled, the first of her old gay sounds that I had heard her make for a long time. 'Give it to Georgie Bedamned – it'll keep her quiet . . . Don't tell Granny, though. It was Lady Lydia who gave it to her as a present long ago and she wouldn't like to think of us giving it away.'

I took the boa from her and draped it round my neck and over my arms as my grandmother used to wear it to church long ago.

'Crikey!' I said. 'What a thing!'

Far below the hem of my short skirt the silk tassels brushed my insteps.

'For Heaven's sake, take it off!' my aunt said. 'You're as like Mother as life, standing there like that! All you need is yon toque with the feathers up the side like a shaving brush!'

I picked up a black cloche hat that I had contributed to the bundle and perched it on top of my hair, then draped my boa-ed arms across my diaphragm. At that moment, Tom and George looked in through the half-open door.

'Kod Almighty!' Tom said. 'I thought it was Her Ould Self that was in it! I havena seen that thing this fifteen year an' more!'

'We're going to give it to Georgie Bedamned,' I said.

'She'll soon make a feather boa of it,' George said, 'but maybe it will keep her quiet until we get the poor laddie buried in peace.'

I took the hat from my head, threw it on to the chair and

138

began to wind the boa up like a clumsy rope into an unwieldy bundle. 'That was the main idea, George,' I said and laid it with the other clothes.

The far end of the room where the chest of drawers stood was quite dark and my aunt picked up the box of matches to light her second lamp, but George took the box from her hand; and as he spoke, somehow we all moved into the half-light at the end of the room.

'Tom and me was thinking that we would turn out for the funeral,' he said. 'And we'll speak to Duncan when he comes up tomorrow. An' Sir Torquil an' one or two o' the Poyntdale men will come, likely.'

Tom now took the box of matches from George as if it were some badge of office to be held by the person who spoke.

'It is not many that will be there, likely,' he said. 'So we are thinking, Kate, if you and Janet would be seeing any of them, like John-the-Smith or Malcolm-the-Shepherd, when you'll be down about the County Road tomorrow, you could maybe chust sort of mention that George an' me will be seeing them at Davie's funeral, like. He was a good, hard-working laddie, Davie.'

There was a brief silence broken by Tom striking the match and George lifting the glass from the lamp.

'Although it is so early in the year,' Tom said, as he applied the flame to the wick, 'you can be seeing the days getting a little longer already.'

The next morning, my aunt and I left Reachfar as soon as breakfast was over. In those days, I was a fairly strong and fast walker, but I was hard put to it to keep pace with my Aunt Kate that morning as she strode down the hill in the teeth of the north-east wind, a large cardboard dress-box in one hand, a basket with butter, eggs and some edible odds and ends in the other, her dark eyes glinting fire. She did not speak until we were on the road above Bedamned's Corner where I had turned back the night before, but then she stopped dead and said: 'By God! I hope that ould

139

Jamie Bedamned is down there!' and before I could speak she was off down the hill like an avenging fury.

Jamie Bedamned was not there, however, and after a moment my aunt said: 'Flora, where's your father?'

'At his work,' Flora said. 'He's working up at Seamuir just now.'

For a moment I thought my aunt was going to explode, to disintegrate in a shower of fiery particles right there in the middle of the cold bare kitchen, but she did not. Instead, she looked over her shoulder at the closed door of the parlour at the other end of the passage, sighed and said: 'Flora, Janet and I brought some clothes for you and Georgie,' and we began to unpack the things we had brought.

We spent the whole morning at the house. We had some difficulty with Flora, who, looking longingly at the discarded grey coat and skirt of my aunt's, said she had to get on with the washing and had no time to try on clothes.

'Flora!' my aunt said harshly. 'Your brother goes to his grave tomorrow! Have you forgotten that?'

Suddenly Flora began to cry for, I think, the first time and my aunt nodded with satisfaction while Georgie began to jump about and jerk her arms and shout: 'Chorchie! Chorchie!'

My aunt swung round on her. 'You sit down!' she blazed. 'Over there!' Miraculously, Georgie obeyed her. 'Here, put this on you!' and my aunt gave her the big black feather boa. Then she turned to me. 'It must be fine to be like her!' she said in a low, vicious voice. 'Not able to feel anything and as vain and pleased with yourself as a peacock! Make some tea for Flora!'

'No!' sobbed Flora. 'Don't light the fire! And there's only enough tea to do till Friday!'

'You hold your tongue!' snapped my aunt. 'Tom is coming down with a load of sticks and I'll make my own tea any time I like. Here, stand up, till I measure your waist!'

It was like a nightmare while it was going on, but the

140

results of it were good. Purged by the tears she had shed, her face bloodless, her eyes almost colourless, Flora two hours later was closer to sanity than she had been when we arrived, and Georgie was still happily admiring herself in a broken looking-glass, the black feather boa twisted into a turban on her head, now, with its long ends trailing down over her shoulders. My aunt and I unpicked and snipped and pinned while Flora stood, sobbing at first, but gradually coming out of her grief and taking a little interest in the clothes, fingering the worn material as if it were the finest cloth of gold.

'And now,' said my aunt towards midday, 'Janet and I are going home to get these things sewn and pressed. Flora, you have to get the house cleaned up for tomorrow, so never mind that washing.'

'My father will—' Flora began.

'To hell with your father! You tell him we've been here and that Sir Torquil and the Reachfar men are coming to Davie's funeral and that he and the boys are to be dressed and ready in time . . . Who is arranging the funeral?'

'Doctor Mackay, and the minister and Sir Torquil are seeing to things.'

'Where are your brothers?'

'At their work. They werena for going but my father—'

'Your father's back—'

'Kate!' I interrupted hastily. 'That's Bill-the-Post coming along the road. It must be nearly twelve o'clock! We'll have to go!'

As we went out, Flora coming with us to the broken gate, Bill-the-Post set his bicycle against the rickety fence.

'My great sympathy, Flora, lassie,' he said, taking off his cap for a moment. Then he reached into his bag. 'But I've something here that may help ye in your trouble. There's two o' them – one for your father and one for you. I couldna help knowing who they're from, for his name's on the back o' them – James Smith, it says on them.'

Flora stared into Bill-the-Post's bleary drunken eyes

141

with her own washed, sorrow-bemused ones and in their depths there began to grow the wonder that must come to eyes that look upon a vision of Heaven.

'Jamie?' she breathed on a faint, questioning note.

I thought she was going to faint, and, apparently, so did my aunt, for: 'Come into the house, Bill!' she said hastily. 'I've got some whisky in my basket. Janet, bring Flora!'

We all trooped back into the house, where Georgie now had her feather boa round her waist and my black cloche hat perched back to front on her head, with one of the tassels of the boa pinned up to it. Round the scarred wooden table, the rest of us had whisky and water out of cracked tea-cups while Flora, trembling, opened her letter and Georgie preened herself anew. The letter was only a few lines on a single sheet, but as Flora unfolded it a slip of thicker paper fell to the floor. I picked it up and it was a bank draft for a hundred pounds. Flora read her letter, pushed it towards my aunt, smiled. Then her eyes filled with glittering tears and she put her wispy head down on the table and cried with a joy that was as intense as had been her sorrow over her brother Davie.

My aunt and I came away and began, slowly, to climb the hill to Reachfar. My aunt was very silent, strangely flat and unlike herself.

'She'll still need the clothes,' I said, 'in spite of the money, Kate. She has no time to get others.'

'Did you see that letter?'

'No.'

'The danged young fool has sent ninety-three pounds back to ould Jamie Bedamned!' Her voice was shaking with fury and then she stopped dead in her tracks. 'Here, I'm going back down there!'

'What for?'

'To take that hundred away from Flora! If somebody doesn't take it and bank it for her Jamie Bedamned will get hold of it!'

And before I could move, my aunt was in full flight back to Bedamned's Corner.

142

I stood on the hillside where she had left me, looking down at the little black house with its broken chimney and the steel-grey, cruel sea behind it and tried vainly, once more, to understand its people – to see why Jamie Bedamned must work every waking hour to hide every penny in the bank and force his sons to do the same; to see why the sons did not rebel as their elder brother had done; to see why Flora was resigned to her life of slavery; to see how she could love the dreadful Georgie as she did. When my aunt came back, I was still standing staring at the house, but I knew no more about the Bedamneds than when she had gone away.

'I got it!' she said.

'What?'

'The *money*, you fool! That Flora's no more all there than Georgie is! She was going to give it to her father! I only got it away from her by saying she could buy things for Georgie with it.'

'Kate, I don't understand about these Bedamneds,' I said.

'Oh, you and your understanding!' my aunt said. 'There's nothing to understand except that that old brute Jamie has bullied the guts out of the whole lot of them.'

'But why should he – should he be allowed to?'

'Who's to stop him?' She glared down the hill at the house. 'Not that I won't have a damned good try one of these days! Come on! We'd better go round by the smiddy and tell John about the funeral.'

'I'll laugh like stink,' I said as we set off up the hill, 'if Jamie Bedamned finds out you took that money from Flora and comes up to Reachfar about it. What in the world will you say?'

'I'll find plenty to say when the time comes, but it won't. Jamie Bedamned will never come back to Reachfar,' she said.

The next day, my aunt left home in the morning with Flora's clothes, came home for dinner, and in the afternoon she and I dressed in our darkest clothes but equipped with clean white aprons which we carried in the baskets with the sandwiches and scones we had made, went down to Bedamned's Corner to serve the cup of tea to the people who came to the funeral. When we arrived, Flora, Georgie, her two remaining brothers and her father were dressed and standing round the bare kitchen in uncomfortable attitudes, but Jamie Bedamned, as soon as he saw us, grunted and went outside to stand by the broken gate. My aunt and I interested ourselves in Flora's altered coat and skirt and expressed our satisfaction with it, and in Flora's wizened little face pleasure in the clothes battled with the sorrowful reason for them. Georgie, seeming to envy the interest we were showing in her sister, pranced about, thrusting first her new shoes upon our notice, then my old white blouse, then the feather boa and, of course, bent over and turned up her skirts to show us her bandaged dog-bite.

'The poor bairn!' said Flora. 'She's so proud o' that feather boa it's a pleasure to see her. And she's as *good* about that sore leg! What brute of a dog could have bitten the poor bairn?'

I found the sight of Georgie far from a pleasure and wished that I were in the company of the brute of a dog rather than in hers. For me, Georgie brought to the bare, miserable house, where the black-coated mourners were now beginning to gather in the untidy garden, a dreadful slant of the macabre, and I had a horrible consciousness that, among these people, even the tragic death of a young man was being robbed by her of the only thing that made it bearable, its last dignity.

The fine weather today had completely given way before the nor'-easter that was blowing in over the Firth, a sharp knife of sleet held in its teeth, as it howled round the pitted walls of the little house. The short service, in the dank, fireless parlour, where, at each shock of the wind, some loosened mortar fell from the broken chimney-top down, pattering, into the hearth, was a shivering nightmare that was soon over, and then George stepped forward

144

to the coffin which lay on a row of three chairs. Tom pushed Jamie Bedamned's elbow and, as if he had been awakened suddenly from some dream, he stepped forward and took his place at its head. Roddie, the now eldest son, took the other side; then George and Hughie took the centre and Tom and Sir Torquil the foot. As instructed by my aunt, I had gone to hold open the door of the house, for its hinges were damaged and it would not stay in place, and as the coffin passed me Jamie Bedamned's face was not six inches from mine. It was as if a dead man walked past. The eyes might have been of dark glass and the face of grey granite. Nothing emanated from him. Walking in his heavy-footed way, as if his mind were miles away, he carried what remained of his son out of his house, raised the head of the coffin to the hearse and turned away, dusting his hands as if he had placed one more stone on some invisible wall he was building and that only he could see. As the mourners filed past me and out through the low doorway I wanted to run, screaming, out into the clean cutting wind, out of this grey creeping miasma that enshrouded the accursed house, but at that moment Georgie decided that too much attention was being concentrated on something other than herself and began to dance, her feather boa streaming in the wind, her skirts held high above her knees as she gyrated wildly among the withered weeds of the garden, half-snuffling, half-barking her 'Chorchie! Chorchie!' After a moment Flora somehow got her into Sir Torquil's car and I shut the door of the house, leaned my back against the inside of it and 'Kate!' I said. 'Oh, Kate!'

'Come, lassie,' my aunt said. 'You and I will have a droppie tea before they get back.'

Part IV
1940

Part IV
1940

With my departure to Hampshire, the whole panorama of my life changed, and very soon Bedamned's Corner, Flora, Georgie and all the horrors connected with that family that had seemed to lie like a black blot on my mental landscape, just as their home was a black blot on the fair countryside by the Firth, had disappeared, away into the surrounding mists of the no longer immediate and therefore half forgotten. I probably did what my father called a 'willing forget' about them, for my father held a theory that one forgot to do a thing only if one was predisposed to forgetfulness of that thing – if, in other words, it was a thing that one did not want to do or did not like doing in the first place. I was probably like this about the Bedamneds. I went away; I put them behind me, and the new way of life which flowed in around me in the south of England conspired to keep all thought of them in the far background. And, certainly, when I came home to Reachfar on holidays during the succeeding years I was at no pains to seek them out.

Historically, as you know without my telling you, the 1930s were a muddled period and I can claim to be thoroughly representative of my historical period at this time, for no young woman drifted along in more of a muddle than I did. In retrospect, I seem to have had no ambitions beyond earning a modest competence in the way that came most easily to hand, and no plans beyond what I would wear that evening when I went out with the young man of the moment. The only thing I can say in praise of myself – and maybe it is no small thing, at that – is that I was, most of the time, very happy. In fact, in the main, I had a wonderful time, so wonderful that my memories of the 1930s are mostly like a group of clouds made of iridescent champagne bubbles, all dancing hither and yon, so that without a deal of concentrated thought I cannot tell you whether it was in Devon in 1931 that I was so terribly in love with Terry or whether it was in London in 1938. In the 1930s, to me, very few things mattered very much.

In 1934, in July, though, a thing happened that did matter and that was the death of my grandparents within twenty-four hours of one another. This was not a sad event. My grandmother was eighty-two, my grandfather ten years older, and after their long life together there was something satisfying and fitting in the one coffin following the other down the narrow, rough, hill road from Reachfar to Poyntdale on the shoulders of my father, George, Tom and our friends, and on to the churchyard in Achcraggan on two of the Poyntdale hay wagons. It was one of the largest concourses of people ever seen at a funeral in our district, and many of the older mourners did not climb the steep hill to Reachfar, but when we reached Poyntdale steading a procession of cars and about a hundred people on foot were waiting, and at the west end of Achcraggan some three hundred more were gathered to follow the coffins up the last little hill to the churchyard. Among these last were Jamie Bedamned and his two sons, and I remember the ungenerous thought crossing my mind that he must have been forced to stop work and come to the funeral, because no work was being done anywhere in the whole district that day.

I also remember that I suddenly realised, when I shook hands with him after the ceremony was over, that Jamie Bedamned was an old man, that he was not only rising towards sixty, as were my father and my uncle, but that he was among the really old – that he was probably older than Tom. Because he was the father of Roddie, who had

150

been in my class at school, I had taken it that he was about the same age as my own father, but this was not so.

'Tom,' I said, on one of the few days I spent at home after the funeral, 'what age will Jamie Bedamned be?'

'He is a good bittie older than myself,' said Tom. 'He will not be seeing seventy again.' Tom was as coy about his exact age in those days as any hopeful maiden lady. 'Why was you asking?'

'I suddenly discovered that he was far older than I had ever thought when I saw him at the funeral.'

'Aye, he began going down the hill very fast a year or two ago. That is the way people is when they get old. Maybe you were too young to notice it in your granny and granda when your mother died, but yon was the time they took the turn down the hill and a-all between one night and the next morning . . . Och, aye, Jamie Bedamned was well on when he married, I mind. We was a-all very surprised at him marrying at a-all, for he had been clarting away on his own down in the housie there, looking after himself for years.'

'I wonder what made *him* take the turn down the hill that you speak of?' I said. 'He's so damn' selfish that I don't see how anything could touch him, much less send him down the hill.'

Tom gave his mischievous snort of laughter. 'It is myself that wouldn't be surprised if it was your auntie!' he said. 'She fairly has the fear o' the devil in him!'

I laughed at this, but at the same time I felt that there might indeed be some truth in it. From the day of Davie's death Kate had espoused the cause of Flora Bedamned. No one will ever know all the reasons for this championship, least of all Kate herself, who, despite her spirited intelligence, has always been dominated by the impulses of her passionate and generous heart. I think she was governed by some queer compound of reasons and feelings, in which Flora's remote relationship to the much-loved Malcolm had a part while, at the same time, Malcolm's defection had bred in her the need for a focal

151

point on which to pour out her scorn for men in general and a more justifiable focal point for this than Jamie Bedamned it would be hard to find. Then, my aunt was the daughter of my grandmother who had always interfered mercilessly – if, on the whole, helpfully – in the lives of other people, and my aunt was Highland through and through, a race notorious for espousing causes long since lost.

At all events, seldom did a week pass without my aunt calling at Bedamned's Corner, and Jamie Bedamned had been known to sit for two hours on a cold, wet afternoon under one of the 'bridgies' over the County Road rather than go into his own house, because he knew my aunt was there. The first, and only, open quarrel between them took place very shortly after the funeral of Davie, when Flora used a pound of her own money, which was deposited at the bank in Achcraggan, to buy a new dress for Georgie from Mrs Gilchrist's Drapery Warehouse. My aunt, on her way back to Reachfar with her basket of groceries, had called at the bereaved house to find Flora and Georgie cowering in a corner while Jamie raved about the sins of vanity and thriftlessness, his anger increased, of course, by the fact that he had not known of Flora's money from America until that very afternoon. It is one of my regrets that I was in the train en route for Hampshire and Islington Hall on this particular afternoon, for ever since the day of Davie's death my aunt had been spoiling for an interview with Jamie Bedamned, and on this day she had her great chance. I know no details, but I am assured by Tom and George that by the time she left the little house it was Jamie who was cowering in a corner and his bullied daughters were trying to shield him from the fury of the pent-up Kate Sandison wrath. Thereafter, he hated her, but he avoided her, which was all she asked, and he was more careful in his treatment of Flora in case the dark, avenging fury from Reachfar would seek him out and smite him once more. In being hated by Jamie, my aunt was no different from other people except in degree. Jamie Bedamned hated

152

everybody. He merely hated Kate Sandison more vehemently than he did the rest of the world, because he was afraid of her.

After my short stay at Islington Hall with Lady Lydia's daughter, I went from job to job about the south of England and London, a very fortunate young woman, attended, I think, by more good luck than I deserved, but few earthly rewards and punishments seem to go by deserts. I turned into something of the same sort of flibbertygibbet that my aunt had been at my age, except that I never had anything approaching her beauty. The only thing in life which I did with any planned forethought was to come home to Reachfar once in every year and this I planned and accomplished by some instinct, without knowing why I did it. I am now aware that my roots were deep in that soil and that I found my way back to it, through an unrecognised need for sustenance, as an animal will find its way to water, but at the time I told myself that I came home 'to see my people' and gave the matter no further thought.

During these holidays, I spent most of my time at Reachfar, going out very little, for I was out of touch with the local people and those of my own age were scattered to the ends of the earth and seldom were at home on holiday at the same time as I was. Alasdair Mackay, a doctor now, was gaining experience in his brother's busy practice in Edinburgh, preparatory to coming home to help his ageing father in the widespread practice based on Achcraggan, but he and I, for once, converged on our homes at the same time, in the summer of 1935.

Alasdair Mackay and I have always had a curious effect on one another, and this is true still although we are now nearer to fifty than forty. As soon as we meet, we seem to revert, mentally, to the age of five, as we were when we first met in the Baby Class of Achcraggan School. In 1935 we were twenty-five years old, but we did not see in each other a potential love affair or even a flirtation, although, in other company, we were both very much to dalliance

153

disposed, especially Alasdair, although he accused me of being 'far worse' than he was in this particular way. No. At twenty-five Alasdair and I did not think of kissing in corners; we thought of things to do that were pretty much on the level of our joint climb on to the church roof long ago. At least, Alasdair thought of them. Left to myself, I seldom climbed on church roofs, for I much preferred trees.

Alasdair, too, at this time, was going through a phase of being a Scottish Nationalist. I have never been able to take seriously party politics in any form, probably because my intelligence is too limited, for I have always been able to take seriously and derive the interest of enjoyment from anything I can understand. To be absolutely honest, I do not think that Alasdair really understood party politics either – especially Scottish Nationalism – but it is a gift given to many people to be enjoyably enthusiastic about something that they do not fully comprehend. After all, look at the people who attend the ballet every night and the old ladies in boarding-houses who fill in these coupons about Association football.

So, in 1935, Alasdair was a Scottish Nationalist and wore the kilt all the time – the kilt that torture would not have made him wear a year before – and had a tendency not to shave if his father had not forced him to do it. Also, in 1935, young Torquil Daviot, who was about our age, had just come home from India where he had been with the Army, to help his father, Sir Torquil, with the estate which he would inherit. Alasdair, who had known Torquil all his life, suddenly saw him through Scottish National-istic eyes as an oppressor of the people and treated me to long diatribes about how the noble sons of the soil had had their crofts burned about their ears in order to make deer forests for the like of Torquil and all that. This struck me, in my friend Martha's phrase, as a lotta hooey, but it was fine summer weather and I wanted to wear my new tweed suit to the Highland Games at Inverness, and Alasdair, even with the beard, was as fine-looking an escort in a rugged sort of way as a well-dressed girl could wish for, so

I sort of went along with this Scottish Nationalism thing for a bit, although pointing out gently that the Daviots of Poyntdale had not been such grinders of the faces of the poor as many families had been.

At the beginning of our three weeks together Alasdair worked out a complex scheme on the six-inch-to-the-mile maps of our district for the partitioning of Poyntdale into crofts as 'it had been before oppression began', while I lay on my back on the short rough grass of the East Moor of Reachfar and watched the larks disappearing into the blue, but Alasdair was never really cut out for a desk or planning job and lost all patience over the question of Bedamned's Corner. The smallest economic unit in his Utopia, Alasdair said, was ten acres, and every crofter was to have ten acres whether he wanted them or not.

'No good giving some of them ten acres,' I said, narrowing my eyes at the dot-and-carry-one flight of the latest lark. 'They wouldn't work them.'

'Don't talk rot!' said Alasdair. 'Given the land, the people would work it – they would have pride in it, the pride of ownership, the pride of—'

'Jamie Bedamned wouldn't,' I said, watching another lark take to wings of song. 'He's got five acres now and they're a wilderness. He's a stone-mason, primarily, and he doesn't seem to be frightfully strong on the pride of ownership and that.'

'You haven't got the sense you were born with!' said Alasdair. 'As for vision! Don't you see, you ass, that a stone-mason's land would be worked by other crofters in payment for mason-work he had done for them?'

'Jamie Bedamned wouldn't like that,' I said.

'How d'you mean, he wouldn't like it?'

'Jamie Bedamned wants *money* for his work, so he can put it in the bank. He doesn't care a cuss whether his acres are worked or not . . . Not that you could do this intensive cultivation thing you are saying about with Bedamned's Corner, anyway, even if you worked your behind out of joint on it. It's mostly sand and rock.'

155

'You are just being obstructive!' Alasdair told me. 'Obstructive and lethargic, the two things that have brought Scotland so low!'

'What's low about it? You don't have to run about in a kilt and give Jamie Bedamned acres that he doesn't want in order to be Scottish. You don't have to get mixed up in politics to be Scottish either. If you all put your Glengarry bonnets on back to front you won't make someone like me anything *other* than Scottish, and if you hoist your sporrans on twenty-foot poles you can't make me any *more* Scottish than I am already. Being Scottish is something away deep inside people, in their blood and bones and minds, just like putting money in the bank is away inside Jamie Bedamned!'

I stood up and kicked my shoes off.

'What the devil are you doing?' he asked.

'I'm going for a paddle down the burn.'

Alasdair put his map under a stone so that the wind would not blow it away and drew the dirk from the top of his stocking as a preliminary to accompanying me on a trip down the Reachfar Burn.

We paddled our way happily down from its icy source on the East Moor, through the deep gully where the bramble fronds hung overhead laden with their ugly, hard green fruit to make a dark tunnel, and on down over the Poyntdale land to the place where the burn had been divided into two streams, the main westerly one going to feed the dam that once supplied the water power for the sawmill farther down, the easterly one being the little bypass stream that I used to come up on my way home from school as a child.

'You know,' I said, 'the only place around here that I don't know really intimately is Poyntdale Dam – I was scared off it by my mother when I first went to school.'

'Wish I had my rod with me – it's stuffed with trout!' Alasdair said. 'If only that poaching old devil Bill-the-Post would leave them alone. Torquil knows he's at it, but ke never can catch him.'

There was no word now of Torquil Daviot being a grinder

156

of the drunken face of Bill-the-Post, if he could catch him at the dam, I noticed, but with the Highland Games at Inverness in mind I did not say anything. A girl has to be tactful, I thought.

'Let's go and have a look and see if the trout are rising,' I said, so we took the westerly stream and paddled on to the sluice that fed the dam.

It is a beautiful place, Poyntdale Dam. It is not very deep, but deep enough to be dangerous to children so that all the mothers, as mine did, try to stop their children going near it. So it has an unspoiled, untrodden look. The long grass round its verges is unbroken; the willow branches hang like a green-gold fringe over the water; the water-hens stare at you perkily for a moment and then go on with their business, and the yellow flags flutter their banners in the little wind between sun and shade. On this day two swans, with their flotilla of four grey cygnets, were sailing, white and lordly, about the still water, leaving behind them a long leisurely arrow of a wake.

'Who's that over at the far sluice?' Alasdair asked suddenly but low-voiced. 'Seems to think he's Mussolini speaking at a Fascist parade!'

I looked across the dam. In the middle of the sluice gangway across the narrow neck that fed the water to the mill-race was someone who was visible from the thighs upwards, his arms waving and jerking, the whole torso swaying this way and that. 'Crumbs!' I whispered. 'I don't know.'

'Let's creep round a bit and have a closer look. He's making a speech – must be dotty!'

'Probably a Scottish Nationalist!' I said, but I do not think he heard me.

Across the water, a sound was audible that was not the chuck-chuck of the waterfowl or the loving summer whisper of the breeze among the trees and grasses. Quietly, Alasdair and I made a detour into the birch wood and re-approached the dam nearer to the mill-race sluice.

'It's Georgie Bedamned!' I whispered as we peered out

157

between the willow fronds, and it was – Georgie posturing, gesticulating and admiring her own reflection in the water below while she smiled and nodded at it, saying: 'Chorchie! Chorchie!'

As we watched, she bent down and picked up from the gangway the feather boa that my aunt had given her on the day of Davie's funeral and a large hat which, I think, must once have belonged to Lady Lydia. It was white and of some light straw, its crown wreathed in flowers. Very carefully Georgie arranged the feather boa about her shoulders, placed the once-elegant hat on her head, then leaned over the low parapet of the gangway and became still, silent and lost in rapture at the beauty of her own reflection. Instinctively, Alasdair and I turned away from the sight and he produced his packet of cigarettes while we looked at one another.

'It's queer,' I whispered, 'when you think of it. Legends that are handed down through the ages either get beautified or uglified. Narcissus is a beautiful legend now, but he might actually have been an idiot just like Georgie.'

Alasdair stared at me and turned away to look again through the willow fronds at the sluice. 'You and I have always approached everything from opposite ends,' he said. 'I didn't think of Narcissus. All I thought was that if the wood of that gangway is like the wood of the east sluice, it's damn' rotten . . . We ought to get her away from there. What do we—'

He broke off as a gruff shout, like the noise that an angry animal would make, came across to us: 'Chorchie! Chorchie!' The light breeze had whipped the big hat from Georgie's head and, hopping and jerking in rage, she was dancing on the gangway, her feather boa coiling about her with a serpent-like life of its own while the hat, like a small island of gay flowers, floated on the smooth water below. Without further ado, Alasdair and I made our way as quickly as we could through the long grass and tangled undergrowth round the crescent of the dam to the sluice.

As soon as Georgie saw us she rushed towards us on the

bank, jerking and gesturing at the hat while she kept up a running fire of 'Chorchie! Chorchie!' and then, recognizing Alasdair as a male, she clutched her arms round his neck and smiled up at him with a dreadful travesty of seduction on her oddly misshapen face.

'Get off!' Alasdair said, pushing and wriggling. 'Get off!'

Like so many of life's tragedies, it had in it a hideous element of the ludicrous, and I, feeling sick and at the same time feeling a desire to seek release in a fit of strident laughter, seized a fallen willow branch and began to fish for the hat. At last Alasdair broke free of Georgie's embrace and came to help me, and after a few moments, which were filled with the repeated 'Chorchie! Chorchie!' from the creature behind us, Alasdair, one hand in mine and the willow branch in the other hand, was able to reach forward and catch the hat by its trailing pink ribbons. We turned round, I to the calves in the water, Alasdair to the knees, still hand in hand, Alasdair holding the absurd hat, to face Georgie on the grass verge of the dam. She had now taken off her upper garments and, with her oddly misshapen body exposed from the waist upwards, the feather boa across her shoulders and held wide from behind her about her out-stretched, spindly arms, she made a jerky dancing gesture of dreadful, mindless lewdness towards Alasdair. His hand that was holding mine tightened almost unbearably and he muttered: 'Oh, Christ!' like a panic-stricken prayer. I, of course, as I always instinctively do in any impossible situation, thought of my dead grandmother.

'Give me that bloody hat!' I said, and, wrenching my hand out of Alasdair's, I picked up the long willow branch that was floating round our feet. I shook it menacingly at Georgie. 'Put on your clothes at once!' I said. 'Put them ON – or I'll beat you! . . . Clear out, Alasdair! I'll take her home!'

'Chorchie! Chorchie!' she said, still coming towards Alasdair, but at the same time, with uncanny vain cunning,

159

taking care not to get her black patent leather shoes into the water.

'Get out of sight!' I told Alasdair.

'But is she safe?' he asked.

'I'll *safe* her!' I said and flicked Georgie about the ankles with the tip of the branch, which made her recoil, snarling: 'Chorchie! Chorchie!' but reach for her discarded clothing.

'Get away, Alasdair, for Pete's sake! She'll be safe enough. Follow us, but don't let her see you!'

Alasdair waded away round the edge of the dam and was soon concealed among the drooping willows, while I dropped my branch and helped Georgie into her clothes, finally admiring the bedraggled hat when it was poised once more on her head. Now that Alasdair was out of sight, she was easy to control. Down the years, I had gathered from my aunt that Georgie could be persuaded to do anything – even a simple, useful household chore – if you praised her fulsomely and appealed to her monstrous vanity. As I walked towards Bedamned's Corner with her, bare-footed across the fields, pointing to my own bare feet and then with simulated envy at her patent-leather shoes, she preened herself and rearranged her hat and feather boa with a disdainful swagger, while Alasdair darted about, level with us, but behind the hedgerows.

It was an extraordinary experience, and it became more extraordinary still when I brought her into Flora's kitchen, for Flora, of course, had been searching for her and began to scold her for running away. Georgie, in the fields a moment ago, had had the intelligence to feel herself, shod and dressed in hat and boa, superior to me with my bare feet, and she had had the power to communicate, by her swaggering gestures, this thought in her mind. Flora did not speak angrily to her or menace her in any way, as I had done at the dam, but as soon as she realised that Flora was accusing her of wrong-doing she lapsed into utter idiocy. The scornful light went out of her eyes, the half-sneer left her face and she became utterly vacant,

160

like a misshapen body that was not inhabited by any mind. I had a resentful feeling that the mind was *there* and that this idiocy was a screen that it dropped at will to conceal its horrible adoration of this hideous body that it inhabited and its filthy machinations for the satisfaction of that body's unnatural appetites.

While Georgie went to a chest of drawers in a corner and began, with many mutterings of her name, to pull out and bedizen herself with various odds and ends of ribbon, Flora hospitably offered me a cup of tea which I refused with the excuse that I had to meet Alasdair Mackay. I stayed for long enough, though, to notice that the kitchen of Bedamned's Corner was a changed place. The dresser was re-painted and reinstated in its 'bonnie' status of so many years ago and bore on its shelves a number of 'art' vases which had been bought, I could swear, from Mr Dickson, Ironmonger and Seed Merchant in Achcraggan. There was a particularly hideous 'three-piece set' of two orange-scarlet vases with raised jet-black whorls upon them that looked as if the black china had been piped on to the red with a confectioner's icing forcer. The third and central piece of this set was a bulbous sort of jar with a grid of brass wire across its top, and piped on to its fat belly, in black, among the black whorls, were the words 'Rose Bowl'. I thought with sadness of the homeliness that yet had an elegance of the things that used to decorate that dresser and thought that surely this period since I had been ten years old had some of the worst taste in all history.

But Flora was filled with pride for her possessions and I duly admired them, but I jibbed when she offered to show me the parlour. I had already exhausted my words of admiration on behalf of the kitchen, and, too, all the 'bonnie' things were still dominated, for me, by what in my mind I still called the 'blackness' of the house itself. I wanted to get away from it, out on to the clear, clean hillside where Alasdair was waiting, healthy and normal.

'My aunt tells me you are hearing regularly from Jamie,' I said.

161

'Yes. Jamie is a good boy and he has done well out there in America. And Mrs Sandison spoke true that night. He has never forgotten his home and he sends me ten pound every month o' the year, regular as the clock.'

She looked round her kitchen with pride, her eyes resting with pride on the three-piece rose-bowl set, then moving on to the picture above the fireplace which depicted a lake of Mediterranean blue, dotted with white-sailed yachts – their white duly reflected in the blue – and surrounded by mountains of deep royal purple under a sky that was half blue to match the lake and half white to match the sails of the yachts. Underneath, in neat print, was the caption: 'Highland Loch', and I decided in my own mind that the reason for all the yachts, such as had never been seen on any Highland Loch, was the desire of the artist to bring home to his public that the layer of blue was water. In a similar way, he had subtly brought out the identity of the white and blue bit at the top as the sky by putting a white bird on the blue bit and a black bird on the white bit. If he had only put a Scottish Nationalist in a Glengarry bonnet on top of one of the purple hills, I thought, he could have done without the caption altogether.

'And when Jamie sent yon first hunder pound,' Flora was continuing, 'I thought at the time that your auntie was terrible hard on my father about it, but maybe it was all for the best, for since he got older, my father, his memory isn't what it was. Sometimes he will be forgetting to give me the housekeeping money quite often and being able to go to the banker, unknowing to him, and get what I need for us all is a great comfort. Of course, the boys is very, very good and give me something every week, but my father doesna know about that. They give *him* something too, chust to keep the peace, but he doesna know how much Roddie and Hughie is making. Wages is up a lot – the boys makes good money.'

'They work hard,' I said.

'Och, surely. They would *have* to do *that*,' Flora said.

'And is your father still working himself?'

162

'Och, yes, with his own way of it. It's not much he can do now, though, but old Captain Robertson is very good to him, and so is Sir Torquil, and he always has a bittie to put in the bank every week. He has always been hard-working and thrifty, my father, and if he wasn't able to go down to the bank with a bittie on a Saturday he would feel something was wrong, ye know.'

I felt that the whole philosophy of Bedamned's Corner, as well as Flora's attitude, was away beyond me, so I edged my way towards the door, round Georgie, who now had on another hat, a red felt this time, with a long, upstanding feather in its crown that I could trace back to Margaret Maclachlan, who was a nurse down in Glasgow. Slobbering 'Chorchie! Chorchie!' with pleasure – a noise like a small child chewing a too-large lump of sticky toffee – she was slavering and drooling down over her chin as she admired her reflection in the small looking-glass that hung by the window. As Flora followed me past her, she looked at the repulsive idiot young woman and said, smiling indulgently: 'Och, look at her, the bairn! You canna help but be taken with her and her so happy among her hats and bitties!'

I said nothing. I could think of nothing to say.

'It was good of you to bring her home, Janet,' Flora said.

'Oh, that's nothing! I'm glad I've seen you, Flora. Goodbye!'

I ran away up the hill beyond the water-spout, impatient to put distance between myself and that house and return to the normality of Alasdair, who was waiting for me up above.

We walked together, south-westerly, on the long slant that I had often taken back from school, back up to the spring at the head of the Reachfar Burn, in a morose silence. I could think of nothing to say and Alasdair's face was closed and distant and, still in silence, we sat down side by side to put on the shoes and stockings we had left there. Having rubbed the soles of my feet on the rough,

163

clean grass, I put on the first stocking and pulled it up over my long leg, reaching under my skirt for the suspenders that dangled from the narrow belt round my waist.

'You know, Janet,' Alasdair began and, turning my head, I looked into his face. He is a red-head, with fair freckled skin, and I noticed that his brow was flushed dark and that his blue eyes were also darkened to a near-black. 'Janet, it's a funny thing. I'd never noticed it before, but you're really sort of beautiful—' he said.

In that split second the relationship between Alasdair and myself 'grew up'. Instead of the innocent, unselfconscious, clear-sighted friendship that we had, without contrivance, preserved between us for twenty years, we were plunged into the complex, self-conscious, muddled, semi-wakefulness of the twenties. We were both afraid of the new thing while our hearts wept for the loss of the old, and we were both suddenly unhappy. Alasdair stared at my legs, which are normally shapely, and hastily I turned away, stuffed the second stocking into my pocket, pulled my shoes on and stood up. We could no longer look at one another without consciousness of our bodies – my five feet eight inches of hillbred, strong-boned womanhood and Alasdair's six feet two inches of Viking-descended bone-and-muscled manhood. I do not remember the words, if any, that we spoke at parting, but I remember that he turned east and strode away down the hill to Achcraggan while I turned west towards Reachfar, and in my mind I was mourning for my lost childhood in that childhood's own words: 'Oh, *dirt* on that Georgie Bedamned!'

But time is an ever-flowing stream that wastes away one thing and brings another thing in its place, and I thought seldom and little about either Alasdair Mackay or the Bedamneds again until the early June of 1940, when I went home to Reachfar on a short leave from the airfield where I was serving with what, at that time, was the Women's Auxiliary Air Force.

164

May of 1940 is a landmark that will always stand up, like a spire on a desolate plain, in the panorama of British history, but it is well known that people who are living in the shadows of great landmarks are, in the main, unaware of them and do not see them in their full shape and perspective until they have moved some distance away from them in space and time. As I remember that time, when I was at Reachfar early in June, there were two recurring phrases at the family table. One of them was like this: 'I heard from Bill-the-Post that young So-and-so is back all right', at which there would be an outburst of happy comment; and the other phrase was like this: 'There is still no word of young So-and-so apparently', at which there would be a few moments of silence. At that time the epic retreat from Dunkirk was a heart-breaking muddle, a horrid tangle that spun round the axis of hope that was fatefully linked to the axis of fear, so that, in the orbit of hope, you still felt upon you the chill breath of the parallel orbit of fear.

My aunt's husband – for she had married before the war Hugh Davidson, the foreman at Poyntdale – was one of the first in our district to be reported safe, and a few days later we heard that my brother Jock, who was in the Navy, had been helping at the evacuation of the troops, but by the first week of June the cold miasma of encroaching fear was beginning to freeze out retreating hope about many of the other men of our district. By this time old Granny Reid, who had heard officially of the loss of her grandson, was more to be envied, I think, than Doctor and Mrs Mackay, who had heard of the death of one doctor son and the wounding of another but had no news at all of Alasdair.

'You'll have to go down and see them, Janet,' my aunt said to me.

'Kate, it's awful! Come *with* me, please!'

'Janet, how can I go there with our own two safe and myself doing nothing? I couldn't! But you're in uniform and, besides, they'll be expecting you to come to see

165

them.' Her voice became coaxing. 'Look, I've got a couple of nice sections of early honey – Mrs Mackay was always awful fond o' honey and—'

'I've nothing to wear,' I interrupted. 'I don't see why the hell you had to go and get all generous with the few clothes I didn't sell! Going giving my tweed suit to that bloody Georgie Bedamned of all people!'

'Don't you use your Air Force bad language to *me*, Janet Sandison!' she blazed. 'And it's the first time I've heard *you* bemoaning a suit that was two years old! Six months or less used to be enough for them!'

'Oh, shut up!'

'I will *not* shut up!'

And so the two of us had a good-going, fish-wife row, just to relieve our nerves, but in the end I set off in my airwoman's uniform, in which I looked like a cross between a too-large bus-conductor and a skinny police-man, carrying a basket with the honey and a dozen eggs, for Doctor Mackay's house in Achcraggan.

I turned in at the front gate at about four o'clock in the afternoon and approached the porch, where, I noticed, Blithe Spirit had just been freshly painted so that he gleamed defiantly gold in the bright June sunshine. Doctor Mackay, his face still its warm, russet colour under his bright silver hair, stepped out of the bushes beside the drive.

'Well, Sergeant Sandison!' he saluted me with his garden trowel to his forehead.

His attempt at gaiety brought a lump into my throat and I looked up at the weather-cock.

'Blithe Spirit is looking very handsome,' I said.

The doctor, too, looked up, and one of the fluffy clouds that were sailing over seemed to be reflected in his eyes.

'Iphm,' he said quietly. 'I gave him a lick o' paint this morning.' He paused. 'The last o' the tin. I don't suppose there'll be any more gold paint for a while now.'

I had a desperate urge to burst into tears, and looking up at the bright prayer that was Blithe Spirit made things

166

no better, but at that moment Bill-the-Post came up the short driveway and Mrs Mackay came running out of the house.

'Anything?' she said.

Bill shook his grizzled head. 'Chust the wan local wan, Mistress.'

'Oh,' she said as the doctor took the envelope from Bill, and then she swallowed convulsively and turned, smiling, to me.

'Janet, how *good* of you to come down, and you with such a short time at home!'

'There's a letter for you at the post office, Janet,' said Bill. 'If I'd known you was here I would have brought it instead o' you waiting till tomorrow for it. Dang it, it's back for it I'll go! It's from John. I couldna help but know it was from him, for it was his name an' number on the back of it and I am knowing his writing whateffer.'

In that moment I could have killed old Bill-the-Post, my lifelong friend, for thus thoughtlessly rubbing the salt of my brother's safety into the gaping wound of the Mackays' anxiety, but the doctor said: 'Aye, you go and get it, Bill, and save yourself the tramp to Reachfar in the morning.'

'Och,' said Bill, 'there'll be another one for Kate from Hugh in the morning mail van. None o' them has any respeck for my ould done legs since this war started.'

He tramped off down the short drive to his bicycle, and the Mackays and I went into the house, into the same shabby old dining-room, where Bella Beagle's Martha was just putting the big brown teapot on the table.

'My,' she said, putting her arms akimbo and looking at me, 'does that blue not suit her real bonnie, Mistress?'

'Yes, very bonnie, Martha,' Mrs Mackay said.

We had just started tea when Bill-the-Post came back up the drive. Martha went to the door and came back with my letter.

'I thought maybe it was a tellygram,' Martha said, 'but it's for Janet, Mistress.'

167

'Thank you, Martha,' I said hastily, and stuffed the letter shamefacedly into my tunic pocket.

'Read your letter, lassie,' said the brave, gentle voice of Mrs Mackay, 'and tell us how John is. He must be finding it very hard at sea and him only twenty.'

I lowered my eyes to conceal the tears, took the letter from my pocket, opened it and began to read it aloud.

'Dear Janet, I hope you got your seven days' leave all right and are at Reachfar by now – I am sending this up there, anyway. My recent service has been very active as I have been weeding the garden at a barracks and have a mobile watering can on wheels which I operate at the short trail. The Ordinary Seaman i/c rake is a very nice fellow who, when there's no war on, is an expert on silver at one of the big auction rooms in London and the A.B. i/c Dutch hoe is a professional footballer, who used to play for, I think, Arsenal. I had a very funny letter from George in which he mentioned Hughie Sheary, but he spelled it "Cherie" for some reason, making Hughie the sheep-clipper sound like a French trawler—'

The usual, silly, cheerful wartime letter went on through several pages and, with heart-rending gallantry, the Mackays laughed at every little sally. I had embarked on the last paragraph, almost unconscious of what I was reading, so much of my mind was concentrated on the old people at the table, and with astonishment I heard my own voice saying aloud: 'I forgot to tell you in my last letter that I saw Alasdair a week or two ago – Alasdair Mackay, I mean. He came off a ship near us with a batch of wounded. He was very dirty but all right and cursing even better than I've ever heard the old doctor do, because there was some sort of muddle about transport—'

I looked up at the Mackays. 'That's what it says!' I said stupidly. 'Honest to God! Here, read it for yourselves!'

Mrs Mackay was sitting bolt upright with the tears coursing down over her pink cheeks, and the doctor pushed the letter back to me across the table.

'Just you read it to us again, Janet, lassie,' he said, and,

168

going to stand by his wife, he laid his hand quietly on her shoulder.

When Mrs Mackay had recovered a little, the doctor called Martha in, told her what had happened and then cut through her sobs of joy with: 'Pull yourself together, Martha, and take this damned tea out of here and bring in that half-bottle of whisky out of my surgery!'

We sat, after that, drinking whisky and water and speculating as to what must have happened to the letters that Alasdair must have written, which, although pleasant, was quite pointless, for the letters might be anywhere between Wick and Penzance, Glasgow and London, or might indeed be in a ship bound for Peru. When we had exhausted the possibilities of this, the doctor poured another round of drinks out of his precious half-bottle, and when I protested he said: 'Special stores. I have given the authorities to understand that this district can fight without weapons but not without whisky.'

'It's got weapons too,' I said and began to describe to them the deadly road-block that my father, George and Tom, who were all in the Home Guard, had constructed on the road up to Reachfar.

'The first thing the enemy encounters,' I said, 'is the most hideous hedge of old reaper knives, fixed up on end in a bed of hard clay and then they come to the old harrow teeth and then—' When we had explored the jungle of the Reachfar road-block, the doctor said: 'They are all air-raid wardens too, aren't they?'

'Yes,' I told him, 'but Tom is very undisciplined. He keeps on feeding oats to the old mare out of his tin hat. My father threatened to fire him the other day.'

'And then what?'

'Tom said he had a good mind to go down to London and join the Fire Brigade, so Dad thought it better to put up with him here as a warden. I must say, though, that Tom's terrific at identifying lights that are showing a long way away. Quite often, looking out from Reachfar, I wouldn't know whether it's old Jockie Croonach's attic window or the Pole Star, but no matter how black the night is, Tom knows exactly who is being careless about the blackout and goes straight down to the Poyntdale telephone, and he's right every time.'

It was nearly suppertime when I at last rose to take my leave, and we all came out to the front of the house where Blithe Spirit was taking on a fiery glow in the westering light. I was facing the gate, the Mackays standing with their backs to it, when I saw another gold being struck to bright red by the evening sun. I was afraid to speak in case this was some trick born of my overtaut nerves as I had read my brother's letter being over-relaxed by the doctor's whisky, but Alasdair began to come up the driveway, nearer and nearer, unshaven, his cap in his hand, his khaki uniform bedraggled and the inevitable respirator and two haversacks dangling from his shoulder.

'Hello, Mother,' he said. 'Sorry I'm later than I said in my letter. I caught the bus all right, but—'

As he saw their astonished faces, he stopped in his tracks. 'What's wrong?' he asked.

There was a sob from Mrs Mackay, a few seconds of silence, and then the doctor said sternly, as he might have said it twenty years ago, but his voice was shaking now as it never shook then: 'Alasdair, what do you mean – worrying your mother like this?'

When the babble of explanation of the letter and telegram which had not got through was over, Alasdair said: '. . . and then I got off the bus at Bedamned's Corner. After all, I was the last person from about here who saw them.'

'Who?' the doctor asked.

'Roddie and Hughie Bedamned, Dad.'

'You mean – they're – they're—' Mrs Mackay could not say the word.

Alasdair nodded. 'Both of them. Hughie was killed on the beach outside Dieppe. Roddie died in hospital at Dover. I brought his stuff – his pipes and that – home. I gave them to Flora.'

170

I left the three Mackays under the lengthening shadow of Blithe Spirit and took my way home to Reachfar.

When I told my family of Alasdair's return and of the deaths of Roddie and Hughie, Tom stared across the table at the fire and said: 'I have never believed, myself, in some o' the things that the ould people would be believing in long ago, but it is chust as if there was a curse on that Bedamned house. When you think on it, there is not one o' them but what has come to a terrible kind of end, except young Jamie, and he ran away from his people to America and never came back and that's not natural-like either.'

'Och, be quiet with your havers, Tom!' my aunt said, with a shiver. 'You and your curses! If ould Jamie Bedamned had been *my* father, I'd have run away too and have never come back! It's poor Flora I'm sorry for. She's spent a lifetime of care and work and for what? To be left down in that hole with an old miser and an idiot!' She clattered the teapot down on its stand and swung round on me, full of fight against Flora's outrageous fortune. 'You'll have to go down there and see her, Janet!'

'Lord above us! Why pick on *me*?' I protested. '*I*'m not the one who's been a one-woman mission to Bedamned's Corner for about twenty years! Go your blooming self!'

'Now, Janet, that's no way to talk—' she began.

'I'll talk how I like! Cripes, you'll be wanting me to go and call on *Jean* next!'

Jean was my step-mother who was living down in Achcraggan and who hated the very sight of me and, to tell the truth, did not care overmuch for Kate, Tom or George either. Indeed, of the whole family, she liked only my father and she could just abide my brother, but I was anathema to her. Her name was, however, always useful for raising at Reachfar when one wanted to change the subject – that is, when my father was not present, of course, as was the case now, for although he spent his days on the croft he went down to Achcraggan for the evening meal.

'Och, now,' said George, 'this war we are having with

171

Hitler is quite enough without you and Jean getting going on another one, Janet. Mind you, I wouldna blame anyone for fighting with her, for she is one devilish aggravating woman.'

'They should put her in a bomb,' said Tom, 'and drop her on Bertie's Garden.' This was Tom's pronunciation of the name of Hitler's country retreat at Berchtesgaden. 'Her and Hitler could be having a fine old set-to and it would keep them from their interferesomeness to other people . . . George, it's your night to go down to Poyntdale and report, mind!'

'I'm minding,' said George. 'Since you got to be in the Air Road Precautions, Tom Reachfar, you're damn' nearly as interferesome as ould Jean!'

'Ach, I dinna mean to be interferesome, George, man, but a body just gets fair seeck, soor, scundered at the young fellows getting killed away there in France and never seeing hint or hair o' a Cherman to be getting a bit of a body's own back on them.' He looked up at the four guns which were still in their rack above the dresser. 'It's myself that'll be wishing sometimes that the booggers might try a landing down-bye and then try to come up the hill . . . My, it's terrible to think on that poor lassie Flora this night, all herself down there with Georgie an' that ould Jamie!'

'And the one o' them just about as foolish as the other,' said George, turning to me. 'Ould Jamie's fair dighted now, ye know, Janet. He spends all his time burying things about the placie – tin cans and ould horse-shoes an' all the like o' that. He thinks it's money he's burying.'

'And him trailing aboot with a lantern in the blackout an' a-all,' added Tom. 'And poor Flora running after him and trying to get him back into the housie.'

'The government is awful foolish in some ways,' George said. 'They never think when they make laws like blackout reggylations that there's people like Jamie Bedamned that has imaginary money to be burying, wartime or not.'

172

'Governments and the law is *always* foolish,' said Tom categorically, 'because they are *there* because some people is foolish and not reasonable. If a-all people was reasonable, there would be no need for the government or for the law at a-all. It is because o' the like o' Jamie Bedamned that the law is *in* it. If a man like Jamie Bedamned was allowed to go his own way, without the law to stop him, he would have made more misery for poor Flora than he has already. The poor lassie – down there all her lone and not a soul going near her!'

Many governments could, with advantage, take tuition in diplomacy, mind-conditioning and propaganda from my family. No matter what subject was raised, they subtly got the conversation back to Flora Bedamned, and, the next afternoon, utterly exasperated with myself and my family, I found myself dressed in the inevitable uniform, taking the basket of eggs and butter docilely from my aunt and setting off down the hill to Bedamned's Corner.

From the outside, the little house looked more tumble-down than ever, for, although Flora had spent some of the money young Jamie sent to her to pretty-up to her taste the rooms inside, the outside repairs were beyond her strength and skill and she had never dared to hire a man to carry them out, because her father would neither 'work for nothing' himself nor would he hear of another man being paid to repair a house that he, a stone-mason, owned. The fence at the front was a tangle of rotted posts and rusty wire, the wall round the remainder of the garden had gaping holes beside which the stones lay in heaps where they had fallen, the slates had slipped from the roof in great patches, exposing flapping rags of underlay and the wood of the joists, and the garden itself was a jungle, except for the little path to the door which was swept clean and bordered by a double row of the blue flower that the country people call 'Love-in-a-Mist'.

I tapped at the door and, country-fashion, walked into the kitchen at the end of the little passage. In spite of the

173

brilliant sunshine outside, the room was utterly cheerless. There was no fire in the grate, only a heap of grey ashes. There was no need for a fire for warmth, but in those days, before the advent of the hydro-electric schemes, it was very rare to find a kitchen in our district that did not have a fire, even on the hottest day in summer. The meals depended upon that kitchen fire, and it might be allowed to burn very low at mid-afternoon, but never, as a rule, allowed to go completely out as this fire had been allowed to do.

On one side of the depressing little black grate, in the old armchair, sat Jamie Bedamned, with his ragged and dirty stone-mason's clothes upon him although he had not worked for several years, his torn tweed cap on his head, his grey hair and beard dirty and unbarbered, his dead, dark eyes staring at the floor beyond his feet in their heavy, unpolished, unlaced boots. On the other side of the dead fire, with her back to the window, sat Flora, hunch-backed, flat-chested, withered, her wispy hair more grey than red-gold now, although she was not yet forty. In the corner, Georgie, a woman of twice Flora's size in stature, was busy at a big wooden box, wearing a jacket of some purple plush material with long silk fringes hanging from it of the type that was called a 'bridge coat' and fixing a bunch of artificial brilliant orange marigolds in her lank, greasy, black hair. The scene, as I stood in the doorway, was the very opposite of a tableau vivant – it was a picture of death in life. The people in that room were all breathing, but they were all dead.

I put my basket on the table, removed my black-peaked cap and laid it beside the basket, and as I put it on the wooden surface the stiff peak gave a small, sharp click. Slowly, Flora turned her head towards the sound, saw me and her dull, dead eyes came slowly up to my face. A small flicker of recognition lit their pale dullness for a moment and then died away.

'Flora,' I said, 'I am so sorry about your brothers. Alasdair Mackay told me.'

'It was good of him to come yesterday,' she said, and

174

then, with a sigh and an effort: 'and it is good of you to come today, Janet.'

'And it helps a little to know that Alasdair – somebody from home – saw the boys—' I said.

As so often before, one half of me wanted to run, screaming, out into the clean sunshine, while the other half was sinking with the Bedamneds into this inertia of death-in-life from which I felt that they would never emerge. I think I would have turned and run before the inertia could gain further ground but that at that moment Jamie Bedamned became conscious of my presence. His dead eyes filled with a dull rage that made them darker than ever and they raked over me from the black service shoes to my forehead and then, staring fiercely into my face, he sprang to his feet with a half-enraged, half-frightened grunt. We Sandison women all resemble one another, and I had a vivid impression that, deep in his decayed mind, there had been a spark of recognition, followed by an upsurge of the fear that my aunt had once inspired in him but which, now, had long been buried in his senility. From the seat of the chair, where it had been concealed between his body and the chair-back, he snatched a cardboard shoe-box, pushed it furtively under his torn coat and half stumbled, half ran out of the house as the heavy, unlaced boots fell away from his feet. From the window, I could see him creep among the tangled bushes of the garden and, scrabbling with his fingers among the earth, make a hole to bury the box.

'You have to excuse my father,' Flora said. 'He is quite funny and childish in his mind now.' She sighed. 'He will always be burying everything – even the dishes and spoons and a-all.' She rose to her feet and took some dry twigs from the corner by the fireplace. 'But he will stop outside now for a while. I will boil the kettle and make a droppie tea. It worries him to see one using the tea and wasting it, and it's a pity to worry him and him so old.'

Her terrible patience of acceptance was like a tightening band round my chest that threatened to stop my breathing

175

and I felt rising in me the rage that this house had always raised in my aunt and recognized it for the struggle of the mind, the wild thrashing about, to escape death by drowning in these waters of hopelessness.

'Flora,' I said harshly, staring at the rain streaks on the pink wallpaper that was bespattered with blue roses, 'whether it worries your father or not, you will have to have your roof repaired! Tom tells me that you're showing light through it at night!'

Teapot in hand, she stared at me. 'That canna be, Janet,' she said. 'It is summer and we are not using the lamp.'

'It won't always be summer and Tom could see your lights from Reachfar last winter.'

'Oh, mercy me! My father—'

'I'll ask Tom and George to come down, if you like.'

'No! Oh, no! . . . It's very good o' you, Janet, but I'll get Robbie-the-Slater. I can pay him. It's not the money. But it worries my father.'

I wanted to say: 'To hell with your father!' as my aunt had said so many times, but I said instead: 'Well, it can't be helped. The roof has to be mended.'

She began to pour water into the teapot. 'Mind you, I don't see how the light gets out. It's Georgie and me that sleeps up the stair and we never take a light up. It worries my father to see a lot of lights burning. It's chust the one lamp we have – in here.'

'Well, the light *does* get out!' I said with the angry vehemence of the unaccomplished liar, for the whole tale of the breach of blackout regulations was only a fabrication, inspired by the thought that one more November gale would rip the entire roof from the little ruin of a house.

This new, practical worry of the repairs to the roof had the effect of bringing Flora to life a little, and while we drank the tea, and Georgie, the silk fringes on the sleeves of her bridge-coat dabbling in her cup, stuffed bread and Reachfar scone into her mouth indiscriminately, we talked

176

of Flora's father and his 'funny ways and childishness' which would have to be by-passed that the repairs to the house might be effected. Flora spoke of him indulgently – without any suggestion of acrimony or complaint – even lovingly, as a mother might speak of a young and unusually trying child.

'You have great patience with him, Flora,' I said at one point, which made her gaze at me wonderingly out of her tired, worried, pale eyes.

'And where would I not have patience with him?' she asked. 'It would be a sin in me to make his old age miserable, for he has been a good-living, hard-working man a-all his life, my father.' As she spoke, she removed the plate that held the scones I had brought from Georgie's reach, and with an angry 'Chorchie! Chorchie!', her face even more distorted with thwarted greed, the idiot beat her fists on the table top and kicked at the legs of her chair.

'All right, then. There's chust one more for ye,' said Flora, putting a scone into her sister's voracious hands, and then, rising, she put the plate away in the cupboard in the corner of the room.

'Georgie is a grand eater,' she told me proudly. 'She has a-always enjoyed her food, poor bairn.'

Half fascinated, half repelled, I watched Georgie stuffing the scone, which she was dabbling in some rhubarb jam on her plate, into her mouth while she snuffled and grunted, and the jam, mixed with saliva, ran down her chin and dripped down the front of the purple bridge coat. I rose to my feet.

'Flora, it's time I went.'

'It was good of ye to come, Janet.' She sighed. 'And the laddies won't come back – och, well, it was chust to *be* that way . . . It was fine to see ye, though. Will ye come again before ye go?'

'I'm afraid not, Flora. I only have nine days' leave altogether and I have to spend two of them travelling. It's not very long.'

'It is a terrible war that is of it,' she said, staring up the

177

green hill towards the water-spout. 'And all the poor people in Holland and places driven out of their homes. It is thankful we should be here in Achcraggan, with none of the fighting coming near us.' She raised a rough, work-twisted hand and caressed the weathered, unpainted wood of the door-frame. 'None of us is ever thankful enough to what we have,' she ended. At that moment old Jamie Bedamned, his head bowed furtively, his arms clutching something he had hidden under the tattered coat, scuttled round the end of the house past the ruins of the water barrel and into the bushes, where he could be heard scrabbling, like some rodent creature that pursues its secretive life in fear of men and the light. I found the whole situation unbearable.

'Goodbye for the present, Flora,' I said abruptly.

'My, you're right smart in that uniform, Janet! Take care of yourself now and come back soon, lassie!'

In a bleak fury, I marched up the hill, my mind an incoherent jumble of incomplete thoughts. 'None of us is thankful enough! Calling me "lassie" as if she were ninety! Somebody should put a shot in that awful old man! What good is he? What good has he ever been? And that abominable Georgie! . . .'

When I got back to Reachfar, I promised myself, I would make it clear to my family that I was doing no more of their sympathy-visiting this leave. After all, I told myself, I and thousands like me were putting up with all sorts of boredom and discomfort and worse in order to try to preserve our homes, and what the devil was the use of it if, when you had leave to spend seven days at the said home, you had to go instead and watch an idiot stuffing her face with scone at Bedamned's Corner? It was all very fine my family saying that I could help Flora by visiting her. Help Flora my foot! Flora did not *need* any help. She had been created specially to be trodden into the mud and was thankful for her lot. None of us is *thankful* enough! Thankful for that slobbering idiot and that selfish twisted-minded old father and for two brothers you have reared

178

rotting in graves beside the English Channel! *Thankful!*

'Hi, Sarge!' said a voice. 'Having a personal interview with Hitler?'

I halted in my angry stride and saw Alasdair and Torquil Daviot under a tree ten yards from the path.

'Did someone pinch your aeroplane?' Alasdair pursued.

'I've been to Bedamned's Corner,' I said. 'Hello, Master Torquil.'

'Oh,' Alasdair said. 'Awful, isn't it?'

'Awful.'

'And damn-all one can do,' Torquil said. '*Your* father, Alasdair, and the Guvnor and I – we've all tried to get Flora to put the old man or the girl or both into homes, but she wouldn't hear of it. And now, of course, since this show started, it's pretty well impossible . . . Cigarette, Janet?'

'Thank you . . . It's no good talking to Flora,' I said. 'I think her mind got stuck at this thing of slaving for that family of hers when she was twelve years old and it's never got any further. I frightened her into getting the house repaired, though, whether the old man kicks up a row or not.'

'Good Lord, how?'

And I told them of the lies I had told to Flora which made us all laugh and lightened the atmosphere a little.

'I say,' Torquil said then, 'let's all go down to the Plough and have one! It's after six o'clock.'

'Have they *got* anything at the Plough?' Alasdair asked.

'Jockie is nearly sure to have something tucked away for special occasions and *we*'re special – he may never see three locals at home on leave at one time again. Come on . . . Your people won't worry about you, Janet?'

'Her people stopped worrying about *her* twenty-five years ago,' Alasdair said. 'Besides, I'll drive you both back with some of Dad's medical petrol. The Reachfar people are never ill so they're entitled to the petrol when drunk and incapable.'

'Jockie probably won't have enough to make a flea incapable,' said Torquil as we turned back the way I had

179

come, but we kept high on the hillside, leaving Bedamned's Corner far below, on our left, on the coast.

Jockie's small public bar at the Plough Inn was crammed to overflowing with Air Force personnel from the sea-plane station across the Firth, naval personnel from a patrol boat that was lying out from Achcraggan, and army personnel from the gun-post on the South Cobbler, for the entrance to the Firth was guarded by two cliffs, called the North and South Cobblers, after two giant shoe-makers who lived and worked, in the days of the giants, one on each cliff and used to share one hammer between them, tossing it to and fro across the deep, mile-wide sea channel that separated them.

'Look here,' I whispered when we were inside, 'it's all right for you coves who're not in uniform, but I'm not supposed to breathe the same air as that Flight Lieutenant over there, according to the book.'

'To hell with the book!' said Alasdair. 'You are in the company of Colonel Daviot and Major Mackay. What'll you have?'

'What has Jockie got?' I asked, looking at old Jockie Plough, who, with his two daughters, was trying to keep pace with the business over the bar.

'Well, so it's yourselves that iss in it!' he said, pushing a tray of glasses aside and planting his elbows on the bar in a leisurely way. 'And how iss a-all the people at Reachfar, Janet? I am hearing that Tom iss getting an extra-special bayonet that will go in an' come oot very easy an' quick-like made at the smiddy . . . There iss nothing but a droppie beer,' he added, getting down to business and looking three sailors firmly in the eye, 'an' ferry poor stuff at that, but you naval boys can haff what there iss off it . . . Bill-the-Post iss waiting for you three ben in the back room,' he continued, turning to us again. 'He hass been there this hour an' more an' will be getting a little blue in the face by this time, although a-always on the blue side at the best off times. Chust go ben and I will be there myself in no time at a-all.'

180

We made our way through the smoke and noise to the back room where Bill-the-Post, old Captain Robertson of Seamuir, and a few other cronies were very glad to welcome us and, shortly, Jockie himself appeared with a new bottle of whisky and a tray with four glasses.

'Cripes!' Alasdair said, staring at the full bottle. 'I haven't seen a sight like that in months!'

'This district around here,' said Captain Robertson with the air of one quoting from a guide-book, for drink always made him pompous, 'is famous for scenery of all descriptions. Be it sea, mountain, moorland or sunlit stream, you will find it in the environs of Achcraggan. It is also justly famed for the unopened bottles of whisky that can always be found by the right people in the back premises of the Plough Inn—'

'Ach, hold out your glass, Captain Robertson, sir, and be quiet with you!' said Jockie. 'It iss a meenister you should haff been and not a farmer with the speaking that iss in you!'

'Sir,' said Captain Robertson, 'I am now, foremost, a soldier once more!'

'Aye, an' the Lord peety us a-all in the Home Guard if the Chermans land the-night!' said Bill-the-Post.

'William,' said the captain with dignity, 'we are in a state of full readiness and merely having a little refreshment while waiting for the hour to strike. We will fight all the better for it. Your health, William!'

'Good health, sir,' said Bill-the-Post and the level in their glasses sank by an inch or two.

It was a most convivial evening. One of Jockie's daughters brought bacon and eggs and scones for Torquil, Alasdair and me about nine o'clock and we saw no reason to hurry away. Bill-the-Post went home and came back with his melodeon, and Captain Robertson and Peter Boatie, an old fisherman, gave some spirited renderings of sea shanties, after which Jockie produced the bagpipes that belonged to his son who was in the Air Force, and Alasdair, marching up and down the passage between the

181

bar and the back room, played a selection of warlike airs.

'You know,' I said, during an interval, 'I've never been really inside the Plough before . . . Alasdair, remember Armistice Day in 1918?'

And we all went back over that great day when Alasdair and I were children, playing outside, while the men of the district celebrated the end of the war till the tide went out and left the coal boat which they had been unloading high and dry on the beach. From there, we went on to memories of the last big Harvest Home at Poyntdale, and after this Alasdair said: 'Here! *You* should be contributing to this programme of entertainment! What about a step or two of the Highland Fling?' And so it was that I took off my heavy shoes, tucked up my airwoman's skirt above my knees and in my respectable, grey cotton, service-issue stockings began to dance the Highland Fling while Alasdair played and the crowd from the public bar surged, cheering, along the passage and into the room. I had reached the seventh step of the dance and the noise was at its height when Alasdair's pipes wailed away into silence and I saw George, Tom, a policeman and Doctor Mackay shouldering their way into the back room.

'It's not closing time yet, Donald, man!' said Jockie to the policeman in a protesting voice.

'It's nothing o' that, Jockie,' the policeman said, 'although, mind you, you're ten meenutes behind, though!'

'Mercy me! Time! Time, chentlemen, please!' Jockie began to shout.

'What's wrong, George?' I asked, sitting down and pulling on my shoes.

'It's Georgie Bedamned – she's out and lost. Flora came up to Reachfar. She thought Georgie must have followed *you*.'

'Me? Why?'

'The uniform, maybe, Flora thought.'

I remembered that I had had to put my cap out of the reach of Georgie's sticky fingers that afternoon.

182

'Was you seeing her at a-all, Janet?' Tom asked.

'No. No, she didn't follow *me* – at least, I don't think so.'

'No,' Torquil said. 'Alasdair and I met Janet at the corner of the Wee Woodie. There was nobody else in sight.'

'Hell!' Alasdair said, pressing the last of the air from the bag of the pipes with a loud, squealing wail and then handing them to Jockie's daughter. 'Well, we'd better get looking for her, I suppose. What a bloody nuisance that girl is!'

'The devil of it is that she may have matches,' the doctor said. 'Flora isn't sure. She can't remember how many were in the box and she forgot to lock the drawer.'

'Matches?' Torquil asked.

'Georgie has taken to lighting fires,' the doctor explained. 'It's just as if the devil were in her. Before the blackout, she never went about setting fire to things as she does now. If she lights a fire tonight, the way things are, Flora will just *have* to agree to put her away. She's a public menace.'

'If she puts fire till a whin bush the-night,' Tom said, 'it'll not be as easy to put out as yon time she put the haystack going in the winter. The grass and heather will burn for miles the-night with the dry weather and the wind that's in it.'

When we went outside, it was after eleven and the full moon was sailing over the clear sky above Reachfar hill, but there was not, anywhere in a radius of forty miles, any sign of fire.

'She must be somewhere in the angle between Poyntdale, Reachfar and Achcraggan,' Doctor Mackay said. 'She has never been out of that area in her life. The thing to do is to keep working between these three points and Bedamned's Corner. We should come on her before too long. You three' – he turned to Torquil, Alasdair and me – 'take a sweep across the fields from here to Poyntdale. You are fitter for the cross-country work than the rest of us. Don't

183

call her name. The little bitch only hides if she hears anyone calling her.'

We set off in silence over the stile into the hayfield on the west side of the Plough, where we fanned out, I crossing the field diagonally and the two men going round the hedgerows and fences at its edges until we converged at its south-west corner.

'Reminds me, Janet,' Alasdair said, 'of that day you and I searched for Miss Boyd.'

'Don't!' I said and shuddered.

'It was you two who found her, wasn't it?' Torquil asked. 'I remember hearing about it when I came home for Christmas.'

'It was Janet's dog that found her really,' Alasdair said. 'She had hanged herself in—'

'Stop it!' I said in a whispering scream and I looked round at the silvery hill and the high white moon and then behind me, as the words 'a frightful fiend doth close behind him tread . . .' flickered across my mind like a shadow over water.

'What's up?' Alasdair asked. 'You got the willies?'

'I don't like this,' I said. 'I don't like it at all. Oh, *confound* these Bedamneds!'

'You can say that twice, chum,' said Alasdair. 'Okay, you two go round the down side – I'll take the up. Surely even *she* won't have gone tramping through standing corn!'

We converged again at the diagonally opposite corner of the field.

'I must say,' Torquil said mildly, 'with this war how it is, I can think of better ways of spending my leave than this.'

'What are *you* beefing about?' I snapped. 'My family had made *me* spend the whole of this afternoon with these damned Bedamneds!'

'It's not the drink that affects her temper,' Alasdair told Torquil. 'She always gets like this when she's looking for anybody.'

184

'Oh, you shut up!' I said, climbing the fence at the field corner. 'Let's get on to Poyntdale as we were told to do. That cow Georgie is probably home by now, anyway.'

I tried to break through the web of evil that I felt all round me by being facetious, and in the voice of Tom I said: 'Chust get on with the chobbie you have to do an' then your time's your own! . . . I hope you have something to drink at Poyntdale, Master Torquil!'

'I wish you would just say Torquil!'

'No. The "Master", to me, is part of your name and I like it.'

I surveyed the field in front of us. 'A very bonnie puckle turnips, Master Torquil!'

'And if anybody thinks I'm going to cross them in the only decent pair of shoes I have they're up in the spout,' said Alasdair and then: 'Hi, it's not very long since these were picked!'

He bent between the turnip drills and came up with about a dozen foxgloves, their stems wrung and twisted, their bells bruised, some of them torn up by the roots. As surely as if she had signed upon them the name that she could not write, Georgie had marked them with her touch. They were the scarred ruin, the mauled carcase of flowers picked for no reason and cast away for no reason, a small part of life condemned to premature death by the whim of the human idiot.

We stood looking down at the broken flowers between Alasdair's hands for a moment, until our eyes were attracted to the moonlit sky by the familiar, drumming sound, a churning, rolling sound, of a diesel-engined aircraft.

'That's a Jerry!' said Torquil.

'Damn and blast him!' said Alasdair.

'Come on!' I said irritably. 'Or do you want to stay here and throw stones at him?'

Alasdair laid the broken flowers on the grass verge of the field and we made our way round its upper boundary and came eventually to the point where the Reachfar Burn

185

divided, the westerly stream going to the dam. All the trees in this area had been cut now and the sawmill had long been disused and abandoned and its roof removed to avoid taxation, but the walls that Jamie Bedamned had built during an earlier war still stood, stark and black in the moonlight on the face of the silver hill. The dam itself, with the clumps of willows about its verges, lay like a silver saucer under the moon, silent, except for the small, contented night sounds of the waterfowl, and that we might not disturb that content we instinctively spoke in low voices.

'It's a very interesting expression,' Torquil said, 'that old saying about making a kirk or a mill of something. That old sawmill might be a ruined church, looking at it from here.'

'A nice problem for the archaeologists of five thousand years hence,' said Alasdair.

As he spoke, the guns on the South Cobbler suddenly went into action with a tremendous crash and the churning noise in the sky seemed to take on the agitation of panic.

'Attaboy!' said Alasdair. 'Let him have it!'

The countryside that had been so silent, its secret life lost in sleep, came awake and the surface of the dam was broken into silver wedges as the waterfowl swam hurriedly from one hiding-place to another. The South Cobbler gave out with a second salvo, the North Cobbler simultaneously opened with its first, and the noise reverberated westwards to Ben Wyvis and came rolling back again. Alasdair, bursting with excitement, jumped on to a tree stump and began to declaim, misquotingly:

'So all night long the noise of battle rolled
Among the mountains by the summer sea—'

And then: 'Christ! They've *got* him! Look! Look! They've *got* him!'

Looking eastwards, we saw the little spot that had once been an aircraft but was now, against the white sky, a dying meteor that trailed behind it a tattered banner of red

186

flame and a cloud of black smoke as it plunged to extinction in the broad waters of the North Sea that lay beyond the Cobblers. When it disappeared from sight, the silence became peculiarly intense, as if even the waterfowl must be listening for the hiss that that flaming mass must make as it struck the water, but no hiss came, and after a moment Alasdair's voice, low and deep, went on with the 'recitation' that he had begun, as if he were unconscious of speaking aloud, as he stared down the hill at the ruined sawmill:

> 'A broken chancel with a broken cross,
> That stood on a dark strait of barren land.
> On one side lay the Ocean, and on one
> Lay a great water, and the moon was full.'

He stepped down from his tree stump. 'Funny,' he said. 'We had to learn that in the Top Class, remember? I've never understood poetry. Funny – I've never seen the picture in these lines until now . . . God, I bet those fellows on the Cobblers are pleased with themselves!'

'I say,' said Torquil, 'there's a Loch Ness monster in the dam! Look! Over there!'

We all stared at the serpent-like, black thing that lay on the silver surface ahead of Torquil's pointing finger.

'Wonder what it is?' Alasdair said and they both moved forward to the water's edge.

I did not follow them. I knew what it was. It was my grandmother's old black feather boa which Kate had given to Georgie long ago and which had been her proudest possession.

They found Georgie's body at dawn the next morning.

Part V
1951

Part V
1951

Time, as experienced by the human mind, is not a progression of minutes, hours, days and years, with every minute and year of the same duration as the minute or year that preceded it. Some minutes are infinitely long, and some years, in the mind, are shorter than many a minute. And space, that other governing factor in our lives, is not statically located or of a single constant significance in our minds either. It is possible, in time of illness and pain, to believe that the space of the whole world is limited to these four walls that contain one's suffering and to believe that this room will always have, in the mind, this character of horror, but when the illness is over the rest of the world reopens to the sight and the four walls become different in this new perspective. The quality of time or space is conditioned by what is experienced in that unit of time or space. It is all a question of when and where you are standing.

In July of 1951, about eleven years after the death of Georgie Bedamned, I was standing in a bedroom of a house in St Jago, which is an island in the West Indies, and between me and 1940 and Poyntdale Dam where Georgie was drowned, there were eleven years of time and some four thousand miles of the earth's space. During the eleven years there had been war and peace, my marriage and making of a home and many other things, and I do not think that, in all this time, I had given a single thought to the house at Smith's Corner. And yet, in space, I had been close enough to it many times, for Twice – my husband's name is Alexander Alexander and I have been guilty of giving him the 'bye-name' of 'Twice' – and I visited Reachfar frequently until we went out to St Jago in 1950 and, when there, we drove very often to Achcraggan with members of my family, passing Smith's Corner on the way; but nowadays I was no longer, mentally, standing on the hill of Reachfar and looking at the immediate countryside. I was now standing mentally in my new home in south-west Scotland with the Atlantic and the West Indies over my shoulder, as it were, so that Reachfar on top of its hill looked like a constant, if distant, beacon and the countryside around it and places like Smith's Corner fell away, insignificantly, into the mists of distance. And when the move from south-west Scotland to St Jago had been accomplished, the focus shifted once more and Scotland, in my mind, was reduced to two peaks that showed over the distant horizon, the peak that was our home in the south-west and the peak that was Reachfar, our home in the north. The little low-lying house at Smith's Corner did not show over my mental horizon at all.

At the end of July 1951 the two peaks on the horizon that were Scotland in my mind were glittering in a brilliant light, for we were packing to come home on our first leave. Or, more accurately, I was packing while Twice was lying on his bed on his stomach with a road map of Great Britain propped against his pillows. We were to travel to Avonmouth by sugar boat and pick up a car there.

'If she docks on the Thursday we can just make that concert in Edinburgh by the Saturday without killing ourselves,' he said. 'And then what? Shall we make straight for Reachfar or go to Crookmill first?'

Crookmill was our house in the south-west.

'LOOK HERE!' I said, sitting down and wiping the sweat from my forehead. 'Are we going to sell Crookmill or aren't we?'

'Oh, don't let's get into that again!' He went to the door and called downstairs: 'Clorinda! Bring some beer up here, please! Heavens, it's hot!'

'It's *always* hot in this perishing island. Now look, Twice, there's no good going on dithering. We are famed for our organization, you and I, what with buying cars and concert tickets at long distance and this and that, and if people knew what fools we are about that house of ours they'd die laughing!'

'What do I care?' said Twice. 'Besides, it's *your* house!'

'Twice Alexander, it's *our* house!'

'I give my share of it to you, right now, free, gratis and for nothing.'

'I ought to clout you on the ear,' I said.

Twice lay on his back and stared up at the ceiling. 'Let's leave Crookmill out of it. There's no point giving ourselves nightmares about selling it to people who will build on a chromium sun-parlour or nightmares about keeping it until it falls apart with dry rot—'

'Now look here, Twice,' I interrupted him sternly, 'it's no use you going on like that. One of the main issues in this trip home is Crookmill. I'm not coming out here for another two years to be driven demented all over again every mail by letters from angry tenants who are being bullied to death by Loose-an'-Daze.'

Lucy and Daisy were two friends whom we had left as caretakers of the house, a duty which they interpreted in such a way that they had worn down and virtually evicted seven tenants in a matter of eighteen months.

'In principle,' said Twice, 'I am in entire agreement with you, but I don't see the slightest point in holding a board meeting about Crookmill here and now. Time enough for that when we get over there. Sit down and drink your beer and stop getting into a frenzy and tempting Providence with too many plans.'

He rearranged his pillows, lay back against them and, taking my glass of beer, I arranged myself in a similar way on my own bed.

'You're quite right, of course!' I agreed. 'Oh, well, cheers!'

We each had a drink of beer.

'On this boat,' said Twice, 'I'm going to drink English beer all day and every day until I get this synthetic island hoss-piss out of my system.'

'You know what I'm going to have – three times a day? Fish – fish and chips, herrings, kippers, grilled sole, fried haddock. Fish that tastes like *fish*, not lumps of slime that have rubbed against fish that have gone bad.'

'And I'm not going to eat one bit of chicken, no matter who offers it to me!' said Twice.

'And not one French bean!'

'I'll have lamb chops for lunch every day.'

'And apples! If anybody offers me a grapefruit or a banana, I'll brain him with it!'

'I'd *like* to see somebody being brained with a banana,' said Twice, who has a very literal, enquiring, scientific sort of mind, being an engineer by profession.

During these last days before our departure, many of our conversations were like this, for our organization for our leave was so complete that we had nothing to do except talk and nothing so attractive to talk about as the leave.

'Maybe the time would pass more quickly if we were one of those couples like the Murphies who discover after they're on the boat that they've left the baby behind and have to come back for it,' Twice said next.

'It wasn't the baby,' I said, 'it was his pot and they had to come back for it because he won't do it in anything else. Thank goodness you don't have a pot. Do we have to take all these pipes? Wouldn't seven be enough? A different smoke for each day of the week?'

'What do you want with all these shoes?' Twice countered. 'Wouldn't seven pairs be enough, a pair for each day of the—'

'Please, Sah,' said Clorinda in the bedroom doorway, 'telegram, Sah.'

'Thanks, Clorinda.'

I began to go on with the packing again. 'If the laundry plant has broken down,' I said, 'wire them back saying to wash the hard way till about November.'

194

'It isn't the laundry,' Twice said after a moment, and at the tone of his voice I went to the bed and looked at the cable in his hand.

'CAN YOU ALTER ARRANGEMENTS TRAVEL VIA NEW YORK URGENT BUSINESS FULL LETTER IN MAIL REACHFAR'

We stared at one another. 'What can it be?' Twice asked after a moment.

'I haven't a single idea.' I stared at the cable form. 'Reachfar,' I read aloud. 'My family has its ways of doing things. They would not have signed that cable that way for no reason. That means a conclave has been held and they're *all* in agreement.'

'Then let's cable back that we can alter.' Twice got off the bed.

'But can we?'

'Our sea passages direct will be snapped up at once. We'll have to go to New York by air, though, and maybe across the Atlantic as well.'

'Oh, damn! I *loathe* that air trip!'

'What else can we do? The family wouldn't have done this without good reason.'

'No, I know. Oh, all right.'

I sat down on my bed feeling that we had indeed tempted Providence with too many well-laid plans.

'I'll go round to the Estate office and phone the cable right away,' Twice said. 'Darling, *don't* be too disappointed! Actually it's rather exciting – I'll soon be back.'

When Twice came back from the Estate office, Sir Ian Dulac, on whose sugar estate we lived and whose sugar factory absorbed much of Twice's engineering attention, came back with him, of course. I say 'of course' because nothing ever happened on Paradise Estate that Sir Ian did not regard as his own personal business. He was dressed, as usual, in white drill riding clothes and high black boots and now drew my family's cable from his coat pocket as if *he* had received it and we had never seen it before.

'By Jove!' he said to me. 'Listen to *this*, Missis Janet!' and he read the message aloud in his best, ex-army,

195

parade-ground voice, then frowned fiercely at me and said: 'What does it mean, eh? Tell me that!'

'Your guess is as good as mine,' I said, 'and probably better, because more far-fetched.'

'Now then, don't you go gettin' like that! Your people wouldn't send a cable like this without good reason, an' they say there's a letter in the mail explainin' everythin'.'

'There'd better be!'

He stared at me for a moment and then turned to Twice. 'Pretty hot today. Tryin' to the temper, very. Any beer in the house?'

Twice went and called Clorinda while Sir Ian turned back to me. 'Now, me dear, you don't want to be all disappointed an' that. If you'd travelled on these sugar tubs as often as I have you'd be glad to fly round New York.'

'I haven't,' I said.

'Haven't what?'

'Travelled in sugar boats as often as you have. I've never travelled on a sugar boat at all and I *want* to travel on a sugar boat!'

'You'll like New York. Great place, New York – finest city in the world. Manhattan Island is the most amazin'—'

'– concrete desert, split into slabs by canyons at regular intervals where the modern troglodyte lives in an air-conditioned cave till he dies of nervous exhaustion,' I broke in. 'That's what you said about Manhattan Island when you were talking about Martha's aunt last week.'

He glared at me and turned to Twice. 'Never saw a woman with such a perishin' memory!' he said. He then took a swig at his beer and turned back to me. 'Come now, me dear, you got relations in New York?'

'No.'

'In America, then?'

'NO.'

'What about your friend Martha?'

'My family wouldn't be having urgent business with my friend Martha,' I told him.

196

'Now then, you never can tell with families. My old uncle in Perthshire once had urgent business with a Kaffir chief and he came to see him with a bunch of his followers with their spears and everythin' and frightened the villagers out of their wits.'

'Maybe Tom and George have been offered a film contract,' said Twice, which did not help matters or my temper in any way.

'Anyway, you'll probably still get to Edinburgh in time to hear that fellah playin' his fiddle,' said Sir Ian. 'I've phoned Pooky Peters and told him I want two seats on every flight from here to New York till further notice. We can cancel up to two hours before the take-off. An' Tommy Fletcher is tryin' to get us provisional bookin's on the next three boats out o' New York. You might have to fly, though. All the ships are pretty full. All we got to do now is wait an' see what's in this letter. Very interestin'. Wonder what it can be?'

For two days this question hung in the air between us constantly, except for the intervals when Sir Ian, at the telephone in the Estate office, rang up the post office and bellowed: 'Ain't that letter I told you about in yet? No, the postmark *ain't* London, ye perishin' idiot! It's Duncraggan!'

'Not Dun – *Ach*!' Twice would say.

'What d'ye mean, Ach? . . . No, not *you*! . . . Oh, I see! . . . Here, you there, the postmark is *Ach*craggan! What d'ye mean *What*craggan? Googorralmighty—'

And at this point Twice would snatch the receiver from his hand and begin to recite: 'A for apple, C for Charlie, H for—'

After such a session, the post office had again told us that the letter had not come in, and Sir Ian, Twice and I had come back to our verandah and were sitting being very hot, short and ill-natured with one another, when little Sandy Maclean, the manager's son, who went to the Estate office every day to collect my letters along with his mother's, cantered his pony up the driveway and called:

197

'Missis Janet, there's a letter for you from home with four an' ninepence in stamps on it an' bags me the envelope, please!'

Life, I find, simply bristles with quirks of this kind, especially life on a tropical island, when the heat is making you feel that you are being smothered by a wet blanket and you want to go on holiday to Britain and you do *not* want to travel round New York. Just to irritate Sir Ian and Twice, I borrowed Twice's sharp knife and opened the letter with exaggerated deliberation and care and handed the airmail cover to Sandy.

'It *is* a beauty, isn't it?' I said. 'And you can read the Achcraggan postmark as distinctly as anything.'

'Awful-lookin' writin' though,' said Sandy critically.

'That's my brother's writing,' I told him haughtily. 'He is quite a distinguished scholar, actually.'

'Looks like a chicken's been scratchin',' said Sandy, unmoved.

'Dammit!' Sir Ian burst out. 'Never mind the blasted writin'! What's in the perishin' *letter*?'

'Dear Janet,' I read, 'We hope that you and Twice were not too much upset by our cable but we were not certain of your sailing date and wanted to be sure of catching you. A tragic thing has happened in one of the local families and it was Kate who first had the idea that you two were in the very position to be of the greatest help. I didn't know the woman at all until now, but Kate says you will recognize her because she was a friend of yours at Achcraggan School. That is going back a bit, but her name is Flora Smith and she lives with her old father at that little house on the shore about a mile west of Achcraggan—'

'My heavens!' I said aloud. 'Flora Bedamned!'

'Flora *who*?' Twice asked.

'Never mind now. Wait a minute.'

I returned to the letter. 'She had a brother called Jamie in the United States – he went out years ago and has never been back. The family is sure you will remember the night he disappeared. Anyway, he and his wife were killed in an

198

air crash about three weeks ago, but four young children have been left behind and what the family is asking you and Twice to do is go round New York, pick the children up and bring them home to their aunt. It seems to me a lot to ask, but Kate says you know what a lousy life Flora has had and that you'll be willing to do this for her. And Flora herself has never been further than Inverness. She seems to me to be the last woman in the world to take on four young kids, but she is crazy to have them so there it is.

'When she got the cable about the death of her brother and his wife, she brought it up here to Kate and George and Tom hit on the idea of getting in touch with Malcolm Macleod, one of the Macleods of Varlich, who is some sort of relation of Flora's. He is with the Cunard company in New York and can do everything about passages for you. This is his address . . . . . . He has been down to Colorado and has taken charge of the children and is attending to everything connected with Smith's estate which, by the way, is considerable. Apparently he was tremendously successful as a building contractor and owned a chain of motels, among other things. If you are willing to go round New York, please just cable us briefly and then arrange everything with Malcolm Macleod from your end to suit yourselves . . .'

I laid the rest of the letter aside and stared out over the brilliant, sun-shimmering, tropical garden, but a lapse in time and space had taken place and I did not see it. What I saw was the bleak, black little hump of Bedamned's Corner as if from the hill road, its sagging roof-tree cowering by the cold grey sea under this latest blow of fate and its ruined chimney standing like a broken rampart against the stormy winter sky.

'The family want us to pick up four young children in New York – their parents have been killed in an air crash – and take them home to Achcraggan to their aunt,' I told Twice and Sir Ian.

'Their aunt? Who is she?' Twice asked.

'My friend Flora Bedamned.'

'Flora what? Have I ever met her?'

199

'No. No, I don't think so. Her name is actually Flora Smith, but she was always known as Flora Bedamned,' I said and I went on to tell Twice and Sir Ian the bare outline of the story of the Smith family that I have been telling here.

By that evening, our air trip to New York had been arranged for two days later and Malcolm Macleod, by telephone, had confirmed bookings for all of us in the next Cunarder out of the Hudson River, and when it was all settled I said to Twice: 'I'm terribly sorry about this, darling. I know you were looking forward to the sugar boat as much as I was.'

'Oh, rot! And look at the fun Sir Ian's had – I shouldn't be surprised if we're booked on this aeroplane as Mr and Mrs Bedamned!'

'Bedamned is right,' I said. 'There's a sort of blight on that family, but I didn't think it could reach as far as this . . . Twice, it's frightening sometimes the interconnectedness there is about life. And yet, too, there is something satisfactory about it . . . You're sure you don't hate all this upset in our plans?'

'There *isn't* much upset, when you think of it. It's only the car to be delivered to Southampton docks instead of Avonmouth and the missing of a concert in Edinburgh, and the compensation seems to be a free luxury trip across the Atlantic . . . Your friend Flora's financial worries seem to be over, anyway.'

'Jamie was always good about Flora. He sent her money every month for years . . . It's a queer thing, the Bedamneds coming up out of the past like this, Twice.'

'It seems to me to have been a *good* thing rather than queer, Flash,' Twice said.

He was not looking at me while he spoke, but looking down at his hands. Twice's face is dominated by his brilliant blue eyes, and when they are hidden, as they were now, I sometimes feel that I am in the presence of a stranger who may express a thought that is quite unexpected. This happened now.

200

'Since we had that letter from Jock,' he said, 'you've been more like your real self than you've been for the last six months.'

'In what way?'

He looked at me now. 'It's difficult to express what I mean. During the last six months or so, if anyone had asked me, I wouldn't have said that you were any different from what you ever were, but this morning, after that letter came in and you began to tell Sir Ian and me about this Smith family, something began to flow back into you – something which used to be there and which I suddenly discovered had been – been sort of in abeyance. I can only describe it as – well, *Reachfar*!'

'Reachfar? Twice, you're dotty!'

'Oh no I'm not! When you were telling us about the Smiths, your mind went back there in memory. Your eyes became different – seemed to get even bigger – and a different light came into them and your voice changed. You described Flora as a trachled little droichan of a craitur and you said the house was more ropach than any tinkers' camp – words you haven't used since we've been out here in this island!'

I laughed. 'I'd forgotten I knew the words droichan and ropach – and I don't really know them. They're Gaelic – I can say them but not spell them. I'm sorry.'

'Don't be sorry, my pet. It's taught me something. I was worried about your health these last few months – you were so damned depressed all the time Martha's aunt was down here – I thought the climate was getting you down, but it isn't that. There's nothing wrong with you that a good injection of Reachfar won't put right. God bless Flora Bedamned, I say, for channelling some Reachfar straight across to St Jago!'

'Poor Flora! She needs all the blessings that can be called down on her. That awful old father of hers is still alive, it seems, and now she's got four kids. Four wealthy American kids. I wonder what they're like? Most of the wealthy American children that one sees down here on

201

holiday are pretty unattractive and there's something incongruous in children of that sort going to Bedamned's Corner.'

'I don't think that the few divorcees' and film stars' brats that we see down here around the hotels can be representative of the young of any country,' Twice said. 'The Smith lot are probably quite normal.'

'No Bedamned was ever normal,' I said gloomily. 'They were all ab- or sub- except Flora and she was super-. Not only super-normal but superhuman as well. Poor Flora! I'm forty-one. She must be forty-eight. She has reared a family already and she has seen them all die, and now she's about to start in all over again. That life of hers is frightening. It has been one long, endless sacrifice. But the old father is the worst thing. He's given me the creeps ever since I was five years old. I've never known why until now.'

'And now – why?'

'I never once saw him smile.'

'Oh, come, Flash, he must have had the odd moment!'

'Not one, odd or even. Jamie Bedamned never smiled. He glowered with anger, he looked sullen with hatred, he looked cunning with miserliness, he looked frightened in the presence of Kate, but never once have I seen him smile.'

'Sounds like a nice comfortable cove . . . I suppose the family's sure it's doing the best thing for these kids, bringing them home like this?'

'It's apparently the only thing. Flora seems to be the only relative. Flora will do her best for them. I feel less worried about the kids than I do about her. Everything, always, seems to come back to rest on Flora, and yet she struggles along through it all and is never overpowered. There is something almost inspiring about her. In fact, now, seen at this distance of time and space, that Smith family has for me a queer sort of – a sort of significance – as if it were a microcosm of the whole pattern of all life. Old Jamie Bedamned married that woman, begot those

202

children and seemed, after that, to be hellbent on destroying them all, physically, mentally and spiritually and every other way. He didn't do it deliberately, I suppose, but he seemed to be driven to it by something inside himself that he couldn't control – just as whole races and nations are driven, even against their will, to all sorts of wars and racial suicides . . . Tom once said that it was as if there were a curse on the Bedamned family and it has an odd parallel in my mind with the curse that seems, sometimes, to be on the human race – the urge towards self-destruction.'

'But this Flora hasn't been destroyed,' Twice said.

'No. And that's a thing to think about. Flora has come through. There is no logical, physical, down-to-earth reason why Flora Bedamned shouldn't be in her grave long ago. She has been underfed and overworked all her life. She has had disappointments and sorrows away above the normal human share. She has never had an irresponsible moment. She has never had a friend. But there she is. She has come through and she is about to start on a new period of service . . . Twice, words are clumsy things, but d'you know what I think?'

'What?'

'That word service – that's the keynote of Flora's whole character – devoted service, blind devotion, complete selflessness. Service, devotion, selflessness – they are all synonymous with love, in a way. I am seeing Flora's life now as a sort of parable of the triumph of that selflessness over everything else – she has never given a thought to herself, and yet she is the one Bedamned who has come through, is still in her right mind and able to tell the tale.'

I left the table where I had been sitting and went to look out into the insect-humming, frog-croaking darkness of the hot tropical night beyond the windows, but I saw there again the little house at Bedamned's Corner, with its broken chimney, sitting humped beside the winter sea.

'I haven't given a thought to Flora Bedamned for ten years and more, and before that, when I did think of her,

203

she always seemed to be the most insignificant person I had ever known. But she isn't. Flora matters.'

'About the only real belief I've got,' Twice said, 'is that everybody matters. Every other belief is a corollary of that. And one can never estimate the full extent of the importance and influence of any one person. Like this Flora. To you, with your knowledge of her and your way of thinking, her life appears to you as a parable, as you said. To other people she will appear in a different light, but she has some significance for everybody who comes in contact with her – your father, Tom, George, Kate—'

'Oh, Kate!' I said and began to laugh, and then I told Twice of how, long ago, Kate had scared old Jamie Bedamned into taking refuge under the 'bridgies' on the County Road. 'Flora simply exasperated Kate,' I ended, 'as you can imagine. Kate used to try to galvanize her into some sort of resistance, but quite without effect. No. Flora may have some significance for me, but she'll never have any for Kate.'

Two evenings later, Twice and I, overpowered by the concrete cliffs of Manhattan Island and by the speed of the traffic between them, as well as by the responsibility that now lay imminently before us, walked into the vast foyer of the Commander Hotel on Fifth Avenue.

'Well,' Twice said after a moment, 'I don't see any large, grey-haired bloke of about sixty looking expectant, do you? We'd better ask over there at the desk with the blonde.'

'I suppose this *is* the Commander Hotel?' I said. 'For my money, it could be the Chicago World's Fair.'

'It says it welcomes us to it on that big board over there, so it must be it.'

'I wish you'd stop saying *it*!'

'This place makes me feel like an it – I don't mean an embryo louse – I mean—'

'A *dig*-it. I know . . . Will you tackle the blonde or shall I? I'm dying for a drink.'

204

'Let's have the drink first,' said Twice, 'and then tackle our responsibilities in a care-free spirit.'

But before we could do or say any more, a male voice at my shoulder said: 'Excuse me, you are Miss Kate Sandison's niece, aren't you?'

I spun round. 'Yes. Yes, I'm Janet Alexander . . . Mr Macleod?'

'Sure!' He shook hands heartily, very pleased with himself. 'I was just going to the desk to enquire and I spotted you. Gee, Mr Alexander, these Sandisons sure run true to form! Might have been Kate standing there!'

Twice looked at me consideringly. 'Janet and Kate are not much alike when you see them together,' he said.

'No, it's not noticeable when we're together,' I said. 'It's a family sort of thing – not a real resemblance between two people.'

In the bar over a drink, before we went up to the rooms where the children were, Malcolm Macleod harked back to this when he said: 'Talking of family resemblances, Janet, how well do you remember James Smith? He was a bit older than you, wasn't he?'

'Not much, although, of course, when we were kids at school he seemed ages older. I remember him distinctly – a dark boy with a round head, very much like his father, old Jamie Bedamned, but without the beard.'

'Well, you're in for a shock up above here,' he said and jerked his head at the ceiling. 'The oldest kid up there, young James, is the very spit of his father and the old man.'

'Oh?' I glanced at Twice.

'And just about as darn surly as well,' Malcolm added.

'The boy has had a terrible shock,' Twice began. 'After all, he's only eight and—'

'This ain't shock,' said Malcolm firmly, 'and he ain't any little baby of eight.' He looked back to me. 'That kid is a Bedamned, Janet, and that kid is gonna be trouble.'

'Oh, lord,' I said, 'what about the other three?'

'A bunch o' honeys – absolute honeys. Very Swedish-

205

looking. They must take after the mother. The twins – they're six – are about the cutest things. And David, he's only four, but smart as a button. But James—' He rolled his eyes at the ceiling.

'But what – what does he *do*?' Twice asked.

'He don't *do* much. In fact, he don't do anything hardly, come to that. He just stands around lookin' and you feel a sorta darkness—'

'That's real Bedamnedness,' I said, finished my drink and rose to my feet. 'Well, will you take us up, Malcolm?'

'Darn it!' he said as he stood up. 'I can't get over it!' He turned to Twice again. 'Say what you like, she might be Kate!'

The elevator took us up to the seventeenth floor, and as we walked along the passage to the rooms Malcolm had taken, he said: 'I'm stoppin' up-town here tonight to see you off in the morning. My apartment's over in Brooklyn . . . Here we are.' The suite of rooms opened off one another, with a bathroom between each, and were all exactly alike, except that the curtains and upholstery were of a different colour in each one, which, in some odd way, made their similarity all the more marked. When we walked through to the third room, there were three children sitting on the floor in the 'cave' under a built-in writing desk, and a large, comfortable, coffee-coloured negress sitting in an armchair reading a comic paper. She rose, smiling, and smoothing her light dress over her ample stomach as we came into the room.

'This is Lula,' Malcolm said, 'and I bet she's glad to see you. Lula don't like New York – huh, Lula?'

'No, sir,' said Lula, but without losing her broad smile.

I shook hands with Lula and then bent down a little to peer into the cave from which three blonde gnomes in blue jeans and white shirts peered out at me, their blue eyes round like coins, their neat mouths, with neater teeth, smiling tentatively.

'Well, *you*'re a cute bunch!' I said to them.

'Yes, *ma'am*!' said Lula. 'These is proper smart kids,

206

ma'am.' She waddled a little nearer to the cave. 'Come on now you, Candy an' Floss, where are yore manners? Come out here and tell Auntie Howdo!'

Obediently, the twins crawled out and stood up at full height, each still clutching a handful of that repulsive grey substance to which children always reduce a quantity of gaily coloured slabs of Plasticine and, behind them, with a red cardboard box clasped to his bosom, came their younger brother.

'And this is David,' Lula said. 'He's a big boy now and going in the ship to Scotland, ain't that so?'

'Ship,' said David solemnly and then smiled benignly upon us all like a genial, round-faced, contented little Puck whose life had held nothing but cream and fun.

They were beautiful children physically and were, I thought, extremely high in personality appeal. The twins, Candy and Floss, shook hands dutifully with Twice and myself, then looked at one another in silent communion for a moment and then, as if a conclave had been held between them, Floss, the little girl, stepped forward to Twice, smiled up at him with conscious feminine allure, held up her lump of grey Plasticine and said: 'Make a plane, huh? Candy and me's been trying but it don't come right.'

Twice capitulated at once, as she had undoubtedly known that he would, sat down cross-legged on the floor and all three gathered round, contributing their shares of the grey Plasticine. Lula laughed her fat, comfortable, liquidly-negro laugh and stood looking down at them.

'And where is James?' I asked then.

She jerked her head at the door. 'In his room. Readin', most like. James is a quiet boy, ma'am, and likes to be by hisself . . . You would like I show you their things?'

'Yes, Lula. Thank you.'

I followed her back through to one of the bedrooms and sat on the bed while she explained in great detail how Candy's clothes were in this bag and this was Floss's favourite doll and that David liked the pyjamas with the rabbits on them best.

207

'Lula,' I said, 'it is going to be very hard for you to part with these children. I'm sorry . . . Tell me, do they know about their father and mother?'

Her big eyes became bright with tears and she sat down opposite to me on the other bed. 'James knows. But, ma'am, you ain't got to worry none about Mr and Miz Smith. They was away nearly all the time. Them kids don't hardly know about Mr and Miz Smith, but they goin' to be askin' you about Sam – that's my husban', ma'am – and maybe they'll be askin' about *me* sometimes.' And with this, the tears overflowed and she began to cry, but after a moment she went to the bathroom and came back, mopping her broad, kind face with a towel. 'When they ask, ma'am, you tell them that Sam an' me is busy 'bout the house like always. Then, by'n by, they'll forget an' not ask any more.'

I began to feel that in a moment I would be in tears myself, so I rose and began to go over the luggage, saying: 'And this is Candy's and this case is Floss's . . . By the way, Lula, what are their real names?'

'Charles an' Flora, ma'am. It was Sam – *he* called them Candy an' Floss.'

'It's nice,' I said. 'Their hair *looks* like candyfloss.'

She smiled and then: 'James is different. James has black hair, like his father. Them three is like Miz Smith . . . You would like to see James, ma'am?'

'Yes, please.'

We now walked back through the room where the Plasticine aeroplanes were under construction and we passed quite unnoticed by the engineers who had now been joined by Malcolm and on through a bathroom into the next room. Lula pushed the door open with a: 'You there, James?' and stood aside for me to enter. As I walked in I was conscious of a furtive movement on the further side of the second bed which flashed into my mind a picture of old Jamie Bedamned scrabbling among the bushes, and I saw standing there, in blue jeans and a white shirt, a miniature of the old man in that mental picture. There were the

208

round, aggressive, cannon-ball head with its dense thatch of rough, straight, black hair, the lowering brows over the dark sullen eyes, and the tightly closed mouth with the surly downward pucker at the corners.

'Here's your Auntie Janet, James,' Lula said. 'And you're all ready to go on the ship tomorrow.'

'How d'you do, James?' I said, holding out my hand.

He fixed his black eyes on mine and put both his hands behind him. I stared back at him, my hand held out. After what seemed like moments, an ugly gleam lit the black eyes for a split second, the mouth tightened even more and then, unwillingly, he came forward and shook my hand. He did not speak.

'Are you looking forward to the ship, James?' I asked.

'That ship can't sail too soon for *me*!' he said and, having cast a disparaging glance round the room, he brushed past Lula and myself and went out.

'Poor boy,' I said to Lula. 'This must have been a horrible shock to him.'

She looked at me for a moment and then turned away. 'James is all right, ma'am. He's just quiet, like his father. He won't give you no trouble . . . Now, these two cases is his, ma'am . . . Not that bag – that's Mr Macleod's – he's sleepin' in here. James won't be no trouble. He dresses and 'tends to hisself. He's got plenty sense. He won't be no trouble.'

I did not argue with Lula, but I felt that I would rather cope with a dozen sets of Candy-Flosses and two dozen Davids than have to be in the presence of one Jamie Bedamned for one moment, and when we went out to the other room again I could see that Twice and Malcolm felt much as I did.

A squadron of Plasticine aeroplanes was now lying on the carpet: the red cardboard box had been turned into a hangar and a newspaper was being torn into strips to form runways.

'Okay,' said Twice, laying down the third runway. 'What now?'

209

'One, two, three – eight aeroplanes,' said Candy.

'How much is that among three?' asked Floss.

'Four,' Twice corrected her. 'Come on, James, want an airline?'

James did not move from the corner where he was standing but a dark wave of scorn and dislike crossed his face.

'Kid stuff!' he said and then he tramped across the airfield, tearing a paper runway as he went, and away into the room where the younger children's luggage lay. Twice and I exchanged a glance as Twice replaced the torn runway with a new one, but the younger children, used to their brother and accepting without question something they had always known, as their aunt and uncles had accepted Georgie long ago, shared out the aeroplanes, three each to Candy and Floss and two to David, and in a moment the room was full of the noise of a busy air terminal.

After an hour or so, Malcolm telephoned and had the children's supper brought in, and James, when called by Lula, appeared silently and sat down at the table with the others, while Twice, Malcolm and I had a drink and Lula had a large, pink ice-cream soda. James was at the table, but not of it, and the three younger children seemed to have developed naturally an attitude to this. They talked among themselves, yet giving a strange impression of being willing to include James should he wish it so, but James did not respond. He remained blackly and coldly aloof, as if his brothers and sister were strangers in whose company he found himself, eating healthily and stolidly and reminding me more and more of the black-avised old Jamie Bedamned who used to come home for his dinner long ago and sit, surly and silent, while Flora placed the food in front of him, then rise, still without speech, leave the house and trudge back to his work. James now, having had his meal, rose in the same way without a word and went away back, with his curiously heavy gait, to his own room.

210

Lula and I now began to put the three younger ones to bed. They did not realise at all the tragedy that had overtaken them, and the fact that their father and mother had been business partners who had, apparently, been more interested in amassing a large fortune than in the personal upbringing of their children was now a blessing. Lula had been a wonderful nurse to them and had discharged her duty with remarkable selflessness, making no demands on their affections, so that they were all independent little people, secure in a background of well-being, who regarded this journey on the big ship as a great, unexpected adventure. They were a little wistful when they remembered that Sam had already been left behind and when they tried to imagine leaving Lula behind on the next day, but their minds were too young and elastic to contain these thoughts for long.

While they splashed in the bath, all three at once, Floss looked up at me and said: 'Sing, Auntie Janet! We always sing at bath time.'

'I'm not a very good singer,' I said.

'Lula'll teach you!' said Candy.

'Lawd! Auntie Janet don't need me to teach her to sing! Auntie Janet got plenty songs for sure!'

'Sing, Auntie Janet!' David commanded.

No understudy, forced to go on stage on a first night, had ever a worse attack of stage-fright than I had now. My palms became wet; my mind became blank and the world contained nothing but three pairs of expectant blue eyes and suddenly I heard my own voice, a little shaky, begin:

'Early one morning, just as the sun was rising,
I heard a maiden sing in the valley below—'

No song could have been less suitable, but the children, in the unexpected way of children, decided straight away that they liked it, and after I had sung the verse through once they were all joining in while Lula, sitting on the seat of the lavatory, rocked to and fro to the rhythm and added the melodious overtones of her negro voice to the chorus.

211

Then, when the baths were over and Lula was drying them for the last time, I went round the bedroom that the twins and David were occupying and tried to 'learn' their possessions, for I felt that, from tomorrow on, this precious security of theirs would be vested in me and that I was a poor substitute for Lula, who knew all the favourite pyjamas and how David's Mickey Mouse just could *not* sleep unless his feet were on the pillow and his head under the sheet. I was standing looking down at the feet of Mickey Mouse, who was already in his sleeping position, when my eye was caught by a scrap of printed paper that just showed below the valance of the bed. Automatically, I bent and picked it up. I think I had been looking at it between my hands for a moment before the purport of the small printed words upon it penetrated to my mind: 'The Lord is my shepherd. I shall not want. He leadeth me—' I suddenly became aware that I was holding a scrap torn from a page of a Bible and, bending down, I raised the valance of the bed. Underneath was a heap of similar scraps and, among them, some torn pieces of black board on one of which was printed in gilt: 'Holy Bible. Presented by the Gideons.'

I dropped the valance, went past the bathroom that contained Lula and the smaller children into the other room, but only Twice and Malcolm were there.

'Where's James?' I asked.

'In the bath,' said Malcolm and nodded towards the other bathroom. 'Said he was goin' to bed.'

'Oh.'

'Listen, Flash,' Twice said, 'there's no good you working yourself up about that kid. He's perfectly all right and quite happy in his own way.'

'I'm not working myself up, Twice,' I said, 'and maybe I've as much experience as anybody here of what you call his way.'

I went on past the bathroom that contained James and on into the room he was sharing with Malcolm. I had remembered the furtive movement when Lula and I first

212

went in there. And, sure enough, under the further bed was another heap of ruins of another Gideon Bible. I went quietly out to the two men.

'Come and see this,' I said, and, staring at me, they followed me in silence.

I lifted up the valance and pointed. 'James Bedamned,' I said.

'Well, for cryin' out loud!' said Malcolm after a moment. 'Why in hell did he have to do this?'

'There's another in the twins' room,' I said. 'He was in there before supper.'

Twice went back to the room we had been using as a sitting-room and where he and I were to sleep and began opening the drawers, but here it was Malcolm who found the remains of the Bible in the bottom of a cupboard.

Twice frowned and then looked at me. 'But *why*?' he asked.

I shook my head. 'How do *I* know?'

'I mean—' Twice hesitated. 'Has the fact that they are *Bibles* got any significance, do you think?'

'No,' I said. 'At least, I don't think so. I don't think he was specifically destroying Bibles. I think he felt like tearing something up, but he's too much of a Bedamned to destroy something of his own, so he destroys what belongs to the hotel, the only thing of theirs that he *could* destroy.'

'That's about it,' Malcolm agreed. 'Like the way he smashed the radio over to my apartment.'

'What do we do?' Twice asked. 'For me, I'd like to tan the pants off him.'

'NO! We don't do a thing!' said Malcolm hastily. 'Let's just take it and say nothing for the sake of old Lula, huh?'

'All right,' I said, 'but, by golly, if there's any of this on that ship I *will*, personally, tan the pants off him!'

'And I'll give you a hand,' Twice said. 'He's the dourest little b— I've ever seen!'

'And you can say that again,' Malcolm said. 'Let's go down and have a drink an' somethin' to eat an' I'll tell them to charge me with three Bibles.'

213

In the course of dinner the incident of the Bibles dropped out of mind, for the talk was all of Ross-shire, Reachfar and Varlich, the home country which Malcolm had left twenty years before and to which he had never returned.

'You've never thought of taking a trip home?' Twice asked him at one point.

'I thought of it three years back, after my wife died,' he replied, 'and then I just thought what the hell. I've got nobody back there now except a few cousins and I never hear from them. We never knew each other much, anyways. And you know how it is when you slip out of touch – every day makes the gap wider by a year and more.'

'That's true – a sort of compound interest system gets working,' I said.

He nodded. 'It's a funny thing. This business of Jamie Smith's death and the kids and meeting you two like this has brought everything back, sort of.' He glanced at me and smiled. 'I think maybe it's you being so much like your aunt – that, and hearing from your brother and so on.'

'My aunt hasn't written to you?' I asked.

'No. Your brother and I have been arranging everything.'

'My brother does most of the family writing these days,' I said, 'especially about anything important.'

'He's up there at Reachfar, then?'

'Oh no. He's down south, but he happened to be up home on holiday when this thing of Jamie and his wife happened . . . My aunt is the moving spirit behind getting in touch with you though, although Jock's doing the writing. Flora Smith's been a protégée of Kate's for years, ever since one of her brothers got killed falling off the roof of the barn at Poyntdale. Kate went down to help Flora organize the funeral and had a row with old Jamie afterwards and from then on she had the fear of death in him – probably still has, except that he's dotty and pretty well bedridden now.'

Malcolm laughed. 'I bet if Kate got mad at him it *was* the fear of death! Have they any children?' he asked after a moment.

214

'Who?' I said. 'Oh, Kate? No. No, she has no children. Hugh, her husband, was killed in the war, in North Africa.'

'Oh? Oh, I didn't know that.' He stirred his spoon round in the nearly empty coffee cup. 'I'm very sorry. I heard about her marriage, but – but I hadn't heard about her husband being killed. I haven't had a letter from home for years. I'm sorry,' he repeated.

'I think it's pretty much of an old song with Kate now,' I said. 'There is nothing of the tragic widow about her, is there, Twice?'

'No, there's nothing of the weeping willow about Kate,' Twice said and smiled at Malcolm. 'In fact, she's an extremely spirited dame of redoubtable force of character who doesn't look a day older than Janet here.'

'She always had plenty of spirit,' Malcolm said.

'If you asked old Jamie Bedamned, he'd say she had far too much,' I said.

Shortly after dinner we all went up to our rooms although it was still early. Malcolm had sent Lula out by taxi to one of the big Broadway cinemas by way of giving her a typical American souvenir of her visit to New York; and although I was tired after the long day that had begun in St Jago that morning, I knew that I would not sleep and that neither would Twice.

'You wouldn't care to run out and have a look at New York at night?' Malcolm asked.

'No, thank you, Malcolm.'

'I could baby-sit,' Twice offered.

'No, really, thanks. You know quite well that I'm no sight-seer, Twice.' I turned to Malcolm. 'I'm the sort that can only take in a little at a time, Malcolm. This hotel and the people in it and the lights beyond the window there are all I can absorb of New York tonight. To drive me along the Great White Way would be a waste of time.'

'Then we'll absorb a little more Scotch and talk a little more about Ross-shire,' he said. 'You'll have to come back to New York another time. Have you any friends in the States?'

215

'Only one, really – my friend Martha – and Twice and I are not so sure about *her* any more. We've just had a bit of a bellyful looking after an aunt of hers who came down to St Jago for a holiday – an awful woman. Oh, I know it's not Martha's fault that she has an awful aunt, but the aura of her – the aunt, I mean – is bad enough to make me not even want to ring up Martha although I believe she's right here in New York this minute.'

'Very unfair to Martha,' Twice agreed, 'but that's how it is.'

'There ain't all that much of what we call fairness in how things go,' Malcolm said thoughtfully. 'D'you ever see the *New Yorker*?'

'The magazine? Not often. Why?' Twice asked.

'There's a guy draws funny pictures in that – one of his favourite captions is "What am I doing here?" an' there'll be a picture of an innocent-lookin' little guy standing scratching his head in the middle of a cactus desert. That artist's got somethin'. Quite often lately I've been sayin' to myself "What am I doin' here?" and I'm darned if I know the answer.'

I became aware that Malcolm had reached that stage in the evening when the whisky he had drunk was making him talk in a fashion less inhibited than was his wont. Also, I thought, he was probably lonely and Twice and I had for him the double attraction of being familiars from his own country and yet having the ephemeral quality of ships that he was passing in the night.

'I never know how I get to anywhere I get,' I told him now. 'One of the things I often wonder about is how I ever came to meet and marry Twice here, and the more I think of it the more certain I become that if I had never met a perfectly bloody woman called Muriel I'd never have met Twice, and it all gives me the creeps.'

'Oh, damn it!' Twice said. 'There's no need to leave Malcolm with the idea that our marriage is a regrettable accident!'

'I don't mean that, you idiot! . . . Malcolm, what I

216

mean is that it's frightening to think that so much that's so important to one should seem to turn on the sort of creaky, rusty hinge that this woman Muriel was. There's nothing regrettable about Twice's and my marriage—'

'I can see that,' Malcolm broke in. 'I'm pretty good at estimating marriage atmospheres. I've got experience. I learned it the hard way. I made a mistake when I married.'

'Oh. I'm sorry, Malcolm.'

'It's water down the river now. Minnie died in hospital – a hospital for alcoholics. Not her fault. My fault as much as hers. And yet, whose fault? Looking back, I can't see how it happened. Just one thing leading to another – all creaking, rusty hinges, like you said. You go around doing the best you can but you don't know what the outcome will be, like us three now with those kids through there. Here they are, somebody's got to do somethin' so we get together and get them back to Scotland to Flora. And then what? We don't know.'

'We don't,' Twice agreed with him, 'except that it's bound to lead to something. If the three of us and the people at home had sat back and done nothing about these children, I suppose they'd have got taken care of somehow. But it isn't human or natural to sit back and do nothing – it's instinctive to try to help. Seems to me we've got to put our faith in that . . . I must say, though, that I *do* wonder what sort of future that black-browed little so-and-so through there is going to have.'

And, with this, the talk turned back to the children, but I was thinking of something else and at the end of a few minutes I had come to one of my snap decisions. These decisions of mine often lead to results that I do not anticipate, but I am like a man who cannot resist treading on banana skins and I never learn better. I rose and said: 'I'd like to send a cable.'

'Who to?' Twice asked.

'Home to Reachfar.'

'Write it out and I'll take it down to the desk,' Malcolm said. 'It's surer than phoning them at this time in the evening.'

217

'I'll go down myself,' I said.

'I'll do it,' said Twice.

'No. I need a walk. You and Malcolm have another noggin. I won't be long.'

I went down in the lift to the big foyer, found the cable office, took the form and wrote on it in large letters: 'KATE DAVIDSON ACHCRAGGAN SCOTLAND GOOD IDEA YOU WRITE FRIENDLY LETTER MALCOLM STOP INTER-FERESOMENESS WELLMEANT LOVE JANET.'

The clerk, when I handed him the form, stopped chewing his gum for a moment, turned the form towards me, pointed with his pencil at the address and said: 'That the complete address?'

'Yes. There's only one of each of them in Scotland.'

'One of each?'

'That's right. One Kate Davidson and one Achcraggan.'

He stared at me for a moment, brought his gum into action, tucked it away again and pointed the pencil at 'interferesomeness'.

'That a word?' he enquired.

'Yes,' I said firmly.

'What's it mean?'

'What you are doing now.'

'How's that?'

'Wellmeant interferesomeness is asking people in a polite way if they are sure they know what they are doing.'

He looked at me in silence for a moment and then his jaws began to work on the gum again.

'Whatever you say, lady,' he said then, calculated the charge for the message and I paid him and went back to the lift. I was aware that he was studying me from behind with care, probably trying to work out whether I was mad or merely drunk, but I felt that I was neither.

But I think that, the next day, I must have indeed been drunk or in some coma, for I can remember no details except flashes of the customs sheds and the quayside until

218

the evening, when the ship was down the Hudson, the children were all in bed and asleep and Twice and I were having luxurious drinks followed by a light supper in the privacy of our own stateroom.

'I feel like a film star,' Twice said.

'I'm extremely conscious of not *looking* like one,' I told him. 'My goodness, what a couple of days!'

'Pretty bad, but they're over. And this voyage is going to be fun, Flash . . . I wonder how much all this is costing?'

'Oh, Malcolm will be getting trade prices,' I said. 'I'll have another martini. Why does gin taste better at sea than it does ashore and whisky not so good?'

'Don't let's question things. Let's just accept them . . . Poor old Lula, it was tough on her at the end.'

'I know. She behaved terribly well, though – there was a sort of nobility when she waddled away for the last time that I'll always remember.'

'I wonder if the kids will remember?'

'It's difficult to say,' I said. 'I should think Jamie would and even the twins – I can remember things that happened when I was six and things before that, even.'

'Your memory *is* a little unusual though, Flash. I think your mind has a bias towards memory, if that makes sense. I mean, I think that when you were a child you were much more aware of what went on *out*side of you than what went on *in*side. Now, black Jamie here, I question if he'll have a good memory for events. It seems to me that he's too busy with some sort of machinations going on behind those eyes of his for the eyes to take in very much of what's going on around him. Flash, I *can't* get over that thing of his tearing up all the Bibles! It was such a – such a *bedamned* thing to do!'

'That's just the very word,' I said. 'It's a terribly queer thing, but his grandfather had that same – I was going to say "gift" but it's a curse, rather – that same curse for doing the one thing that would damn him in the eyes of the people around him. Like the time old Jamie came to

219

Reachfar and accused me out of thin air of stealing his money. Dad and George and my grandfather, at that time, had a lot of influence and controlled between them a lot of the work that was going in the district and they had been kind to old Jamie in lots of ways, but after the money incident they'd never have any dealings with him if they could avoid it. And it was like that with everybody. His hand just seemed naturally to be against the hands of all men. I think everybody either hated him or was afraid of him – except Flora, of course. Flora neither hated him nor feared him. I don't think she loved him either. Or maybe she did – does. But it is more that she accepts him – and I suppose she is still accepting him and he'll be taking a bit of accepting now. He must be as dotty as all get-out by now and seems to be bedridden as well, which will be pretty ghastly, for he was always pretty unshaven and dirty and scruffy, anyway.'

'What sort of a woman *is* this Flora?'

'I wish you wouldn't keep on and on asking that! I've no words for Flora. She's vaguely what I think of when I think of some of the female saints, a thing I don't do very often. I haven't much in common with saints and martyrs although my conscience tells me I ought to admire them . . . She's small and thin and faded and wishy-washy and generally inefficient at anything she does and you'd think a puff of wind would blow her away, but she's stood up to more hardship physical and mental than any other woman I know. How she's going to cope with these four kids as well as that dotty old man I don't know. In common reason it's an impossibility, but yet I know that Flora will do it – better than you and I together could. She's a sort of miracle – saints *are* miracles, anyway. You don't believe me. I don't blame you. Wait till you see her. Not that you'll be impressed then either, you still won't believe what I've told you about her. But the fact remains that she *has* come through the most appalling life and she'll go on coming through and bring those kids through with her!'

'Here's to Flora!' said Twice, raising his glass when I stopped for breath.

'Yes, indeed. Here's to Flora!' I agreed. I looked round the luxurious stateroom. 'Yes, in very deed, here's to Flora! I would have said she was the last person in the world to make a dream of mine come true, but she's managed to do that too.'

'Oh! What was the dream?'

'When I was a youngster living on Clydeside with Aunt Alice and Uncle Jim and travelling up and down to Glasgow by bus every day to the university, this ship was being built in John Brown's yard at Clydebank. She was known then as Number 534 – the Five-Three-Fower, the shipyard workers called her. Then the trade depression came and work on her was stopped. In the bus in the evening, when the sun was going down in the west and I was travelling westwards, her great big steel ribs used to stick up, black against the sunset, like the skeleton of hope that had died. Clydeside was terribly sad at that time. I used to sit in the sad bus looking at that huge skeleton and saying to myself: "Work will start on her again! It must! *One* day they'll finish her! She'll be launched, she'll sail the seas!" It was a sort of prayer, really. I felt that if I kept on saying it, it must come true. And sometimes I'd say: 'And maybe one day, when I get a job and get on and get rich – maybe one day *I'll* sail in the Five-Three-Fower!' That was a prayer too, in a way . . . Well, here I am, sailing in the Five-Three-Fower, but it's not through any effort of my own. One's prayers get answered in roundabout ways, it seems. And unexpected instruments get chosen to achieve unlikely ends. Who would have connected Flora Bedamned with the Five-Three-Fower?'

Twice spoke with his back towards me. '*You* are the link between Number Five-Three-Four and Flora Bedamned, Flash. You know, I often think you have been endowed with a most happy gift. You were born under a lucky star.'

'What d'you mean?'

He turned round. 'You never forget the prayers you

221

have made and you never fail to recognize the answers when they come, and you feel grateful for the answers no matter how long they have been delayed in transit. I think a lot of us pray and then forget, if there's no immediate response, but you remember and even if it's twenty years before the answer comes you give your thanks by recognizing the instrument – Flora, in this case.'

'Maybe I remember because I don't pray very often,' I said, 'and yet I do, but not in a very orthodox way. No matter what looks like going wrong – even if it's only a cake I'm making, I find my mind saying: "Please, God, don't let it!" . . . And there's nothing flippant or careless about it. I've done it since I was a child. I suppose that's the effect of many an hour spent listening to the Reverend Roderick Mackenzie. There were two great powers in my life as a child – God and my grandmother. Between them, they could cope with everything. That was before my mother died. After that, there was only God, because my grandmother told me God had taken my mother and I knew that my grandmother would have stopped Him taking her if it had been possible . . . Twice, does it seem wrong – or sacrilegious or anything – to you to regard sailing in this ship when one never expected to as an answer to prayer, as a sort of affirmation of divine power? I mean, ought one to hope for an answer to a prayer about a thing like sailing in a ship?'

'I think one has the right to hope for an answer to any sincere prayer,' Twice said.

'To travel in a certain ship is not a proper thing to pray for, though. I wouldn't – I *couldn't* – pray for a thing like that now.'

'No, perhaps not. But at twenty, you could and did, and I have a feeling that in the circumstances, then, it must have been what you call a proper thing to pray for. The sailing in the ship was your sort of symbol of hope in the future or something of that sort, probably. I *am* convinced that if it hadn't been a *proper* thing to pray for, you wouldn't be sitting in this ship right now. My faith is a very

222

muddled affair, as you know, but it is there. I think what we can only call the wrong or *im*-proper sort of prayers – like prayers for bloody vengeance on an enemy and so on – either get ignored or lost somewhere in the stratosphere or come back like a boomerang to smite the person who prayed them, but the proper sort of prayer, made in the right spirit, for *it* God always has a Flora sitting waiting to convey the answer to you when the time is ripe. The important thing *then* is to do what *you*'ve done and recognise Flora's part. I think God will accept that as your gratitude.'

'Then God bless Flora,' I said and I meant it.

'Yes, indeed, God bless Flora,' Twice repeated.

Twice and I, who have no children of our own, had been chary of admitting to one another, even, the weight of responsibility that we felt about tackling this voyage with the four little Smiths, but the journey as arranged by Malcolm for us led to the position where we could have easily felt like so much excess baggage attached to the children on their trip. Candy, Floss and David were so personally attractive and such social types that at the end of the first day at sea they were the hub around which the nursery games revolved and they politely but firmly gave us to understand that they were going to have lunch with their own new friends at a time earlier than the grown-up lunch-time. Jamie made no friends with anybody, but pursued his solitary way, having his meals sometimes with Twice and myself and attending, sometimes, the children's meals, but being equally aloof and uncommunicative at both. The only times in the day when Twice and I were in demand were in the morning, to find clothes or toys and tie hair ribbons and shoe laces, and again in the evening, to sing 'like Lula' at bedtime, and thank goodness that Twice has quite a good voice so that the pride of the Cunard fleet breasted the Atlantic to a fine rendering of 'Early one morning—' each evening.

The few days slipped by in a luxurious, leisurely, first-class ship routine of idle chat, drinks, lunch, a little reading perhaps, tea, drinks, dinner, all punctuated by visits to the nursery or the playdeck where our charges treated us in an off-hand manner and obviously wished that we would not interfere, even in so much as by looking in at them through the nursery windows.

'Everything's always easier than you think,' said Twice.

'I hope four days by car from Southampton to Smith's Corner will be easier than *I* think with no playdeck or other kids,' I said.

But even the long trek north by road from Southampton was not too difficult. Twice suggested that it might be happier to let the silent, black-browed Jamie sit in front with him while I sat behind with the three little ones, and this was how we travelled. We broke the back of the journey on the second day by reaching Carlisle before we stopped, and the children were so tired that the three little ones were asleep before we could undress them, but Jamie, although exhausted, was our silent and disapproving companion at dinner, when he made a meal of tinned beans and ice-cream. On the third day the little ones became a little restive, but we reached Perth in time to let them play in the garden for a little while with a friendly dog before bed and that compensated in their happy, resilient minds, it seemed, for the long, tedious day. On the fourth day, of course, I could dangle before them the bunch of carrots that was journey's end. Immediately after lunch, when we got into the car again, I said: 'A hundred more miles and we'll be at Smith's Corner,' and Candy, Floss and David took this up as a chant, so that every half-hour or so one of them would say: 'How far now, Uncle Twice?'

'Eighty, now.'

'*Eighty* more miles and we'll be at Smith's Corner!' the three shrill voices would pipe. '*Seventy* more miles and we'll be at Smith's Corner!' and the black-browed Jamie would turn in his seat, glower back at them and say: 'Can it, you kids!'

They took no notice of him and, with a curious, listless

224

frustration, he seemed to accept the fact that they did not, but he never failed to issue his scornful command as if it were some lip-service of loyalty that he had to pay to the contumacious spirit that was contained in him.

At long last the road turned eastwards at the foot of the Ben and met the shore of the Firth, and: '*Five* more miles and we'll be at Smith's Corner!' I chanted with them, and then there came the junction of the Poyntdale Road with the County Road on which we were travelling, and: 'Less than *two* miles and we'll be at Smith's Corner!' we were singing and then the milestone and: '*One* more mile and we'll be at Smith's Corner!' and very soon the little house came into sight round the bend of the road by the waterside.

In the golden light of the summer evening, with the ripening corn in the fields on the hill beyond it, it shone white and gay and glad with welcome and was no longer the grim little black humped defiance with the ruined chimney like a broken rampart. Its rooftree was straight under the repaired slates, the chimneys stood proudly firm at either end, the walls were strong and clean with their coat of white rough-cast, and the bright-red paint of the windows and door shone behind the seed-packet brilliance of the neatly fenced garden. As we approached and drew in to the house, Flora appeared at the gate and then, behind her, I saw on the path the members of my family – my father, George, Tom and Kate, dressed as they would be for only one reason. They had been to a funeral. I knew it before the car had stopped, and I sprang out and went to Kate.

'Old Jamie,' she said, even before I had asked the question. 'We have just got back from the funeral. I made Flora change out of her black dress because of the bairns.'

She at once turned away and the outburst of greetings began.

The three smaller children had poured out of the car behind me and, although my family had not seen Twice or myself for eighteen months, the eyes of my father, George and Tom were all for Candy, Floss and David, who, in that moment especially, I dearly wished were my own. The sun on their blonde hair, Floss between her brothers, they stood in a row, looking up at the strangers with their wide blue eyes, the small confiding smiles of good faith in life forming round their pretty mouths.

'Well, now,' said George, looking down at them, 'you are a right fine bunch o' Smiths!'

'I'm Floss,' said the eternal feminine, realising that her charm had already begun to work, 'and this is Candy and he's David.' She dealt George a glance of killing coquetry. 'I'm the only girl,' she announced.

'That's chust the very thing I was thinking,' said George, whereupon she sidled up to him and placed her small hand in his large one.

I was looking at Flora. She was wearing a pretty blue silk dress that hung loosely and unevenly from her thin shoulders, and on her tired feet were large, flat, red suède slippers, lined with sheepskin that turned down round her thin ankles, giving me a reminder of the clumsy big boots of long ago. The blue of the dress and the red of the slippers were the only colours about her. Everything else was faded. Her lips and skin were not pale – pale was not the word that came to mind, I mean – the wispy hair was not grey, the eyes were not dulled with age, but lips, skin, hair and eyes were all merely faded. Yet, behind this faded façade there was, as she looked down at the children, a strange vitality, so that she reminded me more than anything of a variety of winter jasmine which hangs about in lifeless cobwebby strands and yet, when the weather of winter is at its fiercest, can suddenly put forth a wealth of pale, starry flowers. I had the feeling that something of this secret life and power was hidden somewhere in this faded wisp that was Flora.

Quietly, she began to go round the three small children, talking to them in her thready voice, her work-worn hand resting on their fair heads for a moment, a look of serene happiness on her face, and then she came to me where I

226

stood between them and the car and said: 'And Janet! It's grand to see you. I have to thank you for bringing the bairns home to me.'

'It was nothing, Flora. They are splendid bairns . . . I am sorry about Jamie and your father—'

The faded eyes filled with tears. 'Aye, poor Jamie and his fine young wife! . . . And my father. It was a pity he didna stop to see the bairns. But he wouldna have known them – he was fair foolish altogether at the last. But I would have liked him to have seen them. Och, well, he's away and it's myself that will miss him. He was a good man, my father.' She drew a hand across her eyes and then said: 'But, wait, where's *little* Jamie?'

Somehow we all looked round at one another before all our eyes concentrated on the boy who was still sitting in the front of the car.

'James,' Twice said, 'come along and meet your Aunt Flora!'

He stepped down from the car, put his hands behind him and looked up from under his down-drawn black brows at Flora.

'You my aunt?'

'Yes, Jamie,' she said in her quiet voice.

'That our home?' He jerked his head at the house.

'Yes, Jamie,' she said again.

'Okay. What we waitin' for?'

He flung the garden gate open and with that curiously heavy, menacing stride of his walked up the path between the bright rows of flowers and disappeared behind the red door.

There was a moment of silence among us all, followed by a quick burst of talk as we all tried to cover the awkwardness we felt, and Twice and I hurriedly began to unload the children's baggage which George and Tom carried into the passage of the house.

'The heavy stuff will come on from the railway, Flora,' I told her.

'Come in and get a droppie tea,' she said.

227

'No, no, Flora.' It was my aunt who took charge. 'You've had a big day and you'll just be fine on your own with the bairns and none of us to bother you. And we have to get back up the hill. There's nobody looking after the place.'

'Oh, well, well,' said Flora in acquiescence. 'You'll come down again to see us, Janet?'

'Oh, surely, Flora. We'll be down tomorrow to see our bairns. They're a bunch of beauties.'

'Aren't they now!' The faded face glowed with pride. 'And the wee ones so fair in the hair – they'll have gone to the mother's side, I am thinking. But Jamie is a *Smith*!' Pride rang now in the colourless gentle voice.

'Yes, Flora,' I said. 'James is a Smith all right.'

'He went up the roadie there and into the house just as though it was my father that was in it!' she informed us all. 'My, it was good to see it!'

We were all at a loss to respond, but we were rescued by Jamie himself, who suddenly appeared in the red-painted doorway, his black brows beetling as he glared down the little flower-decked pathway at us.

'Hi,' he growled, 'what's about somethin' to eat? I'm *hungry*!'

'Oh, my!' said Flora, delighted. 'I must be off! Just listen to that!' and she went clopping up the pathway in her big loose slippers without even pausing to wish us good night, while Candy, Floss and David, three laughing little gnomes, scampered after her, eager for this latest adventure.

Without words, Twice, my family and I piled higgledy-piggledy into the car and drove home to Reachfar.

That evening, and on many subsequent evenings, a lot of local friends came up to Reachfar, and Twice and I were out a great deal during the days and very soon we had to leave Reachfar for our own house in south-west Scotland and from there we went down to the midlands and on to London. Four months' leave from a foreign country to the

228

homeland is not very long to do all the things that have been planned and to see all the people who have been mere signatures on letters for eighteen months, and we did not give much time or thought to the family at Smith's Corner after the first few days. That family was self-contained now and did not need Twice and me any more. And when these first few days at Reachfar were over, I had something nearer home to think about.

Mine is, I think, a silent family – silent in its depths, I mean. Life at Reachfar, as I said before, is a deep-flowing river with, as it were, a pebbly channel on one side where the waters of everyday life go by in a ripple of small, pleasant chatter, carrying with them a light straw of local news here and a little thorny twig of family argument there. But, alongside this shallow, pebbly channel, there is a deeper flow which slides along under a shelving bank, in secrecy from the eyes of everyday, and in these waters there are hidden whirlpools and hazards of emotion that seldom see the light. At the end of about the third day that Twice and I were at Reachfar I was aware of a whirlpool forming in this deep channel and the awareness was not mine alone. At the centre of the vortex was Kate, my aunt, and occasionally an angry little wave would rush across from her to me; there would be uneasy glances from the rest of the family and then the little wave would slide quietly and harmlessly past and on downstream and Kate's dark eyes would avoid mine for an hour or two.

On the last night before Twice and I left for the south, however, the little vortex seemed to me to reach a point of momentum, as a result of a few words spoken by Twice which, on the surface, were not in any way relevant to the real trouble.

George and Tom are the least egotistical people I know. They seem to live entirely outside themselves and can never have enough of hearing of the experiences of other people, so that, every evening after my father had gone down to his cottage in Achcraggan, they would hark away from the farming subjects which were the everyday talk of the household, to ask questions about St Jago, New York, our Atlantic voyage or the road journey from Southampton.

'Tell me now,' said Tom on this evening, 'when you came up in the aeroplane from St Chago to New York, was you coming in to this place that they will be calling Idlewild?'

'Yes,' Twice told him. 'We did, Tom.'

'And that is the name of it?'

'Yes.'

'And what is it like now?'

'Pretty much like any other airport, Tom, but pretty big and busy. Why?'

'It is my opeenion,' said Tom, 'that Idlewild is a very, very foolish name for an aeroplane place. Aeroplanes is neither idle nor wild neither, when you think on it.'

'I think perhaps the name was there before the aeroplanes, Tom,' I said, 'like this being Reachfar airfield if they made one here.'

'That is not the same thing at a-all,' said Tom categorically. 'Aeroplanes reaches far and Reachfar is a fine name for a place for them.'

'*You*,' said my aunt in an impatient voice, 'think that Reachfar is a fine name for *any*thing!'

And in her words I felt the swish of that little wave from deeper waters, and so did George, for his voice was far too colourless as he said: 'And when you landed you came to this hotel with a-all the storeys on it?'

'That's right.'

'Man, Tom, it's a peety you an' me canna go to New York. I'd like fine to put in a day going up and down in that lift contrivance through all them storeys.'

'Not me,' said Tom. 'If I was to go to New York, I would be wanting to see this wifie that's called the Statue o' Liberty. They tell me the size o' her is something terrible.'

My aunt rose and began to clear the supper table. 'The two of you needn't bother to make any plans,' she said curtly. 'You're no more likely to go to New York than I

230

am!' and swish came the little wave out of the darkness again.

I began to help her to carry the dishes through to the scullery while Twice, once more, tried to describe the hotel, its rooms and its food to George and Tom, and somehow he came to the story of Jamie Smith's destruction of the Gideon Bibles, for the little incident had made a deep impression on his mind.

'*Three* of them he tore up?' George asked.

'Yes. Into scraps no bigger than pennies.'

'The weecked little deevil!' said Tom. 'What a thing to be doing, tearing up the Bibles that this people put in the hotel for people for nothing.'

'What on earth did you do?' my aunt asked from the scullery door while I began to wash the dishes at the sink.

'Well, I'd have liked to beat the pants off him, Kate,' Twice said, 'but Malcolm didn't want a fuss so he told the hotel people he would pay for the Bibles.'

My aunt shut the door between scullery and kitchen and in that moment I became aware of the uncanny silence that lies at the heart of a Reachfar vortex. I took my hands out of the sink, shook the water from them and turned to face her. Her dark eyes were flashing fire, her defiant chin was up and thunder rode upon her broad brow.

'Malcolm didn't want a fuss!' she threw at me in a low, vicious voice. 'Why did you send me that cable?'

'It seemed like a good idea at the time, Kate.'

'A good idea! I – I could *kick* you!'

'Did you write to him, Kate?'

All the rage went out of her and she sank down on the scullery chair. The only window in Reachfar that looks to the north is that little one in the scullery and the chair was beside it. She looked out of the window, away to the far hills beyond the Firth. In summer, in Ross, the sun sets as much to the north as to the west and the evening glow caught her pale skin and kindled fires in the depths of her big eyes.

'Yes, I wrote,' she said, 'by airmail. I haven't had an answer.'

231

'Kate, he hasn't had very long and—'

'Long enough!' She sprang to her feet, the momentary mood of bowing to life completely gone. 'Malcolm didn't want a fuss! Malcolm never wanted a fuss – Malcolm always wanted everything his way – the easy way – everything to drop into his lap! If it didn't drop, the next best thing would do! Any old thing, as long as there was no fuss!'

'Kate, I haven't talked about this. You didn't ask me and I didn't want to interfere—'

'You've interfered enough!'

'Kate, wait a minute. Maybe Malcolm *did* want everything his own way but it didn't turn out to be the easy way. His wife was a drunkard for years. She died in a home. He didn't get it very easy, Kate.'

'Is that my fault? Is *that* why you sent me that cable?' She seized a towel and began to dry the dishes with trembling ferocity. 'I wrote that letter. I feel like – like this dishclout! I feel like an old rag lying on the ground for people to tramp over! I feel like – like Flora Bedamned!'

'Kate!'

'Oh, hold your tongue!'

'Well, I can only say I'm sorry.'

'Sorry! . . . Oh, there's no good in my going at *you*!' she said then. '*I'm* the fool! I should know better at my age than to make a doormat of myself like Flora Bedamned!'

She threw down the dish-towel, went out and I heard her feet go up the stairs to her bedroom.

The incident put a blight on the start of my holiday, but I soon forgot it – after taking perhaps the hundredth decision in my life not to give way to these impulses of mine, one of which had led to the sending of the cable – in the excitements into which we were plunged when we left Reachfar for the south and London, but in November, when we came back home before sailing again for St Jago, the blight returned and settled over my conscience as soon as I saw my aunt. This was not her fault. The storm

232

of emotion that had held her in those days in August had slipped into the past, it seemed, and she had regained her old serenity, with all the fires damped down behind her dark eyes, and she went about the work of the house with all the old vigour and efficiency; joined in the gossip of the countryside with all the old interest and was as warlike as ever in her attitude to the family at Smith's Corner when I asked about them.

'Ach, Flora's down yonder clarting away among the four bairns, and their clothes in tatters and their hair needing cutting and them all as happy as pigs among dirt. The place is in a muddle as if you'd stirred it with a stick – the same old muddle as in the old days.'

'Flora was always a muddler,' I said. 'Of course, when you think of it, she never had a chance to learn to do anything in the house – she was just plunged into having to do it.'

'Och, but anybody with any sense could plan the thing a little better! But it's my belief she's happier in a muddle like that, just the same as she's never happier than when she's down-trodden. I just *canna* understand her. The three littlest bairnies would go to the heart of any woman, you would think, but it's not that way with Flora. That black-headed little devil Jamie rules the roost down there, never speaks a civil word to her and yet he's the apple of her very eye!'

'Oh well, Flora's a bit old to change her ways now, Kate.'

But my aunt had not yet learned to accept things or people who did not suit her. She never has learned. She still tries to put the world to rights.

'She's a foolish, feckless little craitur, that's all she is!' she said. 'Say what you like, if we were all like Flora, things wouldn't get very far.'

'I suppose she gets *some*where in her own way, Kate.'

'Where? I'm damned if I can see it . . . Here, take an end of this sheet and give it a good pull – it's as twisted as a dog's hind leg with that wind I got on washing-day.'

233

I did as I was told and as, between us, we pulled the sheet into shape, I changed the subject and said: 'Are you going to this meeting in Achcraggan tonight that Dad and Tom and George are going to?'

'Me? Are you off your head!'

'I don't think so. What is the meeting about anyway?'

'It's the Young Farmers' Club.'

'The *Young* Farmers?'

'That's right. But there's no show without Punch – George and Tom are members and your father goes because it gets him out of the cottage for the evening, I think.'

'Well I'm darned! No wonder Twice is so keen to go, if Tom and George are the life and soul of it.'

'You should go yourself,' she said. 'Girls and young women are in it too. Och, I've gone once or twice myself when Sir Torquil was starting it, just to encourage the younger ones, but it's well on its feet now and they always have a good turn-out. You should go down tonight with the rest.'

'Probably I will,' I said.

I did go, and it was a lively meeting, with discussions about all sorts of things, followed by an interval for cups of tea about eight o'clock, after which a documentary film on farming in Canada was to be shown. It was a cold, clear, frosty evening, although it was warm and cheerful in the little village hall, and as George laid aside his teacup, he said: 'Tom, I don't think I am likely to be emigrating to Canada to start farming over there.'

'No, nor me neither, George, man, forbye and besides,' Tom agreed. 'If we should emigrate at a-all, it is to New York that we'll go.'

'That's right, Tom.'

'And so you would rather go to the Plough for a drink than see this film?' Twice asked, catching on.

'Now that is a very good idea of yours, Twice, lad,' Tom said.

'Tom and me is better at the meetings and the speaking nowadays than at the farming itself,' said George.

234

'But I'll offer a standing prize of a fiver to any member of the Club that can beat them at hoeing turnips!' said young Sir Torquil.

While the young farmers rearranged their chairs to view the film, my father, George, Tom, Twice and I left the hall and walked the few yards down the street to the Plough Inn on the shore, and when the landlord had served us he drew aside the curtain and said: 'I hope there isn't a draught from this window. It got broken today.'

The two lower panes of the window were filled with cardboard.

'I'll get it fixed tomorrow.'

'What happened to it?' I asked.

The landlord was a young Englishman, an ex-officer of the Air Force, who, with his wife, had taken the lease of the inn at the end of 1945 when old Jockie Plough died.

'Oh, some boys throwing stones at one another,' he said. 'Their aim wasn't so hot.'

'It was that wee boogger Jamie Bedamned that's home from America,' said old Bill-the-Post who was nursing his evening dram by the parlour fire. 'Myself saw him doing it. And the other boys wasn't there at the time at a-all. He was chust throwing stones for pure badness, that's what he was.'

'But the other boys *were* calling names after him,' said the landlord's pretty young wife from behind the bar. 'I heard them, when I was coming home from the shops.'

'They was only shouting Jamie Bedamned at him, Mistress,' said Bill-the-Post, as if this were the most reasonable thing in the world. 'His father and his grandfather and his great-grandfather afore that a-all went by the byename of Bedamned and the name is bound to follow him, looking like a Bedamned, the way he is. And he's a weecked little boogger, Mistress, begging your pardon, and don't you be going wasting your sympathy on him. There never was a Bedamned yet that needed sympathy.'

'What about Flora?' I asked.

'Och, aye, Flora, the poor craitur. But ye couldna call

235

Flora a proper Bedamned – not as ye might say a *Bedamned*, like.'

The landlord and his wife looked a little mystified at this and Twice said: 'Evidently there are Bedamneds and *proper* Bedamneds!'

'Evidently,' they agreed and laughed.

'What's the difference?' Twice asked old Bill, but he was at a loss for the words to explain what he meant.

'Well,' Tom said after a moment, 'the way I see it is as follows. The proper *right* Bedamneds kind of brings things on themselves, like, a-all the badness and a-all—'

'And the other poor Bedamned craiturs gets the badness brought *on* to them and chust has to suffer it,' George rejoined.

'Yes, that's chust about the way of it,' agreed old Bill-the-Post.

After another round of drinks, my father went home to his cottage, and the rest of us got into the car and drove west out of Achcraggan on the way to Reachfar. There was a bright, frosty full moon and already there was a silver mail of snow on the high hump of Ben Wyvis away west at the head of the Firth, which lay like a black cloth streaked with threads of moon-metal between the hills that were sleeping under shawls of hoar-frost lace. As we approached Bedamned's Corner, it presented to us its back, east wall, ghostly grey under its slate roof that looked black against the frosty sky. The gay little house of August, with its white walls, red paint and brilliant flowers seemed to be something I had dreamed and this black, defiant, sullen little hump was the reality. Our headlights raked over it and it seemed to cower away from the white brilliance, glad to slip back, almost furtively, to our left and away behind, and, when it was past, the countryside before us seemed to lighten, to become more clearly brilliant now that that small but telling black emphasis on a bright picture had been left behind.

We turned off the County Road and began to climb the

farm road towards Poyntdale steading. Behind us lay the broad, glittering waters of the Firth, on either side of us the winter trees stood stark and bare, and as we topped the first shoulder below Poyntdale Farm we could see to our left the ruins of the old sawmill and the smooth waters of the dam, like a great silver tray reflecting the light of the moon.

'What's that building?' Twice asked me.

'The old Poyntdale sawmill.'

'I've never noticed it before – I suppose the trees have been in leaf or it's been too dark. I thought for a moment it was a church.'

'In some lights,' I said, 'the difference between a kirk and a mill is pretty subtle.'

'The difference is probably *entirely* a question of light,' Twice said and the dam and the old mill fell away behind us as we approached the farm steading while, at the back of my mind, words formed:

'A broken chancel with a broken cross
That stood on a dark strait of barren land.
On one side lay the Ocean, and on one
Lay a great water and the moon was full . . .'

– words that, somehow, were inextricably entangled in my mind with the little house at Bedamned's Corner.

As we ran through Poyntdale Farm square, George said to Twice: 'Watch the hill road tonight, Twice, lad. It'll be treacherous further up'; but when we had left Poyntdale behind and were on the rougher track for Reachfar, Twice said: 'There's been a car up here ahead of us tonight.'

'A car? Who would that be?' Tom asked.

'Probably Monica,' I said, for my friend Monica is the wife of young Sir Torquil at Poyntdale and a frequent visitor at Reachfar.

'No,' Twice said. 'Something bigger and heavier than Monica's car. Anyway, it's still up there so we'll soon find out.'

When we came round the granary gable into the yard

237

there was indeed a large black car sitting outside the barn.

'An American car,' Twice said as he pulled up.

'An *American* car?' said the two voices from the back seat.

I clutched Twice's arm as the dogs gathered round to welcome us and then said to George and Tom: 'All right, boys. Shall I go in first and see who it is?'

'Chust you do that,' said George, 'and Tom and me will be helping Twice to put the car by for the night.'

George and Tom were old enough now to distrust the unexpected, but I went into the house confidently, for, somehow, the visitor was not, to me, entirely unexpected.

'Malcolm!' I said. 'You might have written to say you were coming!'

And I looked at my Aunt Kate. She was over fifty now, you know, but her big dark eyes were like spring stars and there was a softness about her mouth that usually leaves women around their twenty-first birthday.

'I'm not so good at the letter-writing,' Malcolm said. 'Long ago, I once made a clumsy mistake in a letter. Only a mutt makes the same mistake twice.'

'So he didn't write, Kate? He just arrived?' I asked.

'Aye,' she said. 'That's right. He just arrived. About an hour ago. Where are the rest of you?'

'Putting the car away.'

She put the kettle on the fire, then went to the dresser cupboard, took out the teapot and set it, with six tumblers, on a tray. She then took the whisky bottle from the cupboard and set it on the side of the stove.

'I'll go and fetch the others in,' I said and then I took the teapot from the tray, put it on the stove and moved the whisky bottle to where the teapot had been. 'Is that better, do you think?' I asked her.

'Aye,' she said breathlessly. 'Aye, that's better!' and she gave a giggle that might have come from an eighteen-year-old. Its happy gurgle followed me out into the frosty yard.

The next morning, in the scullery over the breakfast

238

dishes, she swung round from the sink suddenly and said: 'Janet, I owe you an apology. I was right wicked to you about that cable you sent and I shouldn't have been. I am sorry.'

'Don't be an ass!' I said. 'You're – you're really happy, Kate?'

'I'm really happy, Janet.'

'You deserve it.'

'But for you, I'd never have got it. Malcolm says it was seeing *you* in New York that – that brought everything back.'

I could think of nothing to say. The silence between us thickened, the silence of the deep waters that lie at one side of the Reachfar stream.

It seemed false to me that my aunt should feel beholden to me in any way for the happiness that had come to her, for I do not believe that happiness ever comes entirely through the agency of another person. This happiness of Kate's, I felt, was something that she had earned; something that had grown and struggled to life out of the soil of her own character in spite of the harsh winds and cruel weather of her own fierce pride. This happiness was her own, as the happiness of Flora Bedamned with her new family was her own. And, as I looked at my bright-eyed aunt across the workaday Reachfar scullery, I remembered that night in St Jago when Twice and I had talked about Flora and I remembered my own words: 'Flora may have significance for me, but she'll never have any for Kate.'

With the deep waters of the Reachfar stream about us, I saw my way back to the shallower edge where the water flows over the pebbly bed of the light chatter of every day.

'Oh, rot!' I said. 'I had nothing to do with Malcolm coming back. If you have to be grateful to somebody, be grateful to Flora Bedamned. I'd never have gone to New York at all if it hadn't been for my friend Flora!'

THE END